CLOTHED

WITH THE

SUN

Then the dragon stood before the woman

CLOTHED

WITH THE SUN

Ω

J.B. SIMMONS

Book Two of the Omega Trilogy

www.jbsimmons.com
jbsimmons.light@gmail.com
@jbsimmonslight

Cover by Kerry Ellis
www.kerry-ellis.com

ISBN 978-1502923981

For Mom

Ω

My name is Elijah Goldsmith. This is my story, and it's the honest-to-god truth. I'm glad you're back to hear more. My dreams still haunt me, but I've seen signs of hope. At least I ended up beside Naomi, in the middle of a desert. What matters is what we choose to do next. I've made some good choices, and some bad ones. You might as well hear all of it before you pick sides.

1

I stood in a narrow valley, facing a small stone cottage. Its roof was thatched, and smoke drifted from its lonely chimney. No other buildings were in sight. No other sign of man. Steep hills rose around me, spotted with dark rock and covered with grasses blowing in the wind. The breeze carried ocean salt. There were a hundred shades of green. This place felt lush and wet and thin—close to the heavens.

"She's in there." The voice behind me was powerful. It almost knocked me to my knees.

"Who?" I asked, my voice quivering like a bowstring.

"Your promised one." It was the voice of a man I knew, but I could not look at him.

"Naomi?"

"You have more than one?" The man sounded amused. "I underestimated you."

"Why are you here?"

"She has my child."

The answer sent a shiver down my spine. "Your child?"

"Come, see for yourself." The man walked past me, toward the cottage. His body was tall and regal. The grasses swept around him at the knees.

I rushed after him. I felt the dense meadow grabbing my legs, holding me back. I struggled to keep up. Just as I reached the cottage, he opened the plain wooden door and stepped inside.

"*No!*" he shouted.

I stepped through the door, breathing heavily. The cottage had a small, simple room with stone walls. A fire was burning bright in the hearth, and another man sat facing the fire. I couldn't see his face.

"What's wrong?" I asked.

The man in the chair didn't budge, but the tall man spun to me and grabbed my throat. It was Don Cristo. I should have known. His face twisted in rage as he lifted me off the ground.

I fought for breath, but none came.

"You," Don growled. "You know where she is."

But I didn't know. I tried to shake my head.

He squeezed harder. "Why did you lead me here?"

I tried to think, but I felt consciousness fading. The man watching the fire seemed oblivious. My eyes closed, with Don's angry face seared in my vision.

"Eli, Eli." Someone else was speaking to me. It was a familiar voice, in a French accent. "Sun's rising soon."

I cracked open my eyes. Jacques's scruffy face was in mine. His breath smelled as musty as a tomb.

"It's still dark," I mumbled.

"Never let the sun get ahead of you." He pulled me to my feet. His grip on my shoulder was gentle, but his hands were strong, like leathery, callused clamps.

I tried to rub the sleep and the dream out of my eyes. Dreams and reality kept blurring in the desert.

"A little rest, a little folding of the hands, and you'll be destroyed, boy." Jacques's whisper echoed in my ears.

I looked around the tent, half expecting to see something different in the first light of morning. But it was the same. Two piles of sleeping blankets, with Naomi curled up under one on the far side of the tent. She was breathing deeply—serene and pregnant.

The tent's canvas matched the light brown sand at my feet. Just days ago my feet had been paler than the sand. Now they were darker, at least between the straps of my sandals. Jacques had given me the sandals. I chose to believe it was a loan rather than a gift, because that way I could pretend I'd be leaving this desolate place soon. Doubtful.

"Quit staring at your feet." Jacques was waiting by the tent's open flap of a door.

I followed him outside and pulled my brown cloak closer. The desert heat would come only with the rising sun. We reached the well, and Jacques handed a wooden bucket to me. It was heavy and tied to a rope that felt like sandpaper in my hands.

"Draw," Jacques said.

The first morning, after Jacques had pulled me out of sleep, he'd shown me how to draw the water. It was simple, but not easy—and definitely not the kind of thing you did growing up in New York City. After a few slips and bruises, I'd figured it out.

I was determined to make this morning's drawing my smoothest yet. I held the bucket over the deep hole in the ground, while my other hand gripped the rope firmly. As I stepped back, I looped the rope around the closest of the oasis's three palm trees. I heard the distant splash of the bucket hitting water. I waited a moment, then began to pull the bucket up.

The rope was taut with the bucket's weight, but the makeshift anchor eased the effort. Hand over hand, I raised it steadily. How long before my hands would be as callused as Jacques'? When the bucket came into view above the well's ancient stone rim, I tied off the rope around the palm. I walked to the bucket, swung it over to the stone rim and untied it. I grabbed the bucket's handle with both hands and waddled it over to the trough. I poured it in, put the bucket down, and looked to Jacques. Maybe I expected his praise, or at least satisfaction.

He looked at me with his ever-amused, ever-tanned face. He had only faint wrinkles at his eyes, but the strands of bright white in his hair and stubble had to mean he was at least forty.

"You learn fast," Jacques said. "Still, your hands shake. They must grow stronger. Now let's get the herd." Part of me smiled inside. That was as close to praise as he'd come.

He led me to the other side of the tents, where the camel herd was corralled each night. The area was tucked within the banks of hills around our dried riverbed, but the camels still had to be bound. Jacques had taught me how to fetter their front legs. All it took was a short cord of cloth Jacques called an *aqal*. We'd bend each camel's front right leg at the knee, then tie the *aqal* around the bend. That kept the camel from going anywhere far. It seemed cruel, making a creature spend the night with only three legs for standing. Jacques had said only, "this is done," when I'd pressed him. He said things like that a lot.

This morning, as we reached the camels, the sun was just cresting on the cloudless horizon. I hadn't seen a cloud since we'd arrived here. The brownish red hillsides around us became stripes of amber and garnet. It made the harsh terrain seem alive.

"*Mierde*," Jacques muttered. "*Grabuge*." He was holding one of the fettering *aqal* ropes. It had been chewed through.

"He's gone?" I asked.

"*Oui*. Pack up. We ride out and find him. Only an idiot tries to escape here." He eyed me accusingly. "The desert is death to anything alone."

2

The runaway camel had left tracks. We'd been following them all morning with no sign of life outside our little caravan of four. Jacques and I were riding camelback over the plains of ragged scrubland, with two extra camels tied behind us. "Never trust one camel when you can have two," he'd said.

We reached the top of a low hill and again saw emptiness sprawled out before us. "Are you sure he went this way?" I asked.

Jacques pointed at the line of tracks in the sand. He looked at me like I was clueless.

"Yeah, I see the tracks," I said. "But how do you know they're Grabuge's?"

"You see other camels?" He gestured to the empty expanse as far as our eyes could see.

I shook my head. "How far could he have gone? Is it really worth all this for one camel?"

"Every camel in my herd is priceless. I have a duty to protect them." His eyes never wavered from the horizon.

"Is that supposed to be a parable?"

"It's no parable, boy. It's a camel."

As if that settled things, Jacques fell into quiet and rode ahead. My camel followed without any nudging from me. I gripped the reins and thought back to my dream. I'd had it two straight nights. Did that mean it would come to be, like my dream of Rome? It should have been less terrifying. There was no dragon—just rugged hills, a cottage, and a couple of men. But one of those men was Don, which made my stomach roil. He'd thought I'd known where Naomi would be, but in the dream I'd had no idea. That made me feel sick, too. The more I tried to untangle the dream's meaning, the more unanswered questions I had.

As another hour passed, the desert's temperature rose. I felt like the proverbial frog in a pot being brought to boil. After a while, I started unwinding the scarf from around my face. I'd rather get a face full of sand and sun than suffocate in this heat.

"Leave it on," Jacques said.

"Why?"

"I said leave it on."

I wound the cloth back around, to cover my head and my face again.

"Good." He drew his camel closer to mine and pulled a canteen from a saddlebag. He opened it and held it over my head.

"What—?"

He dumped the water on me and let out a muffled laugh. "The wet cloth cools. Breathe deep, boy. You're still very soft, but these lands harden even you."

"Whatever, man." I was shaking my head, but the water did feel good. "All I need is to get back to my home."

"Your home is soft," he said. "The world is soft, makes soft men. The desert makes real men." He formed a fist and flexed his bare arm. The tanned muscles looked as steady as the rocks scattered at our feet. "We trust in our bodies and in the Lord, not in precepts and governments." He tapped his temple. "Five years since I used mine. My mind is free now, just as yours can be if you keep your precept shut off."

"You have a precept?"

"*Oui*, disconnected. It was once essential."

"Essential to what?"

Jacques smiled. "Any other questions?"

"Lots of them." Every other time I'd tried to ask about his past, he'd given me some chore to do. Now we were stuck tracking a camel in the middle of nowhere, so I fired away. "What did you do before you came here? How did you get into this religious order?"

He stared ahead, as if he hadn't even heard me.

"You don't seem like the order's type," I said. "Neither does Camille. Did you bring her here? And why the Moroccan desert? Were you running from something?"

"The water has gone to your head," he mused. "Was it

curiosity that made you a seer?"

His question made me think of my Mom. She always used to say I was curious. "Nothing made me a seer. That's just a label your order made up."

"Did we make up the dragon that you saw in Rome? The dragon that attacked your plane and made you crash here? The dragon that killed Bart?"

I shuddered at the memory. No, the order had not made that up, and my dreams had grown only more vivid in this wasteland. "You haven't answered any of my questions," I said.

"You find my camel, and maybe I'll answer one."

"Fine." I scanned the desert around us. No camels. The tracks disappeared over the crest of the next hill in front of us. "*Grabuge!*" I shouted, as if calling for a lost dog.

"Shhh! Quiet boy. Are you trying to scare him away?"

"No one can hear us out here. He'll come if he hears my voice." I looked out over the empty desert. "*Grabuge!*"

Something hit my side like a truck, knocking me off the camel's back. Next thing I knew, I was flat on my back, gasping for air. Jacques was on top of me, gripping my throat in his fist. His eyes were flat, grey and firm.

"*Quiet,*" he whispered. "You hear me?"

I tried to nod and he let go. My mouth burned as I gulped down the hot air. The sky was an enormous blue mass pressing down on me, squeezing me between the earth and the heavens. I just laid there on the sand for a while, defeated. I slowly rose to my feet.

"Next time, you listen, yes?" Jacques gazed at me

coolly.

I nodded, keeping my face blank despite a flicker of fear. His grip had felt like Don's in my dream. I stood no chance against this guy, and it was just the two of us out here. I should have known better by now. This man was no joke. He was a rock. What had he been in the past?

His eyes shifted to the right, looking past me at something. A grin spread across his face. "Grabuge," he said with the affection of a father greeting a son. "You wily boy."

I turned to look, just in time to catch a giant, wet lick from the camel's tongue. "Ack!" I hopped back, but Grabuge nuzzled his head into my chest. A new camel was at his side.

"He likes you, boy." Jacques ran his hand over the new camel's face. "And he brought a friend. Your lucky day. You found two camels, so maybe I answer two questions. We return now, yes?"

I nodded and brushed the sand off my back. Better not to mention that my shouting had worked. I mounted Grabuge as Jacques tied the new camel to our caravan. We'd gone from four to six. Jacques took the lead again as we headed back the way we came, the sun high overhead.

3

We rode a long way in silence. Between the hot sun and the swaying camel, I found it hard to keep a straight line of thought. My mind wandered to Naomi. Right now she'd be helping Camille with chores around the camp. I could envision her slender hands molding oats into honey cakes. Her face would be focused. Everything she did seemed elegant, even out here in the wilderness, even with a baby growing inside her.

She insisted she was a virgin, and that some kind of miracle or technology had done this. I believed her, though it was little comfort. My thoughts drifted back to the dragon and to last night's dream. Was Don really the father? How was that possible? With a single touch? I had learned better than to doubt my dreams, but I couldn't imagine how I'd lead Don to a remote place like that cottage. I puzzled over the man who'd been in the chair, watching the fire. Why hadn't he turned when Don shouted?

After a while, Jacques interrupted my inner rambling. "Earlier you ask if I bring Camille here?"

"Yes, and who were you before coming here?"

"You ask many questions," he said. "I pick two. This is how it works."

"Okay, so did you bring her here?"

"Camille is magnificent woman, yes?" The French-lover look in Jacques's eyes made me squirm.

"Sure."

"Her beauty belongs in palaces, not deserts." Jacques sighed, gazing ahead as if drifting into the past. "That is where I met her. Six years ago, in Versailles. It was a banquet of my country's most powerful and famous. In this gathering where everyone has privilege, Camille was like a diamond in a pile of quartz. She'd worn a white dress clinging to her every curve. On first sight, I knew my life could continue only with her. I needed to feel her thin waist in my hands, to pull her chest close to mine, and to drink deeply from her mouth." Jacques trailed off, still looking ahead.

This was getting awkward, but I had to admit it was intriguing. I'd never heard Jacques say so much at once, and he sounded nothing like the others in Naomi's order. "So what happened?"

He smiled. "*Oui, it* happened. We married within the week. We moved here within the year."

He made it sound like his life's greatest accomplishment. "That was fast," I said. "How did you convince her to marry you? And why did you come *here*?"

Jacques winked at me. "A man who knows his calling and pursues it—well, God gives to that man. My hair had no white in it then. My position and presence were," he shrugged, "difficult to resist. I will never forget Camille's face when I declared my intentions to her, that she would be mine that night and forever. She was amused, enticed, and vulnerable. You see, Camille was known in France. She was a model and a film star. No man could claim a woman like her. No man but me, for God had prepared me. And Camille was ready. She was addicted—to fame, to wealth, to drugs. Her life was unmoored. Her soul cried out for help, to be tied to a fixed pillar." He looked at me with an intense gaze. "I became the pillar."

I felt blood rushing to my cheeks at the not-so-subtle implication of his metaphor. "So you and she, you know… it all sounds a little too hot for people like you."

"People like me? You mean a leader of the Order of John? A God-fearing man?" He paused. "Well, my God created passion. You know my God, you are Jewish, yes?"

I nodded. Better to keep him talking than to test what he meant by "knowing God." I knew enough now to believe there was a God, but he wasn't gaining any favor with me after letting the dragon loose.

"You know the stories of the Torah?" Jacques asked.

"Some of them," I said, but not like I did with V's help. Every memory seemed fainter without her in my mind. I wondered if I'd ever get to reconnect my precept.

"The God of our patriarchs had a simple view," Jacques explained. "Ever heard this, from your Torah and my Bible: *And Isaac brought Rebekah into his mother Sarah's tent, and he took Rebekah, and she became his wife; and he loved her.* Just so, but in Paris rather than a tent, Camille became my wife." He turned to me expectantly.

"Interesting." I didn't know what else to say.

He studied me, with a slanted smile on his face. "You want to marry Naomi this way, yes?"

"*What?*" I shook my head. "No. I mean…no." He'd caught me off guard. So I'd fallen for Naomi. Maybe I loved her, but he'd gone too far. *Marriage?*

"But she is with child," Jacques said.

"Not my child!"

"This is known, Eli, but I see you with her. You smile at her voice. Your eyes reveal desire as plain as day." Jacques leaned over and squeezed my shoulder. "Keep at it, and maybe you can take her into a tent, eh?"

I pulled away from his arm, my face flushing again. "No, I…"

"It is okay," Jacques said. "Maybe this is one reason why Camille and I come here, to this place. We wait for you and Naomi. Now we hide you and teach you. We show you how to love."

4

As we rode on quietly in the desert, I tried not to think about Jacques's words. But I failed. Was he serious? Marry Naomi? That was ridiculous, especially when the world was unraveling around us. But did she ever think about it? I remembered the words she'd said but forgotten as she'd died in my arms on Patmos: *I love you.* Did she really have no memory of that? What else had been erased with the miracle that brought her back to life? I'd been over this a hundred times and gotten nowhere. It was no use rehashing it again.

I tried not to think at all. I held up my thumb and studied it. The skin was darker that I'd ever seen it, with a touch of sun-burned red and a layer of desert sand caked around my thumbnail. I set the base of my thumb at the horizon. I positioned it so that the setting sun was at my thumb's tip. It formed a bright flower, casting out glorious orange and red pastels into the blank blue sky.

"Beautiful, yes?" Jacques broke the silence as our caravan made its way down the last hill toward the hidden oasis.

"I guess so," I shrugged, "but I miss the color green."

"You mean her green eyes?" Jacques asked, just as Camille and Naomi came out to meet us. I did not respond, probably because he was right.

"A new camel!" Camille said as we reached them. I could see it now. Her curved figure. Her pretty face. Her long dark hair. She would have looked more at home in Versailles than here. So would Naomi.

"Grabuge found a mate," Jacques announced. "You two lovely women find shade today?"

We climbed off our saddles and stood before Camille and Naomi. They both wore white linen dresses without any dirt or dust from the day's work.

"We did," Naomi said. Her gorgeous face was still glowing, and not just because of the sunset's light. "Camille showed me how to make lentil stew. I also learned more about medieval history." Her bright eyes turned to me. "Elijah, did you know Camille was an actress? She was in a movie about the French crusades."

I nodded. "Jacques told me a little about that today." Maybe he and Camille were coordinating their releases of information to us. It was almost frightening how much we depended on them out here.

"Come now," Camille said, with her hands planted on

her hips. "You boys are filthy. You wash, then we eat."

"It's lovely to see you, too, *mon amour.*" Jacques grabbed her around the waist and they spun. I glanced toward Naomi, who smiled and rolled her eyes. "*Très belle,*" Jacques said, glancing from Camille to Naomi. "Both of you. Your hair is oiled, your fragrance is sweet, your dresses are flawless. To what do we owe this honor?"

"My dress *was* flawless, until a camel herder took hold of me." Camille's voice feigned disappointment, but she held tight to Jacques.

"Maybe you can help me?" Jacques winked.

"Someone has to keep you clean," Camille replied.

"Aye." Jacques glanced at me. "You can wash up after you tend to the camels. The herd must be fed before its masters can eat, yes?"

He walked off with Camille without waiting for an answer, without any doubt that I would obey.

5

"That was awkward."

"What? French lovers?" Naomi asked. "Okay, yeah, that was a little awkward." She grabbed my hand, without a care for the dirt. Her touch was a jolt of electricity. I hadn't been away from her this long in a week. "Shall we?"

"We shall feed the camels."

"Such a noble duty," Naomi said, as we headed toward the tent that held supplies.

"Maybe you heard a few too many of Camille's stories about the knights and the crusades today."

"Whatever it takes to get my mind away," Naomi sighed. "The days out here are long."

"Long and exhausting."

"And boring."

"You miss your precept?" As much as I missed V, what

I really missed was my sync to Naomi. I'd gotten used to knowing her heart rate whenever I wanted.

"I miss it every hour that goes by," Naomi answered, as we began filling feed bags with oats for the camels. "I've never gone so long with so little information."

"Same here. But aren't you supposed to be getting answers from God or something?"

"Oh, I'm listening," she said, without a hint of doubt. "His voice is closer than ever, nudging me, but still…"

"What?"

"I'm worried." She slowly dropped a handful of oats into her bag. "About Chris and Patrick, and everyone else. It's hard not knowing what is going on out there, especially when I'm certain it's bad. Really bad. The memories of what happened still haunt me…especially from Patmos."

"I know," I sympathized. The images of the dragon's killings were seared in my mind. Chris and Patrick had rescued us from Patmos, and they'd left us here. "Jacques gets a message from Chris every day. Don't you think Chris would tell us if there were major news?"

"Maybe," she said. "But he tells Jacques so little."

It was true. Each night we'd seen Jacques checking his old school transmitter outside his tent. He flipped it on, then off a moment later. He told us the messages from Chris just confirmed all was well, and that we should hold our position. Naomi and I had discussed this before, but I had to ask again: "How can you be so sure Jacques is telling us everything?"

"He's an honest man." Naomi paused. "And he's kept

us safe out here so far." She sounded like she was trying to convince herself.

"The order trusted Gregory, too."

She winced. Maybe my words were harsh, but his betrayal could not be forgotten. As I'd reconstructed the events on Patmos, I'd realized the British prince must have helped the dragon and Jezebel the demon track us. The rest of the order stayed off the precept network, and Naomi and I had not connected our precepts anywhere from Rome to the island. Gregory had led them straight to us.

"There may be more like Gregory." Naomi's voice came out quiet and stiff. "He was one of the order's best. Evil likes nothing more than taking down the best." She was shaking her head, staring off at the sky. "And the order is not the same without Bart. I could always trust him. Now, well, I don't know. But, I just—"

"What?" I urged.

"We can trust Jacques, right?" Her moist eyes met mine. "We are hidden among these tents. We haven't been attacked yet, and at least we're together. Maybe there's a purpose to our time here."

I took her hand, the one still dusted with oats. "You are even better without the distractions, you know?"

She smiled at me with her innocent green eyes and freckled face. "I admit, that's nice to hear. I've been worried"—she bit her lip—"about what you'd think of me now." She pulled her hand away from mine and to her stomach. "With this change."

"That should be the least of your worries," I said. "You

know how I feel about you, and after what we've gone through, I want nothing more than to be with you, to protect you…even in the middle of this wasteland."

"Thank you." Tears filled her eyes again. She'd been crying a lot these past few days. "I've been praying for answers, for guidance. I don't have an explanation for this." Her eyes looked down to her stomach, then back at me. "Any more visions?"

"I had the dream again last night."

"Did Don say the same thing? He thinks *he's* the father?"

I nodded.

"I will not believe it." She sounded strong, until she sniffed again. "God wouldn't let this happen to me. Would he?"

I pulled her into my arms. "It'll be okay," I said, holding her tight. "You keep saying it will work out for the good. I believe you."

She looked up at me and nodded, then shook her head, with conflicting emotions on her face. "I know, it will," she whispered. "Listen, I have to tell you, I think God is nudging me to leave. I can't just stay here and let all this come to me. No matter how logical it seems, safety can't be my main concern. I trust Jacques, and he's wise, but he's no Bart. He's alone out here, operating on Chris' old instructions. I need more information. We will have to leave this hideaway eventually."

That made a lot of sense to me. She seemed to be shifting away from the blind obedience she'd had when I met her. She seemed to be shifting closer to me. I asked, "Why not leave sooner rather than later?"

She hesitated, then looked down at her stomach again. "Maybe it would be better to get out before it's more obvious."

"Agreed," I said, trying to imagine her with a melon-sized belly, "but I doubt Jacques would let us do that. He thinks this is where we must stay until the order tells us to leave."

"You're right." Naomi's voice was somber. "Maybe we should leave without asking. You'll come with me, right?"

"Of course." I wiped a tear from her cheek.

"Thank you. Let's give it some time. That's one thing we have plenty of out here."

The monotonous, deserted days became countless. Each morning Jacques woke me before dawn. I drew water from the well. We fed the camels. By then Camille and Naomi had a fire going. We ate oat cakes for breakfast. We washed them down with camel milk.

Jacques and I led the herd out to graze on whatever shrubs they could find along the dry riverbed. Jacques taught me survival skills. How to build a fire. How to detect water deep underground. We even did hand-to-hand combat training. I left each time with bruises and another ounce of fighting instinct. With each passing day, I became more convinced the man had been some kind of soldier.

Despite Jacques' stoic face, I would have sworn he enjoyed my company, except when I asked him hard questions. He never answered them.

Each day ended the same way: we led the camels back to the tents and the three-palm oasis as the sun fell toward the vast horizon. Camille and Naomi would have dinner ready. Lentil stew, dried figs, and more camel milk. Jacques and Camille would fawn over each other. Naomi and I would pretend we didn't notice. Then Naomi and I would find a place where we could talk as the sun set. The stars would appear. We talked about ISA, the dragon, the order, and whether the world was really ending. We came up with few answers and plenty of guesses. We would go to sleep then, in our separate beds. I would dream until Jacques woke me again. And so it went, day after day, night after night.

The simple routine left Naomi and me more and more anxious to get back to the real world. Maybe ignorance could have been bliss in this no-man's land, but not when you've grown up in the modern world. I wanted to connect my precept, though I feared what I would learn. Unanswered questions haunted me. Had there been more disasters? Had anyone else seen the dragon? What was ISA-7 doing? Was Don expanding his control? Was Don really who the order said he was?

If the world was ending, maybe it would be better to stay hidden…as long as I had Naomi. We were growing even closer. Our sync was disconnected, but something stronger was forming as we weathered the harsh climate together. I knew it as we talked in the evenings. I knew it from the way our hands rested together, the way all felt well when I looked into her eyes.

The problem was: the more we fell for each other, the more apparent was the final wedge between us. It wasn't enough for her that I now believed there was a God. She pressed me to go further. She talked about big ideas like resurrection and salvation. Some of it sounded intriguing, but part of me resisted. If I had to pick sides, sure, I'd take God over the dragon. But if God made everything, didn't that mean he made the dragon? No matter how many ways Naomi tried to explain how God could be good despite the dragon and all the other disasters on earth, I couldn't get over that wall.

I might have tried faking it—pretending I believed—but Naomi knew me too well for that. I also figured we'd have time to work through it all. I figured we'd have weeks before any hard decisions had to be made.

But one night the time ran out.

"We leave tomorrow at first light," Jacques announced over dinner. He bit off a piece of fig cake and stared at me over the flickering fire.

"Where are we going?" Naomi asked, with a hint of excitement. She looked to me, and I shrugged. Jacques hadn't hinted anything about this.

"You are not going, *petite amie*," chided Camille. She was lounging beside Jacques on the other side of the fire.

I could sense Naomi tensing. It drove her crazy when Camille talked down to her like that. I hid behind a sip of camel's milk. A little sour, as usual.

"That depends," Naomi said. "Who's going, and where?"

"Elijah and I are going," Jacques answered. "Our food supplies need refilling. With four of us, plus an extra camel, we can't afford to wait much longer. Zag is a long and hard day's journey. I'll bring back enough oats and figs for a few more months."

"Zag?" I asked. "What's that?" The prospect of a long, hot caravan with the Frenchman was far from appealing, especially without Naomi.

Camille laughed. "A village, Eli. We trade camels, we get food for a few months. And maybe a new blanket for our bed?" She batted her eyes at Jacques.

"*Rien pour vous*," he said smoothly, stroking her hair.

"*Mon amant*," she purred.

Naomi and I shared a look of amused disgust.

"Seriously," I said to them, "why can't Naomi come?"

Camille stared me down. "A baby is a gift from God. Not every woman is blessed with such a gift. This is not something to risk. We must protect her and the child at all costs."

"I'm not some doll," Naomi said. "We would be careful. I want to stay with Elijah. Wouldn't it be safer if we traveled together?" She posed the question in her most convincing tone. The tone I couldn't resist.

"For the travel, maybe," Jacques replied, "but not for Zag. You must stay hidden from all eyes, Naomi. No one could fail to notice you."

Naomi shook her head. "I'll remain covered."

"We cannot risk the questions," Jacques said. "Even taking Elijah with me brings danger. This is a job for men."

"Oh, for men?" Naomi scoffed. "Because how dare a woman be competent enough to ride camels and trade for food. That's ridiculous, Jacques, and you know it."

He shrugged. "Men know how to follow orders."

"Are you ordering me to stay here?" Naomi pressed.

"If that's what it takes," Jacques snapped back.

"You have no authority over me." Naomi met Jacques's stare, unflinching. "Why should we trust you?"

"I am one of the twelve," Jacques said. "You trust in the Order of John, so you must trust in me."

"I trusted Gregory, too."

Jacques shook his head. "All have sinned and fallen short of the glory of God."

"Exactly," Naomi said. "What are you hiding?"

Their leveled stares stayed locked as silence mounted. It was like a battle of wills. Jacques was tough, but my money was on Naomi. I was right.

Jacques sighed. "You never make things easy, do you?"

"This is not a time for *easy*," Naomi replied. "It's a time for truth."

"Okay," Jacques said. "Here's the heart of it: Eli will not be coming back."

7

"*What?*" Naomi gasped, as my jaw dropped open. *Not coming back*—that meant escape from the desert. But I couldn't leave Naomi behind.

Jacques held up his hand. "Let me explain. You always knew your time out here would be temporary. This place is a refuge from the battle raging in the world. Eli must return to the battle. He will go to DC, where Patrick will provide instructions."

"Patrick?" He was in the order, and in ISA-7, but I still didn't trust the guy. "What about Chris?"

Jacques shook his head. "I fear Chris has been caught. I've received no message from him the past two days."

"Really?" Naomi sounded unconvinced. "If that were true, then you'd let me go, too."

"Your mission is to stay hidden and healthy while your

baby grows. We are still trying to determine your role. You will return when the time is right."

"And who determines that?" Naomi challenged.

"The order."

Naomi opened her mouth to speak, but stopped herself. I could see the defiance in her eyes. She had to be fuming inside about Jacques holding back some contact with Patrick. That was no way to win her trust.

"Look," Camille said, interrupting Jacques' and Naomi's deadlocked stare. The French woman was pressing her finger into the sand and idly drawing. "We do not force anything, and we would avoid separating you two if we could. I've seen enough these past weeks to know how you feel about each other."

"We have little choice," Jacques agreed. "I learned just this evening that Don is moving faster than we thought. He is gathering the world's leaders in a just over a month. We have to be ready to counter him…" Jacques trailed off, gazing into the fire.

"And?" Naomi pried. "How did you learn this? You've got to tell us what you know. Everything." She hesitated, glancing to me. "This doesn't explain why Elijah must leave."

"As I've told you," Jacques continued, "I use an encrypted network once every day to receive confirmation from Chris that all is well. Anything more would risk us being discovered. Tonight, when I connected, Patrick was waiting for me—in a live video link. He warned that the security of my connection may have been compromised.

He said he had to sever the connection, but just before he did, he gave me this message: *The pastor is lost. What was unbound is growing. He rallies support from the powerful and the richest. He will call for Elijah. This is our best chance to get in. Send him to us.*" Jacques paused, turning to me. "That was all."

"Okay," Naomi said, "so Elijah will go. But that says nothing about me. You know Elijah and I are connected, and you know what he can see." Her voice lowered. "We need each other."

Jacques' stare settled on Naomi. "True as that may be, our highest priority is to protect you. Your baby is somehow central to Abaddon's plans. The child must be hidden and safe. Let me be clear: You. Will. Not. Go."

"You have no right—" Naomi began.

"Wait," I said, studying Jacques, "what makes you think Naomi would be safe here?" I thought of the dream with the valley and the cottage, and of what Don had said in it: *She has my child.* If that's really what Don thought, I still couldn't understand why he left us for the dragon to attack. Unless maybe he knew she'd survive? In the dream, Naomi hadn't been in the cottage. But Don thought she was there, and alive.

"No one knows where we are," Camille volunteered. "Even Chris and Patrick erased this location from their precepts. I will keep Naomi safe while you are gone, and then Jacques will return and protect us."

"We are hidden," Jacques agreed, turning to Naomi. "Many prayers shield us. We have the advantage out here. I know this desert better than anyone. Will you obey?"

"You leave me little choice," Naomi said, rising slowly to her feet. Her voice was meek, but eyes were still defiant. She held out her hand to me. I took it and stood beside her. "Give us some time, some space," she told them. "This may be our last night together for a while."

"We understand," Camille said.

"Eli, be ready at dawn," Jacques added. "The evil one grows in power now, but he *will* lose. What has been separated will be united in the end."

"May the end come soon," Naomi said.

Jacques nodded. "*Maranatha.*"

Whatever the word meant, it brought the first smile to Naomi's face since Jacques had said we'd be leaving. She squeezed my hand, and we turned together and walked away.

"You know where you're going?" I asked, almost struggling to keep up with Naomi's pace. Her strides seemed full of indignant anger.

"Nope." She didn't slow in the slightest. "I figure we can just follow the riverbed. I want to get far enough away so I can think clearly. I've been out of sight from the camp only a handful of times since we arrived."

"You're not missing much, unless you haven't gotten enough sand yet."

She stopped and grinned at me. Her glow was unmistakable, as if someone had bottled up the sun and poured it over her skin.

"Me," I continued, "well, I've had enough sand, enough French accents, and enough camels." I motioned to the desert around us. The only living things in sight were a few wilted bushes hugging to the cracked ground. It looked like water might have flowed here when dinosaurs roamed the earth.

"How about me?" she asked, drawing my eyes. "Have you had enough of me?"

"Not possible. Besides, it's a moonless night. How would I see out here without you shining the way?"

She laughed but quickly fell quiet. She held out her arms and studied them. "Weird, isn't it? I feel normal, if a little queasy sometimes. Why would my skin look like this?"

"Is this like when a girl asks if she looks fat?" I asked with a smile. "Smart guys know better than to answer questions like that."

"Maybe, but the *smartest* guys have answers."

She had a point, and I had my guesses. "Don and that other guy touched you," I said. "Not like I would touch you, or anyone else. I was right there when they did it. They touched you like they were accomplishing something. Whatever they accomplished, it made you glow."

"Like impregnating me? Just with a touch?"

"Yeah, I guess. Don thinks he did it. Maybe he's wrong, though." I ran a hand through my hair, at a loss for an explanation. "You have any better ideas?"

"Maybe," she said. "I'm a pregnant virgin. Either someone artificially inseminated me, or I need to talk to Mary, the mother of Jesus. I still think it could have been the Lord who saved me on Patmos. Who else could have brought me back? Who else could have stopped the dragon?"

"An ISA agent," I ventured, "or maybe a super hero."

Naomi smiled. "You said he looked plain."

"Fine, he didn't have a cape," I said. "But he didn't look like God either."

"You know what God looks like?"

I shrugged. Good point.

"Let's say I'm right," she said. "Let's say it was Jesus Christ. Even if He saved me, I doubt my child is his. It wouldn't make sense for him to do this to me, and none of the stories say Mary's skin glowed."

"What do they say?"

"Angels came to Mary to announce the news. No one has announced anything to me. Plus, I think I'd feel different. What if my baby is just a normal child?"

"Then why would you glow?"

"I haven't figured that out."

"Any guesses?"

She hesitated, bit her lip, then nodded uncertainly.

"Go on," I encouraged.

"I trust your dreams, so I think Don really believes the child is his. He could have inserted some micro-drone to impregnate me. That means—" A shudder coursed through her body.

I put my hand on her shoulder, trying to comfort her.

She took a deep breath and continued, speaking fast and quiet. "My baby could have his genes. Maybe Don's trying to one-up the immaculate conception. But then the Son of God came to us. His miraculous touch could have saved not only me, but also the baby from whatever Don did. Couldn't something like that leave me glowing?"

"I guess so," I said. It was a fascinating theory. "Why haven't you told me this yet?"

"I'm still figuring all this out, still praying for answers." She sighed and breathed in deeply. Conviction replaced uncertainty in her gaze. "I also need to make sure you're with me, fully."

"How could you doubt that?"

"Because you doubt my God."

"I'm still figuring things out, too. But that doesn't change my loyalty to you. I'll do everything I can to help you."

She nodded, as if momentarily satisfied. "You see why I have to learn more? Jacques knows this baby has an unusual origin, but he can't figure out what, not without the rest of the order's help." She put her hands to her stomach. "He and Camille want to hide me until they know more. I have a feeling it will be too late by then. The order has many other wise people. I need to reach them." Her smooth face revealed no emotion as she looked at me.

"You're ready to run away?"

"Yes." There was no doubt in her voice. "I won't blindly follow a man's plan when God is leading me somewhere else. And I'm not letting you leave me alone with Camille in the middle of nowhere."

"So how do we do it?" I asked. "Don will be searching for us. He controls the world's connections—the satellites, the precept network, everything. He'll find us. Or the dragon will."

"You're still having the dream, aren't you?"

I nodded. I'd been having variations of the dream with the cottage over and over.

"What did you see most recently?"

"The same thing as before. I was with Don. We were looking for you in that remote, hilly place. He thought you were in the old stone cottage, but when we looked inside, you were gone. He was furious." I shivered in fear at the memory. "We have to keep you away from him."

"That's all? What about the baby?"

"I don't know. We didn't find you in the dream. But Don told me again that the child was his."

"Have you had any more dreams with your mother, or with mine?" Naomi asked.

I shook my head no, thinking of my father. The last time I'd dreamed of my Mom, we'd watched as a wave flooded New York City. Dad had drowned. She hadn't even tried to save him. That couldn't be true. He was my only family left. She wouldn't let him die like that. What was her role in all this?

"What are you thinking?" Naomi pried.

"About my Mom."

"She speaks to you in dreams, just like my Mom did. Why do you think they do that?"

"They both told me to protect you." I envisioned the two women together, reflecting the same radiant light as in my dreams. "They were both so spiritual, and they both died when we were eight years old. It seems like more than just a coincidence. What if they met before they died? What if they're trying to help us now?"

"How? What are they trying to tell us?"

"Every time, they've warned me about something. Your Mom told me not to let Don touch me, maybe suggesting it was okay for him to touch you. My Mom showed my Dad drowning in a flood. She told me I had to learn to fly to avoid his fate."

"You think he really died?"

I shook my head. "He's too strong. He wouldn't go down like that." I glanced down at Naomi's stomach. "My Mom also told me to protect *both* of you. I think she meant the baby. She must have known."

"Any other hints about the baby?"

"Not really, but my Mom didn't seem afraid. She called you the woman clothed with the sun. What does that mean?"

"I don't know. It's a verse. Some say she's a symbol for Israel…it could mean a lot of things." She looked up into the night sky. The thin arcs of her chin and neck caught the moonlight. When she lowered her head and looked back into my eyes, I almost staggered back. Her face glowed with a shining, confident resolve. "We leave tonight, in quiet, in secret."

"Won't Jacques try to stop us?"

She nodded. "We can do it together. Jacques said it was a long day's ride to the nearest town. They have plenty of camels. We'll take four and ride hard. With a night's head start, we'll reach the town well before Jacques. From there we'll make our way back to the U.S., reconnect our precepts, and link up with the order."

I hadn't expected her to want to reconnect her precept. "Does this have anything to do with the ISA?"

"No. I don't think it would be safe to go back there, though maybe Patrick has learned something. The point is, if the world is ending, I'm not going to sit on the sidelines waiting to see what'll happen. I'm going to fight against Don and whatever he's doing. Are you with me?"

"Yeah, I'm with you." My smile met her stern face. She was so tense. I tried a joke. "You sure I can't take you into my tent before we leave?"

She laughed lightly. "You're such a boy, Elijah." Her expression grew solemn. "Prove yourself as the man you're called to be"—she took my hands in hers—"and then maybe we'll talk of tents."

9

I stayed awake in my bed for a long time. Naomi and I had agreed we should wait until we were sure Jacques and Camille were asleep, but depart as many hours before dawn as we could. That meant fighting off sleep, despite my heavy eyes. I tried to lay calm, listening to the desert night. It was silent, interrupted only by a camel's occasional stirring and my own breathing.

Eventually the sounds lulled me deeper into my mind. I drifted to a town of low, adobe buildings. I stood in the center, where two sandy roads crossed. Military men ringed around me. They wore helmets and dark visors. On their chests were the bright blue letters "UN."

I started to walk out of the town's center. As soon as I moved, the men raised their guns. They were laser guns, like the one I had fired on Patmos. One more move, and I might have a red beam burning a hole through my heart.

"I need to leave," I said to the men, as if they cared.

"You wait here," answered one of them.

"Wait for what?"

The soldier pointed his gun up at the sky. My eyes followed the line. I saw a dot in the distance. It was approaching, and fast.

"What is it?" I asked.

Some of the guards laughed. "Bow down," one of them commanded.

I shook my head. I stood straight.

Then a gun slammed into my back from behind. I fell forward, face first onto the ground. Pain gripped me as I tried to rise up. A fierce wind swept over me. Sand stung my eyes when I tried to look around. I rubbed at them fiercely, trying to see.

Then the wind stopped. The sand settled. A sense of horror gripped me as I cracked open my sand-burned eyes. Inches from my face was the dragon. It was even bigger than I remembered. Its slitted red irises were almost as tall as me. The creature coiled its neck back—a motion I knew spelled my death. But this time it extended its head smoothly forward and rested it on the ground before me.

Only then did I see the rider. He climbed off the dragon's back. The serpent had black scales, the military men had black uniforms, but this man wore a white linen suit. He approached me and pulled off his sunglasses.

It was Don. He spoke with a smile: "Time to reconnect, Elijah. Where is she?"

I opened my mouth but something clamped over it before I could speak.

"Elijah!" came a soft whisper in my ear.

Naomi. She smelled of honey and starlight. In my half-awake state, I pulled gently on her arm, as if hoping she'd lay beside me.

She pulled her arm back. "Come on," she insisted. "Time to go."

"What? Leave now?"

"Yes, for Zag. You fell asleep," she accused. She rose and moved liked a ghost out of the tent.

I followed after her, trying to be silent, but the light shuffles of my steps sounded loud compared to her deft glide. Nothing stirred in the camp except for us. My adrenalin pulsed as I thought of Jacques sleeping in his tent. Could we really slip away without his noticing? It seemed wrong, but Naomi was right: this was the only way we were leaving together.

We approached the herd of camels slowly. Four of them were linked together in a line, which meant Naomi had already been out here, preparing. The front two camels had saddles strapped across their backs. A full moon and a billion stars were overhead. The pale light made the camels look like hairy ghosts.

Naomi touched my shoulder to get my attention. She held out her slender arm, pointing to Grabuge at the front of the caravan. I moved toward him and climbed onto the saddle as quietly as I could. The camel did not make any grunt of protest. Maybe he wanted out, too. Naomi climbed onto the camel behind Grabuge without a sound. My heartbeat sounded like the loudest noise in the desert.

I pressed my heels lightly into Grabuge's sides and off we went. The camel footsteps were like distant drumbeats. I looked back and studied the tent where Jacques and Camille were sleeping. There was no sign of movement.

We crested the low hill around the camp and ventured into the empty desert, heading south.

10

My body stayed tense and alert as we rode. The moon fell lower in the night sky to the west. The rocks and sand drifts around us were still and lifeless. The camel's swaying steps might have put me to sleep, if I hadn't expected Jacques to show up behind us any moment. He was not going to be pleased when he woke up.

Hours passed before the first hint of day appeared to the east. I watched the sky turn from grey to yellow to orange to blue. Every glance back revealed Naomi riding like a goddess, curls draping her shoulders.

She caught me staring at her when I glanced back again. There was a mischievous smile in her eyes. "I think we made it," she said.

I smiled back. "Thanks to you. Ever consider a career as a spy?"

She laughed. "I'm a little surprised. Nothing seems to get past Jacques. I felt sure he would've heard us leaving."

"We've put distance between us now." I looked past her, over the barren landscape. Nothing moved anywhere between the horizon and us. "Maybe we should take a quick break?"

"How about once we've passed that hill." Naomi pointed to a gentle slope in the distance. "With daylight arriving, the camels can see better. Let's press them. We're not free yet."

"Okay." I turned forward and dug my heels into Grabuge. He sprang ahead. We rode on in silence.

By the time we crested the next hill, our whole caravan was exhausted. In the desert, everything was further than it seemed. We untied the saddlebags full of water and food. We ate quickly and quietly. Then Naomi and I moved the saddles to the other two camels and climbed on. The whole break was maybe half an hour, and then we were riding again at the same fast trot.

"We have to slow down," I said, after another stretch of riding. "We can't burn out our camels."

"I'm not worried about that," Naomi said. "We don't have to preserve energy for the return trip. We can make it in half the time Jacques said." She peered forward and nodded. "It should be just a little further. See?"

I studied the empty expanse stretching before us. "No, I don't see anything."

"Look, there." She pointed toward the distant horizon.

I squinted my eyes and glimpsed little black dots

moving about against the bright blue sky. "Birds?"

"Exactly," she said. "And birds mean a town. We are getting closer."

As we advanced on the birds, I began to see more signs of life. A stunted tree here and there. A rusted out vehicle half covered in sand. The sun kept rising steadily and was almost directly overhead when I first glimpsed the low buildings of the town.

"I know we're trying to make our way back home," I said, "but what exactly are we planning to do once we get to this town?"

"Sell the camels and buy a ride to the next largest town." There was no doubt in Naomi's voice. "We cannot risk spending a night here."

"What if someone is there, on the lookout for us?"

"What do you mean?" Naomi asked, fixing her green eyes on mine. She suddenly had the tone of an ISA spy.

"The plane we were on," I explained, "the order's plane, it probably went down not too far from here. It would not be hard for Don to figure out we're nearby. Wouldn't he post guards to search for us?"

"Did you see something?" Naomi asked.

I shrugged.

"Another dream?"

"Yeah."

"You have to tell me!" she said. "Your dreams are your gift. What we need most from you is your vision. Please, from now on, tell me as soon as you have one."

"Okay. I wasn't trying to hide anything." I looked away

toward the horizon, feeling guilty. "You have to admit, it was an unusual wakeup. In the rush of escaping the camp, I kind of forgot about it. You know how dreams drift away with the day?"

"Elijah, you know how important your dreams are." She pulled her camel to ride closer to me. "Please."

"I know, you're right. Anyway, last night while I was trying to stay awake, I drifted off. I was in the center of a desert town. I don't know which one. There were UN guards all around me. The dragon came, and Don was riding it. He asked where you were. I woke up before I could answer."

"That doesn't sound good," Naomi said. "Do you think it was Zag? What do you think it means?"

"I wish I knew. These are the kinds of things the order is supposed to figure out."

"But maybe this was another literal one. Some of your dreams are just previews of what will actually happen."

That was not exactly true, but it was close enough. "You think we should turn back?"

"No, but we have to be extra cautious." She paused, thinking. "You should ride into town first, while I hang back with one of the camels. Sell the other three camels, try to find us a ride out of town, and then if all looks safe, come back for me."

"I don't like this."

"You'll be back in just a couple hours. Last time you dreamed of the dragon and Don in Rome, and then they came. We know from your dreams that Don wants my child, and now you've seen him coming to a desert town. Shouldn't I avoid walking right into a trap?"

"Let's say he shows up. What will you do then?"

"I'll see anything flying toward the town from here—at a safe distance. I'd at least have a chance of getting away."

Her lips were pressed tight, the way she did when she'd made up her mind. I still didn't like it. "Okay…so where are you going to hide?"

She pointed to the hull of an old truck several hundred yards to our right. "We should part here. Seen anything better than that for hiding?"

"No, but that also makes the truck stand out."

"It's the best option we have," she said. "If someone sees us both approaching, they'll have more questions. We're running out of time. You got this, Elijah?"

"Of course." I would have been a lot more confident if I had my precept, but no worries. Sell some camels and pick up a ride. Who couldn't do that?

"Good. Stay safe." She put her hand to my cheek.

"You too. I'll be back soon." I leaned forward and kissed her forehead, then rode away with my gaze fixed ahead. I would be strong.

11

The ride to the town was not far, but it seemed to take forever. Maybe because each swaying camel step took me farther away from Naomi. I hoped she was right that this was safer. I hoped this dream turned out wrong.

My caravan of camels advanced steadily, and I stayed vigilant. As the low, sand-colored buildings came into closer view, nothing seemed out of the ordinary. The town looked like it might hold a couple hundred people, at most. There were no power lines, though a handful of solar panels gleamed along the rooflines. Scattered palms rose alongside the buildings, so there had to be water somewhere—probably deep underground.

The first person I saw was a woman hanging clothes on a line to dry. She wore a black robe covering everything but her eyes. Those eyes studied me with curiosity as I approached. My sparse beard probably gave me away as a foreigner. Yet, as I rode past, she turned back to her work without a second glance.

Smooth start. Now I just needed to find someone who wanted to buy some camels.

After passing the woman, I dismounted Grabuge and led the three camels onto a paved road that looked like a main street. There were a few more people ahead. I guessed I could find a market that way.

I started to feel very out of place as I walked on. No other camels were in sight. A pack of four young boys rode past me on rusted bicycles. They pointed at me, laughed, and said something I couldn't understand. I felt eyes staring at me all around.

The crowd grew thicker as I guided my caravan forward. The road led to an intersection. It looked familiar, like the town center of my dream. I checked the sky. No clouds. No dragon.

I wiped the sweat from my brow. My breathing became faster and heavier. I did not want to enter that intersection, even if everything around me looked as peaceful as it could. It was more disturbing than comforting that my dreams had not misled me so far.

I made a split-second decision and turned off the paved road just before the town's center. It was a sandy alley. I leaned against the wall and considered my options. I needed to find a market. I needed to find someone who spoke a language I knew.

Holding the rope connecting the camels, I walked to

the end of the alley and studied the surroundings. I saw one familiar looking sight: a rusted, dented Coca-Cola sign hanging outside a two-story building. The bright red of the sign was like a beacon among the pale yellows and browns of the town. Tables and chairs were lined up outside, with a few people sitting and eating. A café. Maybe someone there could help me.

Before stepping out, I glanced behind me. A dark figure ducked into a door off the alley. Had the person been watching me, following me? There was nothing I could do about it now. I led the camels out and went to the café.

I found a pole and tied the camels to it. Surely someone would pay for them. Maybe they were the only ones in town—a rare commodity. Right?

I walked past the patrons seated outside and entered the café's open door. My eyes had to adjust to the darkness inside after the day of bright desert sun. A middle-aged man was wiping down a counter. A younger girl, also covered head-to-toe in black cloth, walked past me with a tray of steaming bowls. They looked like lentils and smelled like curry. I was starving.

"*Vouloir quelque soup?*" the man asked me. Good, he spoke French. I could work with that.

"*Parlez-vous anglais?*" I asked.

The man shook his head but then nodded past me. The waitress girl walked back in.

"*Oui*, yes," she said, with a thick Arabic accent. I could see only her eyes. They were pretty. "Would you like—"

she hesitated—"table?"

I answered slowly, enunciating each word: "I need to sell my camels. Is there a market here?"

She turned and said something to the man. He laughed and shook his head. They talked then for half a minute—way longer than it took to tell me about a market. The man eyed me with a concerned expression. It made the hairs on my neck stand.

I walked out, and fast.

"Sir!" said the girl, following after me.

"A market," I said to her, as I started untying the camels.

"Yes," she answered, "I show you."

The people eating at the café tables were watching us. This was too much attention.

"Okay, take me there."

She nodded and began walking down another road leading toward the town's center. I followed after her with the camels, my senses on high alert.

"Where you find camels?" she asked.

"In the desert. Does anyone trade them here?"

"We have camel trader, but camels not worth much."

"Why not?" I asked.

She turned onto a narrower road, this time away from the town's center.

I paused before following. "Where are we going?"

"A camel trader," she said, beckoning for me to come.

I had little choice at this point. At least we were heading away from the crowds.

The road ahead of us was empty and quiet. We were halfway down it when the woman stopped.

"What?" I asked.

Her eyes glanced over my shoulder.

I turned, but it was too late. Something pricked my neck.

A dark figure was there. I could see only the person's eyes. My last thought, before everything went black, was that the eyes looked familiar, like Aisha's.

12

Helicopters. Jets.

Their sound thrummed in my head as consciousness returned. My eyelids were heavy. I kept them closed and listened. I tried to stay perfectly still, with my head drooped to the side.

I was sitting in a chair, somewhere indoors. My hands and feet were untied, but something covered my mouth. Maybe duct tape—perfect for restraining any noise. I stayed calm, breathing through my nose. The air smelled dank but spicy, like a basement full of curry powder and saffron.

The sound of engines began to fade into the distance. I stayed motionless, trying to ignore my throbbing head. The room was quiet, but men yelled in another language outside. Their harsh voices came from above. I heard their footsteps directly overhead.

Then they passed.

There was a slight shuffle near me. I thought I heard a breath, as if someone was leaning close to my face. I considered a surprise attack—blinking my eyes open and pouncing on whoever it was. My fists clenched.

"Eli," whispered a girl's voice. "You might as well open your eyes."

I did. It *was* Aisha.

I hadn't seen her since the day of the ISA-7 test in Washington, DC. Now all I could see were her black almond eyes. That was enough. They showed fear. We were in a tiny cellar, empty except for my chair.

"Stay calm." Her voice was soft as a feather. "UN guards in town, looking for us. You've been out an hour. Help is coming."

If UN guards were in Zag, so was my dream. Had they found Naomi? Was Don here?

"You okay?" Aisha asked.

I shook my head, raising my hands to my mouth.

"Here." She grasped a corner of whatever sealed my lips between her fingers. "If you're loud," she said, "if you cause a stir, I'll kill you." She held up a small gun. "Understood?"

I nodded.

She slowly pulled away the tape. It felt like it ripped out every whisker from my scraggly beard. I winced but made no sound.

"So?" she asked.

"I didn't come here alone."

"What do you mean?"

"Naomi's out there somewhere."

For once, Aisha did a poor job hiding her surprise—or maybe it was a look of concern. Her eyes drifted away. I'd almost forgotten how it looked when someone accessed a precept in front of me. I definitely wasn't going to try accessing V. Not here, not with the UN guards around.

"I don't believe that," Aisha said, her eyes focusing on me again. "We've detected no sign of Naomi."

"Who's *we*?" I asked, my throat tightening. How was it possible that they hadn't found Naomi? Was Aisha lying? I stood slowly and met her stare. My head grazed the earthen ceiling. "What are you doing here?"

"The whole world is looking for you and Naomi. You're among the group of UN-designated 'living but missing' from the earthquakes. President Cristo learned that Naomi is in ISA-7, and he wants to find her. He knows as well as we do that your plane went down near here. I've been stationed in another town nearby. When you waltzed into Zag like a lone American cowboy, it didn't take long for someone to report you. I came immediately."

"Thanks, I guess." I didn't say that leaving was Naomi's idea, or that *President Cristo* cared about Naomi for more reasons than ISA-7. If Aisha was being honest and had no idea where Naomi was, maybe it was better to keep it that way. Could Jacques have found Naomi and taken her back? I kept my face blank. "You still haven't told me who's with you."

"You'll find out soon," she said. "How did you survive in the desert?"

"I was lucky."

She didn't budge as she held my gaze. Apparently she wasn't going to answer my question.

"Why are *you* here?" I asked, prying at a different angle.

"To help get you out."

"Why?"

"Because that's what I was ordered to do."

"Who ordered you?"

Aisha hesitated. "It's complicated."

"Somebody gave you the order. Who?"

"The Captain."

I kept my expression flat, but the thought of the bald instructor from ISA-7 brought back a flood of confused emotions.

"We're going back to Washington, Eli."

I shook my head. "Not without Naomi."

"She's not here." Aisha sounded almost sad. Her tone could not have been more different than the last time we'd talked, when we were in Washington. She had relayed a warning from Charles, to keep my distance from Naomi. Charles. My breath froze. How could I know Aisha wasn't a corpse, controlled by Don?

"You remember when you came to my hotel room a few months ago?" I ventured.

"Yes, why?" Her eyes showed no surprise, no uncertainty about my question.

"What did you tell me?"

"Don't you remember?"

"Repeat it."

She stared at me like I was crazy. "I warned you. I told you not to trust Naomi."

I breathed easier knowing that she remembered, but a new series of questions flooded my mind. "So a few months ago, you told me not to trust Naomi. Now you kidnap me and claim to be searching for her, trying to protect her. What's going on?"

"New challenges bring new alliances."

"What alliances?"

"Those of us against President Cristo. Charles and I doubted Naomi's loyalty when we discovered her connections to a group of religious fanatics. But then we lost Charles, the earthquakes came, and Cristo seized more control. Everyone in ISA-7 fears what he's doing. We are monitoring him closely. But I'm especially worried, because like Naomi, I have my own faith. I trust in the Mahdi, and he says Cristo is a forerunner, a sign of worse things to come."

"Like what?" This was more information than I'd received in weeks.

Aisha fixed her Persian eyes on mine. "I think you know better than any of us, Eli."

"Why do you say that?"

"ISA-7 gathered some images from your precept while we were in training." *Not good*, I thought. "One of the images," Aisha continued, "showed an earthquake in Rome, with St. Peter's Basilica destroyed. And then it happened. The images from your mind matched almost exactly the images from the Vatican."

I shrugged. There was no use denying it. "So?" I said. "Could be coincidence."

"Always skeptical, aren't you?" She seemed to wear a grin under her head covering. "We're going back to Washington. We'll reconnect your precept on a safe network and see what—"

A knock on the floor above cut her short.

13

Aisha rushed to where the knock had sounded. It looked like a trap door on the ceiling. A tiny device with a blinking red light was beside it.

Three metallic taps came again on the door.

Aisha tapped her fingers three times in response.

Then five more taps from above.

Aisha pressed her finger beside the blinking light. It turned green and the door fell open.

A drone flew in. It hovered like a tiny helicopter, just like in the ISA-7 simulations.

"All's clear," came a hushed and familiar voice from the drone. "We must go now."

"Patrick?" I asked.

"It's me," he said from the drone. "We'll talk later." His voice was abrupt, stiff. "We have intelligence that

President Cristo is coming to this town personally, and soon. I've secured an escape route. Follow me."

The drone flew out of the room. I stood there for a moment, stunned. Patrick knew the whole story. He was in the order. He'd sent a message to Jacques just yesterday. This seemed like my best chance for finding Naomi. I felt my hopes rising.

"Come on," Aisha said, grabbing my arm. "We have to get out before the President's force arrives."

I nodded, and we climbed out of the cellar. The drone was waiting by the door and took off as soon as we saw it. Aisha and I sprinted after it, as it zoomed through a labyrinth of alleys and buildings. Hardly anyone was in our path, and no one tried to stop us.

We reached the edge of town—looking out the same way I'd entered, with empty desert spread out before us. No sign of Naomi or her camel. I leaned over, hands on my knees, trying to catch my breath.

"Stay here," said Patrick's voice from the drone beside us. "Run when I signal."

The drone flew forward with impossible quiet. A few hundred yards out, it stopped and lowered to the ground. For an instant, everything was still. I glanced up at the sky. The late-day sun was the only spot among the immense blueness.

A bright flash drew my eyes down. The drone blinked a light on and off in quick succession, like a mirror reflecting the sun.

"Run," Aisha said. "Now." She took off at a sprint,

without a glance back.

I sucked in a huge breath and charged out, racing after Aisha. My sandaled feet threw up clouds of loose sand as I closed the distance. My heart pounded, my legs burned.

I'd almost reached Aisha—and the drone—when an immense rumbling began in front of us. The ground shook, then rose. A huge round shape emerged, covered in sand.

A plane.

Just before we reached it, a door slid open. The drone flew in, and Aisha and I dove inside after it.

The door slammed shut and the plane jerked into motion. We were soaring away before I could stand. The plane stabilized and I took in the surroundings. We were in a small supply room, with a door leading to a tube-shaped aluminum hall. It looked like the inside of the plane Chris and Patrick had been flying when they picked up Naomi and me on Patmos. Not a pleasant memory. *Where was Naomi?* I wondered, growing frantic.

"Did they see us?" Aisha asked, her eyes on Patrick's drone.

"Of course they did!" It was the Captain's angry voice, coming through the plane's intercom system. Hearing his voice again sent a shiver down my spine. "Come to the cockpit," he ordered. "Now."

"This way," Patrick said from the drone. The little hovering machine tilted, as if gesturing for us to follow.

We hurried after it down the hall. There were no signs of others. It was strangely quiet. The cockpit was a mirror copy of the other plane. Images of Bart and Gregory and the dragon flooded into my mind. I could still see the cracked windshield and Bart falling toward the desert in the dragon's jaws.

"We got lucky. They sent only a scouting force." The Captain's voice was coming from the plane's control panel. Beyond it, through the glass, were the blues of sky and ocean racing past as we flew forward. The Atlantic? "The UN will know we were there," he continued, "but it's safe for now. You'll be back soon."

"Are you sure?" I asked, thinking of my dream. "Only a scouting force?"

"Were you expecting a dragon?" asked the Captain, in a mocking voice.

"No." I kept my face smooth. If I had any chance of helping Naomi, I had to learn more. "Were you?"

"That depends on you," he said. "Patrick told me what happened to the last plane. A shame, too. We have only three of these left, and the Chinese won't be selling any for a while. They lost half their fleet to a tsunami, right after they'd sold a dozen planes to the UN."

I said nothing, puzzled as to the Captain's point.

"You know why you failed the ISA-7 test, right?" Patrick's voice sounded sympathetic, while his drone showed the emotion of a toaster.

I shook my head, surprised by his question. For once, I wished I could see Patrick's face. How was the ISA-7 test relevant? "No one told me anything," I said.

"It was my decision," said the Captain. "It didn't matter what you scored. I wasn't going to let in an unstable kid with images of disasters in his mind. But that was before your visions started matching reality. I want to know what else you've seen."

So that's it, I thought. This man had failed me out of ISA-7, and now he wanted to use me? Someone had to be lying to me, and the President of the UN and a dragon were trying to kill me. I took a slow, deep breath. This was not the time to fight. I had to preserve my options.

"I might be able to help," I said. "What's your plan?"

"We have a secure link back in Washington," the Captain answered. "We'll reconnect your precept there. You can see more then. What matters now is that we're on the same side. We want to find Naomi, just like you. ISA-7 knows now that President Cristo is a threat, even if we disagree about why." He paused. "You can understand why I questioned your sanity, right?"

I shrugged. "Maybe."

"Well, now I'm starting to think you're not crazy." The Captain did not sound entirely convinced.

Nor did Aisha look it. She had pulled off her head covering. Her beautiful face studied me with skepticism. "There must be a reasonable explanation for what is happening, and we will find it."

"Some things cannot be explained with reason," said Patrick's voice.

"We'll see," said the Captain, "now that Elijah's back on board."

14

I left the plane's cockpit to shower and shave. The little bathing chamber was far better than the desert's well water. I set the pressure settings high enough to wash off a month of sand. Then I changed into a black suit that was waiting for me on the plane. It felt tight and foreign compared to Jacques' loaned desert garb.

Where was Jacques now? I could think of no better explanation for Naomi's disappearance than her seeing danger and fleeing back to him. If Aisha and ISA-7 hadn't detected her, and Don hadn't been around, where else could she have gone? But would she have abandoned me like that? Surely Jacques had followed us and found her. He would be mad, but he was still a leader of the order. He would keep Naomi safe. I had to believe that. And wouldn't Patrick warn me if it weren't true?

The questions plagued my mind as I returned to the cockpit. Whatever Aisha and the Patrick-drone were talking about when I entered, they stopped abruptly.

"Anyone want to catch me up on the past month?" I asked, forcing an innocent tone into my voice.

Aisha met my eyes and, with her lips pressed tight together, shook her head slightly. What, she wanted me to stay quiet? Or she couldn't answer here?

"We've gone into full resistance mode against the ISA and the UN," piped in the Captain's voice.

"Who? ISA-7?"

"Yes."

"Why, and what is resistance mode?"

"It's a result of many things." The Captain's voice was clipped and stern, like always. "Here's one you know. Charles came back to ISA-7 after you were with him at the Super Bowl. He gave us false intelligence and then he disappeared, totally off the grid. After that, it did not take us long to discover his death. His body is probably at the bottom of an ocean. Don had been controlling him. No one does that to one of my agents, not even the ultimate commander."

"We believe this is happening across the world, not just to ISA-7," said Patrick's voice.

"Mostly to world influencers," added the Captain. "Just two days ago, another U.S. citizen disappeared. He was a major religious leader who had gone to Geneva for a UN conference. Patrick had warned us that this man might be taken. Remind me, what was his name?"

"Christopher Max," said Patrick.

"Right. Well, we couldn't do anything to stop it."

"So you say," replied Patrick.

"Keep up the good reports," said the Captain, "and you might regain my confidence. We can't lose another plane."

"I told you, we were attacked. I was lucky to survive. So were Naomi and Elijah." There was heat in Patrick's voice. "You have to let me try to infiltrate the UN."

"The time is not right," said the Captain. "And *you* may not be the right person."

"*We*," Aisha intervened, "have to focus on building the resistance. We cannot risk any direct missions against President Cristo. Not yet."

"Agreed," said the Captain.

It was not much longer before I saw the Washington Monument rise up on the horizon before us. I felt a surge of hope that it still stood there, unchanged. The plane soared toward the city and came to a stop over the Pentagon. The simplicity of the desert felt very far away.

"Welcome back," said the Captain's voice as the plane lowered. "Best time of year in the nation's capital."

It had been weeks since I'd left Washington en route to Rome. The city had exploded into bloom. Through the plane's windshield I could see pale pink blossoms powdering the shore across the Potomac. The river was a magnificent ribbon of glistening ripples. Maybe I'd be okay never visiting a desert again. I'd missed water like this.

"Come to my office," ordered the Captain. "Patrick,

open the roof door for them. Don't let anyone see you."

The plane's lights blinked off. The Captain had ejected from the link.

"See you in five," said Patrick's drone, as it came to a rest on the ground and went motionless.

"Let's go," said Aisha, leading the way out of the cockpit. "Things have changed around here."

15

Once we were outside, a fresh cool breeze played upon my skin—at least it felt cool compared to the desert. The greens and blues around me were overwhelming after the month of browns.

Aisha tapped my shoulder to get my attention.

"Precept disconnect," she said under her breath, to turn hers off. She held my gaze and leaned forward to whisper in my ear. "*Don't trust the Captain.*"

That would be easy enough—I never had. "Okay," I said. "Why not?"

Aisha spoke with fast, clipped words. "The Captain is past his prime. Even if he gets some things right, he is missing the bigger picture. President Cristo has outwitted him at every move. They are both trying to use you."

"Why?"

"I'd say your visions," she answered, "but the Captain doesn't really believe in those. I bet he thinks you can get him into the UN, that you can help him figure out which side Naomi is on. You're rich. You have access to places reserved for the elite."

Her words brought more questions than answers. "Like what places?" I asked. "And what's in this for you?"

"My family..." A faint smile touched her lips. "My people's leader. He is our best hope. I will introduce you. You will see. We will work together."

"Hey!" Patrick climbed out of a door in the Pentagon's roof. "Over here." He motioned for us to come, holding the door open. I'd forgotten how tall he was, how blond.

As soon as we reached him, Patrick grabbed Aisha's arm. "What is it this time?" he demanded. "You turned your precept off again. What did you say to Elijah?"

Aisha yanked her arm away. "Ask him."

They both turned to me. "So?" Patrick asked.

"We talked about Aisha's leader." It seemed like a safe starting point, but apparently it wasn't.

Patrick's face grew red as he faced Aisha again. "Your loyalty is here!" he shouted. Then he stopped, as if catching himself. He smoothed his face and continued calmly. "Please, try to leave your leader out of this. Our numbers are dwindling. We need you."

"Leave them out of this?" She was shaking her head. "Haven't you been listening to me, Patrick? The Mahdi has reappeared."

"What's a Mahdi?" I asked.

Aisha glared at me, but Patrick answered first. "She thinks her people's leader is some sort of redeemer of Islam. They believe he comes before the end of times. Well, the Iranian king, apparently he disappeared over a thousand years ago and now he's back." Patrick shrugged as if it was crazy. "The royal family, Aisha's family, they embraced him, put him on the throne. They say he's this *Mahdi*."

"It is known," Aisha insisted, with hands on her hips. "He is the Mahdi. His forehead is high. His nose is long and curved." She carved the arc of her elegant nose. "The faithful unite under him. He is no king. He is the Imam and Caliph. He fills the earth with fairness and justice. This marks the seventh year of his reign. Isa will come soon. Together they will slay Dajjal and rid the world of evil."

"Who's *Isa*?" I looked from Aisha to Patrick, and back again. "Who's *Dajjal*?"

Aisha shook her head. "For a boy with visions, for a prophet—you know nothing."

"Yeah, I know," I admitted. It seemed all the religions were coming up with some way to explain what was happening in the world. But none of them could explain the dragon I'd seen.

"Isa is Jesus in Islam," Patrick said. "Dajjal is the false messiah. It might be Don Cristo."

"Cristo is the Dajjal," Aisha agreed. She pointed to her eye. "He is blind in the right eye. Isa will come. He will pray behind the Mahdi, and they will kill Dajjal."

"Great," I said. "So why don't we just relax?"

"Prophecy must be earned. We cannot *relax*," Aisha said, through gritted teeth. "If we do, Don will kill us. Just like he killed Charles. He is killing the world."

"You think he caused the disasters?" I asked.

Aisha nodded. "His power is growing."

For once Patrick seemed to agree. "Have you heard what happened to New York?" he asked.

"No." In my dream, my Mom had shown me the city flooded, and my Dad had died.

"A tidal wave hit it just a few days ago," Patrick said. "The city still stands, but the death toll is in the thousands."

"Hear anything about my Dad?"

Patrick shook his head. "Our missions have been abroad, searching for you and Naomi. I just heard about the wave. A smaller one hit LA, too. Scientists say it's because of the earthquakes, and that they might get worse."

"It will get worse," Aisha added. "All the checks on Don Cristo's dominion are crumbling. ISA is fully in his hands, and ISA-7 can hardly monitor him anymore. We have to set up defenses in Iran, a ring of protection around the Mahdi."

"We can't just defend," Patrick countered. "We have to infiltrate Geneva. We have to rescue Chris." Patrick paused. "But you are right, our resources are limited."

"What you have to do," said the Captain's voice, "is come to my office. *Now*." His drone was hovering behind me, without making a sound. I wondered how long he'd been listening.

"Coming," said Patrick and Aisha together. They shared a look of distrustful respect. It seemed their feelings about the Captain were all that united them. We followed after his drone into the building.

The halls of the Pentagon reminded me of ISA orientation. Normal looking people scurried around doing normal looking things. The ceilings, floors, and walls might have been a century old. Modernity had barely touched this place. There was comfort in the drabness.

The comfort ended when we walked up to an anonymous looking elevator. It was tucked away in a remote corner, with no one else around. Its door was plain steel. There were no markings around it. Patrick and Aisha each reached out and pressed their hands onto the metal. The door slid open.

We stepped inside the grey box. There were no buttons. The door slid closed and down we went.

"Remember," Patrick said to me, "almost no one knows ISA-7 exists. Our badges and files show that we have random desk jobs in ISA. I checked yours. They show you'll be a summer intern for the administration bureau."

"So does this mean I'm in ISA-7 now?"

They both shook their heads. "No, but you should be soon," Aisha replied. "You still have to pass the test and survive initiation."

Survive? She sounded dead serious. "What if I don't want to take the test?" I asked.

The elevator stopped and the door opened.

Patrick stepped forward and looked back at me in disbelief. "You're still pushing, still trying to be special. We'll let you talk to the Captain about that. Speaking of, I'd avoid bringing up anything related to Naomi or her friends."

"Why?"

He stared at me, as if I should know the answer. Was he talking about the order? "Trust me. This way." He motioned for me to follow. We were in the same long hallway where we'd been attacked on our first day of orientation.

As we walked, Aisha asked me, "Does this place bring back fond memories?"

"Absolutely," I said. "The décor is so uplifting, really. And it's tough to beat the robot arms dropping from the ceiling."

Aisha grinned. "It's good to have you back, Eli."

We stopped in front of a plain door. Patrick leaned his face toward a red sensor. It blinked green a moment later.

"Guests first," Patrick said, as the door opened.

I walked right in. No use being timid now.

The smell of rubbing alcohol hit me immediately. The room was spotless. The cleanest looking room I'd ever seen. The floors, walls, and ceiling were white. Total-absence-of-color white.

"Sit," the Captain ordered without turning around.

He stood facing the blank far wall. A bundle of wires emerged from the ceiling above him and connected to the circuit board on his bald head. Because his completely white outfit blended in with the walls, his head looked like a cantaloupe suspended from the wires above.

There were six chairs. Five of them facing the one nearest to the Captain. There were no other pieces of furniture in the room. In fact, there was nothing else at all in the room.

"Take the middle seat," Patrick said to me. "This meeting is about you."

I did what he said.

Aisha and Patrick sat on either side of me.

We sat there in silence for a few moments. A question came to me.

I looked to Aisha. "Why did you come in body to Zag, if the Captain and Patrick came in drone?"

She put a finger to her lips and shook her head.

"I ask the questions in here." The Captain reached up and pulled the wires out of his head. He turned to me. I had not missed that hard glare. "Where's Sven?"

"How should I know?"

The Captain's eyes stayed locked on me as he sat slowly

in his chair, planted his hands on his knees, and leaned forward. "Who asks the questions in here?"

"You ask the questions," Patrick said. "Sven will be here in two minutes."

"Good. Before he comes, tell me Elijah, why would President Cristo let you and Naomi go in Rome, but now want so desperately to capture you?"

"How should I…"

"Answers!" shouted the Captain. "Give me answers. Save your questions for another time and place. And, '*I don't know*' is never an answer in this room."

I wanted to ask, *who do you think you are?* But I didn't. Maybe it was fear. I had a feeling this guy would just as well kill me as eat his breakfast.

"I've heard several theories about Don," I said.

"Spare me the theories." The Captain pointed his stubby finger at me. "I want to know what *you* think."

How was I supposed to answer that? *You see, Captain, Don is either the devil incarnate or a demented UN president who's a savant with technology and has a pet dragon.* No, that wouldn't work. And I certainly wasn't going to mention Naomi's baby. "Cristo wants power," I began. "For one reason or another, he thinks Naomi can help him gain more power."

"Good try," the Captain said. "At least you're not completely lying. But why Naomi, and why you?"

"Probably because we're in ISA-7." The words collided against the Captain like a stream against a dam.

"*She's* in," he said. "You're not. What about your visions? What do they mean?"

"I don't know—"

"Answers!" He jumped to his feet, his shout echoing around the room. "Do *not* say that again. Give me answers. Everyone knows enough to state an opinion."

"Don has some great power in his arsenal."

"What kind of power?"

Before I could answer, the door behind me opened.

17

"Hey-o Captain!" announced Sven. "Elijah, great to see you again. How about those earthquakes, eh? I hear you were right there in Rome. You've got to tell me more. How did it feel?"

"That can wait," interrupted the Captain. "Can you repair his precept's sync to our system?"

"Can I?" Sven bowed like a performer. "Have I not earned more faith, oh Captain my Captain? Of course!"

"Good. Do it now." The Captain looked at me. "Over there." He pointed to the wires hanging from the ceiling.

"Not wireless?"

"There's nothing like our wires," touted Sven. "Come on, you'll see."

I stood and walked to where the Captain had been standing. Everyone's eyes were on me as Sven stood behind me, poking and prodding my head.

"Yes, right here." He tapped a spot behind my left ear. "Stay still."

Sven grabbed the bundle of wires. He plucked one from the bunch, like a needle from a haystack.

"Very still!" he said with a smile. "No peeking."

I hardly felt the first little prick against my skin, but then came another, and another. Something felt lodged against the base of my skull. Wires tickled behind my ears. Then, all at once, my mind was hit by an avalanche. I was covered in so much information I could not think straight.

"All done!" Sven said, hopping back and holding a wire like a kid holds a lollipop. "Your precept is rebooted, with a secure network link and a carefully curated data dump."

"Good." The Captain moved to face me. "I can tell you're not going to give me anything today, but that'll change after you process this upload."

"That's it?" I asked. "You're not going to tell me more?" My mind tried to dig out of the information overload. There were thousands of pictures and videos of people and places, all of them with reports. It would take me a week to get through all of it, even with V's help. Having my precept back made me feel like an addict in relapse. "This must mean you expect me to come back," I managed to say, as the flood raged on in my head.

"Process the data you just received," he said. "Then you'll understand more. You'll come back when you learn that we want the same thing. We must stop President Cristo. He has taken over ISA. Without an independent

ISA, the UN has no oversight and will trample whatever remains of national resistance. We in ISA-7 are the last chance of fighting Cristo from the inside. Even if we fail, we might reveal more of what he plans so that others can stop his rise. The UN and the ISA have starved my group of resources, but we still have the best minds."

"That's why you were searching for Naomi and me," I said, as distant words came to me from my orientation here a lifetime ago. The Captain had lectured, *We watch every nation. We watch every world leader.* And so ISA-7's eyes would be on Don. And so the Captain might tolerate anyone who would serve that purpose.

"I've already said more than I should," the Captain replied. "I need you to find out everything you can about President Cristo. I believe he will contact you. We'll be watching for that. Come on, time to go."

I hesitated, looking to Patrick and Aisha. They had been strangely silent. "You're in on this?" I asked.

"Yes," Aisha answered. "We have our differences, but the same goal."

"You can trust us," Patrick agreed. "We have a shared bond. My mission is the same as yours: to find out more about Cristo's plans."

I could agree with that, but it left out my main goal. "We still we have to find Naomi."

Patrick's face tightened. He shook his head almost imperceptibly, as if warning me not to bring her up.

"I'm searching for her," Aisha said.

"We're all searching for her," the Captain added. "We

do not take missing agents lightly, especially not after what happened to Charles. I'll find her by the time you return."

"How can you be so sure?" I pressed.

"No questions. We've already said too much." He took my arm as if to escort me to the door. "You'll remember Wade Brown from orientation. He is waiting outside and will take you to the station. Your train leaves for New York within the hour. I suggest you take the ride to start on the data and form some opinions for yourself. It's best if ISA-7 gives you space for a few days."

I shook my head. "I don't understand."

An almost sad looked passed over the Captain's face. "It's in the packet," he said, running his fingers along the circuits on the side of his head. "But fine, I'll tell you now. It's some coincidence."

He hesitated.

"What?" I asked.

"That we found you today, just in time for your father's funeral."

18

My Dad. Dead. Another nightmare coming true.

Wade took me from the Pentagon to the train station. He was as friendly as I remembered, but it didn't help. I followed him onto the train in a daze. I was eighteen and alone. Both of my parents were gone, and I had no idea where Naomi was. At least I was going home.

"There's your seat," Wade said, pointing to an empty row. "I'll be across the aisle." He paused, studying me. "This will be a good time to think, process things. If you need me, I'm here for you, Eli."

I nodded, sat in my seat, and closed my eyes. As the train began gliding forward, tears pooled under my eyelids. Back to New York. Alone. I looked outside at the buildings and trees racing by in blurred lines of grey and green. The speed blurred everything almost as much as my unwanted tears.

My mind pored through the mountain of information from ISA-7. V was back in my head, but I'd told her not to speak to me. Maybe the Captain was right—some words were better to read than to hear aloud.

I blinked twice and then pressed my eyes closed again. Images flashed in my mind. V went straight to the briefings on Rome, Jakarta, San Francisco, and Tokyo—just a few of the dozens of cities hit by earthquakes or storms or tsunamis over the past month. I watched Don's speeches for each one, calling for unity and support for the disaster zones. He explained these were the consequences of a vengeful earth. He explained how people could sync with the UN's systems for immediate help. Nothing about his words sounded evil to me. If anything, they resonated. His voice made something click in my mind like never before, as if welcoming me back to the real world.

Next V took me to the briefing about my home, New York City. Suddenly I was looking out from the city, over the bay. The approaching wave rolled up like dark blue carpet in the grey light of dawn. The water came at the city like a double-decker bus. The view shifted to somewhere above, maybe from a camera on a building. I looked down at the water's onslaught. Anyone and anything on a street or the bottom floors got slammed and ripped away in the frothy turmoil.

The view's source changed to something flying through the city after the wave had struck. The buildings still stood, but the streets were like a ghost town. Most lower-level windows were broken. Cars and trains were flipped and shattered. The video panned along the avenues, scanning the destruction in fast-forward. Then signs of life emerged. A few people ran out of buildings, some crying, some screaming. They mostly looked unharmed—probably those who had been on the higher floors.

News headlines followed, with the cover photos. They ticked across my mind's eye:

New York City Swept Away.

LA and New York: Who's Next?

Wave Spares Neither Poor Nor Elite.

The next day's headlines took an optimistic turn.

The Survivors Return, Rebuild.

Mayor Seeks UN Assistance.

UN Androids Begin Repairs.

But then came a punch to the gut: *Ari Goldsmith Missing.* My father's face was below the headline. *Banking Titan's Body Found. Goldsmith Heir Is Missing.* There was a picture of me.

Then today's headline showed, May 9, 2066. It was underneath an advertisement for Mothers' Day flowers—special irony for me—*Who Will Claim The Fortune? Ari Goldsmith: 2005-2066.*

A video obituary started to flash in my mind. It began by zooming in on my Dad's smile.

"V disconnect," I said between deep breaths. I'd had enough precept for one day.

19

My knees were weak as I stood from my seat. I walked down the aisle of the train, using the shoulders of chairs for support. I came to the bathroom at the end of the train car. The door slid open. I stepped inside, locked the door, and started splashing cold water onto my face.

The water dripped down my cheeks as I stared into the mirror. Black curls hid my brow. My eyes looked like black holes rimmed with red spiderwebs. For some reason they reminded me of the dragon, which reminded me of the dream of my mother. She had warned me, but she had dropped me. Now I'd fallen into this mess, and my father was gone. I didn't even have Naomi with me anymore.

I sagged against the wall and slid to the floor. I curled up in the tiny square room and sobbed. The train stopped and started again. How many more stops?

A while later someone knocked on the door. I ignored it, figuring they'd go away. They knocked again.

"Occupied," I said, surprised by the anger in my voice.

The knocking stopped. The tears didn't. The train went through two or three more stops.

Eventually I forced myself to stand and face myself in the mirror again. I wiped away the tears. I smoothed my hair into some semblance of order. I straightened my black tie. Aside from my bloodshot eyes, or maybe because of the eyes, I looked like a scion ready to mourn his father and take over a financial empire.

With a deep breath, I gestured for the door to open. Wade Brown was standing there. Maybe he'd heard me. Maybe he'd been keeping others away from the bathroom. Wade was a good guy.

"You okay?" He clasped my shoulder in sympathy.

I nodded.

"I'm so sorry for your loss. Is there anything I can do?"

I tried to keep my face blank. No emotion. If I was going to pull myself together for what lay ahead, I might as well start practicing now. I met his eyes evenly. "How many will be at the funeral?"

"You didn't make it through all the information?" he asked. "No, I guess not. It was a lot to process in so short a time. Besides, I'm sure you saw all the important stuff. At the funeral? About a thousand. The press will be there in droves, of course."

"The press?"

"Yeah, it was in your info package."

"I didn't make it past the disasters and the news about my father."

"Okay," Wade sighed. "Well, the press has learned about your return. Someone must have seen us, and word traveled fast. They know you're on this train. Everyone wants to hear from you. It's not everyday a new trillionaire is made. Did you see our suggested talking points?"

I shook my head. "V reboot." I started to move forward. "I'll review the rest of the package on the way."

Wade held up his hand, as if to stop me. "Penn Station is crawling with them, I'm sure."

I nodded and told V to bring up the ISA talking points. I closed my eyes and they appeared. Just a few sappy lines about how sad I was, about how much I'd miss my dad, and about how important it was to keep serving our country and the world through ISA. It was nothing like Don's speeches that I'd just watched. In the face of disasters, he mesmerized his listeners. His words still snaked through my mind, as if shaping my thoughts. Or was that V? Whatever the cause, part of me suddenly yearned to have influence like Don, not to be a pawn.

I opened my eyes.

"You okay?" he asked, taking a step back, as if surprised by what he saw on my face.

"I'm ready," I said. It was time to start doing things my way. I'd had enough of doing whatever ISA and a religious order thought was right. I stepped past Wade to face the world.

20

"*Elijah Goldsmith!*" they shouted. "*Elijah Goldsmith!*"

Lights were flashing in my face. The reporters amassed on the Penn Station platform, forming a ring around me, as if the train were my stage.

"*Where were you?*"

"*Elijah, how are you feeling?*"

"*When did you last see your father?*"

More and more questions rang out.

I held up my hands. The questions stopped. The flashes continued.

"The world should know," I began, "that we will rebuild. I will use my inheritance to protect our cities from more destruction. It starts with New York City. We will clean up and grow back even stronger. Yes, the past year has been a tragic one. We should mourn the disasters. We should help the less fortunate and all those who have suffered from the earthquakes and more. But we humans survived the ice age, we New Yorkers survived other attacks, and we will survive these disasters. We get knocked down, then we get on our feet again. That's how my father would have wanted it. That's what he worked for: to leave me this legacy, so that together we can leave the world a better place."

Their faces were priceless. Jaws and eyes open wide. Maybe they'd expected more mourning. Some of them started clapping.

I sprang off the train and onto the platform. Wade rushed to my side and helped clear a path through the pack of reporters and out of the station. The cameras and questions chased after us.

"What are you going to do to protect New York?"

"Will you go straight to the funeral?"

"Who are you giving money to?"

Good, I thought, as more questions bounced off me like pellets. Their focus had shifted to my plans, instead of my past. It was safer that way.

I followed Wade to a limo waiting on the street outside. A chauffer was holding the door open. Wade and I ducked in. The door closed and a moment later we were cruising through the city, leaving the reporters behind.

"What was *that*?" Wade asked, staring at me.

"*That* was what a wealthy scion would say in the wake of a disaster." And it was the last thing a guy would say if he'd spent the past weeks hiding in the desert from a dragon.

"But today of all days?" Wade challenged. "You should be mourning."

"We all have our ways of dealing with loss." I'd done my crying. I mourned the years of lost opportunities with my Dad as much as I mourned his death. Now I could pretend there was no pain and make the most of it.

"Your way is strange." He hesitated. "Are you sure you're okay?"

I nodded.

Wade studied me, as if deciding whether to challenge me further. "This is not a game, Eli. I suggest you take more care. The guidance of ISA-7 is not to be ignored."

"I know what I'm doing."

"I hope so."

I stared out the window. Maybe I had no idea what I was doing, but apparently neither did the world. It was a beautiful late spring day, which made the devastation of the city all the more jarring. Familiar streets and buildings looked exactly as my precept had shown. The buildings still stood but their ground floor windows were shattered. Most trees lining the streets were uprooted or broken. Bright green leaves still poked out of the dying branches on sidewalks, as if blissfully unaware that their source of life was disconnected.

The limo arrived at Temple Emanu-El, across Fifth Avenue from Central Park. Its giant stone façade was brilliant in the bright sun. Its stained glass windows had survived the flood, as they were just above the wave's high-water line.

I climbed out of the limo and pressed through a group of people gathered outside the tall temple doors. I stepped inside and froze. The temple was a light-filled cavern. It had the damp smell of a tomb. Every seat seemed to be filled—a sea of people in black.

It was just as I remembered it from my last visit, after my Mom died. Eight years past, and now my losses were doubled. I had a feeling she was watching me from somewhere.

21

"You have a seat up front," whispered Wade into my ear. "I'll wait here by the door."

He nudged me forward into the temple. One step followed the next as a thousand eyes began turning to me. The few familiar faces almost made me stumble. I pulled my gaze upward to the giant panes of stained glass on the far wall. The seven windows at the top were like the seven-branched menorah, blazing in blue, red, and yellow as the sun streamed in.

After what felt like an eternity, I reached the front. To my left was an empty seat beside my uncle Jacob, aunt Sharon, and their five kids. Jacob was my Mom's brother. My closest living family. I hadn't seen him since freshman year. New York was a long way from Jerusalem.

"Glad you're here," he said, motioning for me to sit.

"Thanks." I sank into the seat and faced ahead.

Maybe they'd all been waiting for me, because a rabbi immediately took up his speaking position. He talked about God and life and death. He said practically nothing about my Dad. I figured that was fitting. It was no secret he'd been an outsider among these people without my Mom. Both of us were. As much as he'd tried to avoid temples, here he was. Death had a way of taking people to places they'd rather not go.

The burial came next. The rabbi wrapped up his eulogy and issued instructions to the crowd. We'd go to the cemetery and bury my Dad. My row left first, which meant walking back through the sea of faces. This time I kept my eyes on the floor. The red carpet squished faintly under my feet. The flood had barely dried, and here we were moving on. What else was mankind supposed to do?

Wade joined my side as I walked out of the temple. I ducked into the limo before anyone could try to talk to me. The hearse was in front of us.

"How was it?" Wade asked, once the car's door was closed.

"Fine."

He didn't ask any more questions. I found myself yearning to be with Naomi. She would know what to say right now.

A few moments later, the hearse began to creep forward. We were the second car in the procession. I glanced back and watched the line of dozens and dozens of cars inching after us through the streets of Manhattan.

The cemetery was a short drive. We exited our vehicles and made our way to the grave. The surrounding grass and the oak overhead wore the bright green of spring. The dirt beside the pit was damp and brown.

My father was in the coffin at the bottom of the hole. Part of me wanted to see him. When was the last time? In his office, over a month ago. He'd been nice that day. For some reason, that stung.

Unbidden tears were in my eyes when the rabbi started talking. The tears were running down my eyes by the time he finished and invited me to dump a load of dirt in the grave. I thought of my Mom. She would have wanted me to mourn, to cry, and even to tear my clothes. *Are you watching?*

I pulled the shovel from the ground and stabbed it into the mound of dirt. I swung it over the grave and dumped the dirt in. Two more shovel-loads and I was done. I stepped back to the ring of people around the grave and watched as others filled in more dirt. It was solemn work. My uncle Jacob went, and then his wife.

I used V to check for any status of Naomi. Nothing. I checked for our sync, but V had no sign of her. She was totally off the grid. I felt alone, alone with V, among an ocean of mourners.

When the ceremony finished, the rabbi told everyone where to come see me, encouraging them to sit *shiva*. "Elijah needs you in the days ahead," he said.

I met his gaze evenly, wishing it weren't true, wishing the lines of tears weren't on my cheeks.

The burial guests formed two parallel lines facing each other. It was custom for me to walk through them. As I did, they recited: *"HaMakom yenachem etchem b'toch she'ar avalei Tzyion V'Yirushalayim."* I didn't need my precept for that translation. They were familiar words from my childhood: *May God console you with all who mourn in the midst of the Gates of Zion and Jerusalem.*

I needed more than consolation from God, but that would be a good start.

22

"Welcome back, Master Goldsmith." Our butler bowed as he held the door open, formal as ever in his white-gloved tux. His aged face and coiffed white hair were a comforting sight. He was as much home to me as this penthouse was.

I managed a weak smile for him. "That's my father's name, Bruce. Call me Elijah."

"Master Goldsmith," he said, "this estate is yours now."

"I suppose it is. What should I do with it?"

His poised features hinted at confusion. "That is not for me to say, Master Goldsmith. I should note, however, that you will have many guests these next seven days. I am coordinating the schedule."

"How many should I expect?"

"Fifty-seven have signed up to visit so far." He bowed his head slightly, the way he did after every sentence. Nothing about the number seemed surprising to him. It was shocking to me.

"Who?" I asked. I couldn't come up with fifty-seven visitors if I tried.

"Tomorrow is mostly family. Then you have some visitors from the temple, from your school, from your father's company, and from Washington. I expect more will sign up. I will ensure you have a break between each visit."

"Thanks." I paused and rubbed my eyes. "This is going to be a long week."

"It is natural to mourn the loss of one's father." He sounded sad, as if he'd lost his own son. I guess he'd been like a dad to mine, like a grandfather to me. "I have prepared the parlor room for the *shiva* calls."

I nodded. "I guess that's the best place." The parlor had parquet floors, crystal chandeliers, and a view over Central Park. It was where my father had mourned Mom. We'd pretty much abandoned the room after that.

"Prepare my bath, Bruce. I'm going to lay down." I stepped past him.

"But Master Goldsmith," he called after me, "you are in *avel*. Custom would have you not bathe or shave or cut your hair."

I turned back and sighed. "Thanks, Bruce. I know, but I need this one exception. Look at me. I'm a mess after today." I didn't mention that after a month in the desert, after losing Naomi, after being abducted by ISA-7, and after watching my Dad buried—God could tolerate a little breach of custom for a bath.

"As you wish, Master Goldsmith."

I moved through the spotless apartment like I was in a dream. My Dad and I had spent so little time here these past few years. It looked almost more hotel than home. I went to my old room. The bed was so huge. Last night I'd slept on a cot in a tent in the desert. Naomi had been there. That had felt more comfortable than this.

I laid down on the bed and stared up at the ceiling.

"Sync to home system," I told V.

"Sync completed," she answered.

"Summary report on my financials."

"Your trust fund remains in trust until you reach twenty-one," V began. "Payments will continue on a weekly basis."

That was already more than I could spend. "And my inherited estate?" I asked.

"Your net worth is now 1.2 trillion dollars, rounded down." V sounded as excited about that fortune as she did about the sync to my home. "The estate is 47% stock, 21% real estate and mineral rights, 12% gold, 9% cash, and 11% other assets."

The *trillionare* title settled in my mind. That was enough to make me a world power. "Did my Dad leave anything to anyone other than me?"

"Yes," V answered. "A portion of his estate was left to other individuals and entities."

I figured he'd picked a few charities. Even a dead man wanted to keep a good image. "Which individuals, and what did they receive?"

"Many of your family members received one or five million dollars in cash. Seventy-four of your father's employees each received ten million dollars in cash. Fourteen of your father's other employees each received fifty million dollars in cash. Your uncle Jacob received one billion dollars in trust for his people. And finally, Donatello Cristo received forty billion dollars in cash."

23

"*What!*" I sprang off my bed. "Don Cristo?"

"One of Donatello Cristo's aliases is Don Cristo," V responded, matter of fact. "He currently holds the position of President of the United Nations."

"I know that, V. Why did my father give him money?"

"Information not available."

That was weird. I began pacing in my room. "What evidence can you find about their connection? Anything about them communicating? Report on anything you find as soon as possible."

As V began analyzing public data and everything in my system and my home's system, I considered why on earth my Dad would leave so much to Don. Maybe it was just business. The UN had major contracts and financing needs. They'd borrowed almost as much as the U.S.

government in the past couple decades. Maybe my Dad believed the UN was working for the good. What if they were? What if the order was wrong? The UN seemed to be uniting the people, taking action after the disasters. The problem could be just Don, a leader going rogue. How else could I explain what he'd done in Rome? Why did he care so much about Naomi, and about me? I remembered my Mom's voice: *you have to trust your dreams.*

"Interim report," I said, too anxious to wait for V to finish her analysis.

"Donatello Cristo has visited this home six times. He last visited three months ago."

"My home?" My mind was reeling. That meant Don's last visit would have been shortly before I'd last seen my father.

"Yes. He met with your father for seventeen minutes."

"What did they discuss?"

"Information not available. Records deleted."

Of course they were. "What else did you find?"

"Your father received several direct messages from Donatello Cristo with the subject line, *Omega Project.*"

"What do you have on the Omega Project?"

"Information not available."

"What about the messages?"

"Following receipt of three messages, your father took three immediate actions. He purchased a large land parcel in Montana. He invested three hundred million in UN robotics research. And he made arrangements to visit Geneva. No further information from the home system.

Analyzing public databases now."

Great, as if that would help. So my father met with Don about some secret project, took his investing instructions, and then left him forty billion dollars in his will? This felt dirty all over.

"Bruce," I called out, "is the bath ready?"

"Yes, Master Goldsmith." He arrived in the doorway a moment later. "Is everything okay?"

"You ever meet Donatello Cristo?"

"Why yes." Bruce stroked his chin thoughtfully, as if relishing the memory. "He was an honored guest of your father some months back."

"That's right. Any idea what they talked about, or why they met?"

"No, Master Goldsmith. As you know, such things are not my business."

"Okay," I said, "but they're my business now."

I went to the bathroom where steam rose from the marble tub. I took off my borrowed black suit and sank into the churning water. The jets made the muscles in my body unclench. I leaned my head back and rested my eyes, breathing the moist air deeply.

My breathing slowed. My mind began to drift.

Then I saw something.

It was rising from the water. A dripping wet sphere of circuitry. It spun and pulsed as if alive. The delicate nanofibers of the sphere wound around each other like a giant rubber-band ball. Ten antennae poked out of the sphere like the spokes of a satellite.

I was not afraid. I wanted to hold the sphere. I could feel its power. I wanted to use it. My bare arms reached out for it.

Just as my fingers grazed the sphere's edge, another shape coiled out of the water. I snapped my hand away. It was the dragon, but in miniature form. It had the same terrible red eyes. The same shadow and smoke coiled around it.

The dragon did not seem to see me. Its eyes saw only the sphere. It opened its jaw wide, unhinging it like a snake. With a swift bite, it swallowed the whole sphere. But the sphere did not go to its belly. It *merged* with it. The ten satellites suddenly became horns rising out of the dragon's head.

The shadows swirling around the dragon concentrated around the horns like black holes. Each hole grew bigger and bigger until they became one enormous ring of darkness. I gazed into the ring and saw a vast city. It was larger than anything on earth, but it looked underground. People crawled over it like ants. I started to reach into it, but something pulled me back. Something shook me.

"Master Goldsmith, Master Goldsmith!"

Bruce was by my side, averting his eyes and holding out a towel.

I shook my head as I woke from the dream. I was still in the bath. The water was cold.

"How long have I been in here?"

"Over an hour, Master Goldsmith," Bruce said. "My apologies for intruding, but...you were screaming."

I stood and stepped out of the tub, shivering. As I wrapped the towel around me, I asked, "Did I say any words?"

"It sounded like you were in pain." Bruce paused. "Once I thought I heard you shout the word '*Babylon.*'"

"Babylon?"

He shrugged, with concern in his eyes. "May I suggest you make your way to bed?"

"I'll have V order some dream pills."

"Please, sir, may I do that for you?"

He would have done it for my Dad. I guess he wanted to feel needed. "Okay. Check my account to find the last ones charged to me. I need them tonight."

"As you wish, Master Goldsmith."

I made my way to bed. Bruce showed up within minutes, pills in hand. I took them and collapsed, asleep as soon as my eyes closed.

24

The first *shiva* visitor was my uncle Jacob.

As Bruce escorted him into the parlor, I was reminded of Jacques. Jacob had the same strong, lean build, and the same salt-and-pepper colored hair. But unlike Jacques, Jacob's hair was cut short, probably because he was still in the military. Israeli special forces. If Jacques's background was like Jacob's, he'd be a good bet to keep Naomi safe.

Jacob sat across from me and looked me up and down. His lips pressed together. His brow furrowed. "You bathed," he said. "You put on untorn clothes."

"I was dirty. And it's good to see you, too."

He did not speak for a while after that. Bruce had arranged the two plush leather chairs by the parlor's high windows. I planned to stay in my chair for most of the week, playing the part of the quiet and somber host. The visitors could come and go, trying to keep me company. I could gaze out over Central Park while V hunted down clues about Naomi's whereabouts and Don's Omega Project. At least having a precept made me feel productive again.

Eventually my uncle broke the silence. "Elijah, you know your father and I never quite saw eye to eye, but I grieve his loss as you do."

"Thanks," I said, doubting whether he knew how I grieved, because I hardly knew myself.

"The *shiva* lasts seven days," he said. "It is right to mourn, to show some grief. That's what will be expected of you. That's what your father would have wanted."

"Does it matter any more what he wanted?"

"No." Jacob's strong hands tightened on the arms of his chair. His tanned skin matched the leather, except for the thick veins crisscrossed underneath. "But it matters what Arella would have wanted."

I met his stare. Of course he would bring up my Mom. He knew my weak spot, because she was everyone's weak spot in my family. "I'll be here grieving. Come check on me. You'll see."

"No more baths. No shaving or cutting your hair." He pointed from his eyes to mine, with the unique intensity of a career soldier. "The world is watching you."

"This is hard, Jacob."

"I know. We have these customs for a reason—to help you." He studied me, his expression softening. "Is there anything I can do?"

I shook my head. "I just need time. All this attention is a heavy weight, especially now, without my Dad."

"He was a force," Jacob said.

"I feel like I should follow his lead. I want to help our city and the world."

"*Our* city is Jerusalem, and it could use your help."

"I haven't been there since I was a boy. New York is my home. It needs my help after the flood."

"Let the UN help New York. It won't be helping Jerusalem, at least not our people."

"What about the treaty?"

Jacob's face twisted in anger. "It's been almost seven years, and that agreement has given us nothing. All it did was increase Cristo's power. Mark my words, his political success will be Israel's demise."

"Why?"

"We are stuck between him and his only remaining enemy, the Persians. They can't stand against Cristo much longer, and neither cares if we get smashed when their forces meet."

He might have been right about that. A contradiction hit me: why would my father leave money to both Jacob and Don Cristo? "You know my father left you money in his will, right?"

"Your father did no such thing," he said.

"You didn't get anything?"

"I received money on behalf of our people, but it's because of my sister and your mother, not your father. She convinced him to do this many years ago, as a condition for her leaving her home for him. She cared deeply about Jerusalem, just as you should."

"I do care. But it just seems like everybody will want something from me now. How am I supposed to know what to do?"

"Times like this turn boys into men," Jacob said, eyeing me curiously. "Whatever is going on inside you, protect your reputation and that of our family. When you don't know what to do, ask for help. We'll be here."

"Thanks. I'll do that."

"Good." He stood and put his hand down on my shoulder. "I'm sorry, Elijah. I'll come again."

With that he left. A few more relatives came after him. A distant cousin brought a chocolate cake. Three old ladies came with my great aunt. They looked like old weathered cranes, and they talked a lot. A good hour of their conversation was about whether I looked more like my Dad or my Mom. My great aunt prevailed in the end: it was Mom's nose and mouth, with Dad's eyes and hair. After they left, I actually found myself feeling better. Maybe the *shiva* calls were doing what they were supposed to do.

Throughout the visits, I stayed mostly quiet and let V continue her work. Even a precept with immense capacity, like V, took time to process the full universe of digital information. The first thing she'd found was a press report in a local Italian newspaper from seven years ago. It mentioned my father's name, and that he'd met with Don about "business." That was before Don was elected President of the UN, and after my mom had died. V kept digging, and I kept thinking about what the connection between Don and my Dad could mean.

My last visitor of the day was the old rabbi from the funeral ceremony. He sat across from me and studied me with his tired eyes for a while. The sun began to set, casting the room in a soft light. The rabbi nodded off a couple times. His dense brows were like lace curtains between us. He didn't wake until Bruce brought in a late meal.

"Lamb and lentils," Bruce said. "Your father's favorite."

The rabbi blessed the food and ate with me in awkward silence. We finished the meal and sat a while longer when I'd had enough of the silent treatment.

"Are you going to say anything, rabbi?"

His bushy eyebrows perked up at that. "Ah, yes, my boy. I've been praying for you." His voice was measured. "I think I have an answer, and it's this: my words won't mean much until you figure out what you want."

What was that supposed to mean? "I—"

He held up his hand to stop me. "Trust me, you don't know right now. Save your words." He stood slowly. "What do you want, Elijah, and what *should* you want? I'll be back for your answer. *Hamakom y'nachem etkhem b'tokh sha'ar avelei tziyon v'yrushalayim.*" The same blessing from the funeral—for God to comfort me.

Then the rabbi left. Maybe he took God with him, because I did not feel comforted in the slightest. The dream pills were some comfort, and so was my bed. It felt impossible that this was only one day after I'd awoken with

Naomi in the middle of the night in the Moroccan desert. Two of the longest days ever, though I doubted anything could top that day in Rome. Everything had changed since then, including me. I'd always wanted to be important, and now, more than ever, a voice in my head said that I was. But something deeper told me the rabbi was right. I wanted something else—starting with getting Naomi back.

25

The following day a dozen of my father's employees visited through the morning. They said thanks more times than I could count. I guess the money my father left for them meant a lot.

A few of them talked about work—banking and the financial markets. "Vultures are circling the insurance companies," one sharply dressed man said. If I was going to run my Dad's banks, I'd get to know this group better. At least they seemed loyal. They'd shown up.

After them came unexpected guests: Naomi's dad Moses and sister Rachel. They stood behind Bruce in the doorway to the parlor, looming like lanky giants.

"Hey!" I said, as I rose and rushed to them.

"I see you know each other," Bruce said, stepping aside. "They were not on the schedule, but they told me you would want to see them as soon as possible."

"Yes, of course."

As Bruce slipped away, Moses and Rachel stepped forward stiffly. Their faces wore no hint of smiles.

"What's wrong?" I asked. "Something about Naomi?"

"Turn off your precept," Moses demanded.

"Okay. V, shut down." She did as I said. "It's off. Is Naomi okay?"

"She is well," Moses replied. "She is somewhere safe."

I let out a relieved sigh. "How do you know? Where is she?" I motioned to the room. "And please, come in. I'll have Bruce bring another chair. Will you stay for lunch?"

Neither of them moved. "No," Rachel said. "We've come to deliver a message."

"What is it?"

"Last night," Rachel began, "a messenger came to us. The messenger had met with Jacques earlier that day." She looked to her father, as if questioning how much to reveal.

"Jacques shared the story of what happened." Moses's voice rumbled. "The messenger told us about how you and Naomi disobeyed clear commands. About how you ran from Jacques, in the middle of the night. About how you left my pregnant daughter by herself in the desert while UN patrols swept the area."

"It wasn't like that—"

His huge hand rose, stopping me short. "You know Jacques is one of our leaders?"

"Yes, but—"

"And you know the devil has already taken Bart, John,

Apollos, and Gregory, and that Chris has been caught?"

I nodded.

"That leaves seven leaders. Naomi was with one of them, and you tried to take her away?"

"No!" I shook my head adamantly. "It was *her* idea."

"Would she have run without you?" Rachel asked.

I opened my mouth to answer, but Moses spoke first. "A man takes responsibility," he said. "And a wise man considers his enemy and his allies. Who is your enemy, Elijah?"

"Don?"

"Is that a question?" Moses challenged.

"No, but this is complicated. You heard about Gregory, right? How could we be sure we could trust Jacques?"

"Gregory failed us, but we had our suspicions. You know a tree by its fruit."

"What does that mean?"

"You ever wonder why the dragon didn't attack you in the desert?" Moses asked.

"Sure," I said. "I don't think it could find us."

"Why not?" he pressed. "You think, just maybe, it was because you had a divinely appointed protector in your midst, praying for you?"

No, I'd never thought anything like that.

Moses clasped my shoulder and leaned close to me. "Hear me, Elijah. This is no battle of mortals. This is *not* about an agency, politics, and some powerful leader. This is about God and Satan. The last battle is coming. You better know which side you're on."

"I'm on your side," I insisted. "My loyalties to Naomi are beyond question."

"That's not enough," Rachel said. "Naomi is *on* our side, but your loyalty cannot rest in a person. You have to be loyal to the Lord."

"I'm working on it," I said, trying to dodge the topic. "What do you want from me?"

"This is not about what we want," Moses said. "Hear the rest of Jacques's message: *Naomi understands her mistake. She says to tell Elijah, please don't try to find me. I'm safe. We must trust the order. Seek the light. When you find it, you'll find me.*"

"I don't believe it," I said.

"It's true. Show him, Rachel."

"The last thing," she said, "is this." She pulled a necklace from her pocket. It was Naomi's. The one with the red ribbon and the golden cross. Rachel placed it in my hand. "She wanted you to have it."

I ran my fingers along the red ribbon, feeling ripped apart inside. Naomi was safe, but *she wanted me to stay away?* What if the order was just trying to manipulate me? I looked up and met Moses's honest eyes.

A slight smile touched his mouth. "Elijah, we all sin and fall short of the glory of God. I have hope for you, son. Naomi does, too."

"Thanks." But I wanted more than hope. I wanted facts. "Do you know where the messenger saw Jacques? Where is Naomi now?"

"We don't know," Rachel said. "It's safer that way.

Only the leaders of the order know where they'll hide."

"Where are the leaders?"

"You have bigger questions to face," Moses said. "I suggest you use this time of mourning to pray and consider your life. Consider why your vision is gifted."

"Or cursed," I said, shaking my head.

Moses's hands clasped my shoulders again. His dark eyes peered into mine. "Gifted," he said, as he pulled me into a strong embrace. He released me and stepped back. "Goodbye, Elijah. I hope we'll see you again."

26

I sat alone, in silence, after Moses and Rachel left. The message hurt. I tried to avoid it, explain it, justify it...but the pain didn't go away. I eventually turned V back on and watched videos of memories. The first day I'd met Naomi, then the night before the ISA-7 test, when she'd invited me to Rome. The memories didn't help. They only made it worse.

I set V researching Jacques. Could I believe everything in his message? My gut told me I could, as did the necklace in my hand. No matter what I felt about the Frenchman, I trusted him to take care of Naomi. He wouldn't have sent her necklace unless she agreed to it. Why had we left him in the first place?

I'd gotten no answers when, later that day, two buddies from my boarding school stopped by: Adam and Hoff. I'd known Adam Moritz as long as I'd known anyone. He looked even more Jewish than I did, and he was a quiet kid. Quiet but solid. We'd grown apart over the years, but sometimes knowing somebody long enough can make a friendship hold even as time makes the connections thin.

Hoff's real name was Dane Hoffman. Everybody at school called him Hoff. The soft sound of the name fit his pudgy body, his flaxen blonde hair, and his round, freckled, and always-scheming face.

The two of them were standing behind the chair across from me. I'd stayed in my seat, as usual.

After some small talk, Hoff asked a hard question: "So where you been the past month?"

"Trying to make my way back here," I said. I'd been preparing ways to get out of questions like this. Half-truths were better than lies.

Hoff grinned. "Think you can weasel your way out of answering me? Think we'd forget? You told us you were going to Rome with that girl you met in DC. The girl you ditched us for a hundred times this spring. Naomi, right? Did she survive the earthquake, too?"

I nodded. "It was a total disaster. Naomi had ISA connections, which helped us get out."

"So where is she now?" Hoff asked.

I fought to keep a straight face. "Wish I knew. Remember, I didn't make the cut for ISA." For once I was glad I'd told them that part. It provided a good out.

"It must have been some test," Adam said, shaking his head. "I still think they were crazy not to take you. But hey, look what happened to Charles."

"Yeah, at least you're alive," Hoff said.

"I've got that going for me," I said dourly. Were they so unconcerned about Charles's death? The memory stung.

"You've got that…and a bagillion dollars," Adam said. "Are you going to try again to get into ISA?"

"Maybe. Sometime after graduation."

"So why not live it up until then?" Hoff asked.

"Come on, man." Adam turned to him. "His dad just died. Would you feel like *living it up* if that happened to you?"

Hoff shrugged. "Yeah, probably would."

Adam sighed and turned back to me. "So how can we help you get your mind away from all this?" He gestured around the room. They were both trying in their own ways to make me loosen up. They didn't know about Naomi or the order, and they couldn't know.

"Way I see it," Hoff suggested, "you need a change of scenery. Quit this sappy crying business."

"I'm not crying, Hoff."

"You know what I mean. Let's go do something fun together. In a week, you'll be back at school, and then we graduate. Let's go somewhere, adventure. You'll need a wingman to beat off the ugly girls. They'll all be after you now, ya know?"

"Weren't they already?"

Hoff laughed at that. "Man, that was pretty good. Glad to see you're still funny behind that grim face."

Grim? I tried to put on a smile.

"So how about it?" Adam asked. "A celebratory trip after graduation? Some cultures do that, you know. Instead of *shiva*, they get everyone together to drown the memories."

"That's exactly how we Irish Vikings do it," Hoff touted, puffing out his chest.

"It's not a bad idea." If Naomi wanted me to stay away, what else was I supposed to do? It might fit others' expectations of a rich heir—a playboy venturing away to blow off some steam. "But can we do that in a time like this? A bunch of people just died in the flood."

"Of course we can," Hoff said. "President Cristo has sent in his machines. New York will be fine, probably better than ever. That guy can solve anything."

"There have been a lot of disasters lately." I gazed out the window. "Some people think the world's ending. Seems like a strange time to celebrate, right?"

"Not at all," Hoff said. "It's the perfect time. This talk of the world ending is crazy. People have been saying junk like that for centuries, but here we are. Besides, even if it is ending, shouldn't we make the most of the final days?"

Classic Hoff. I looked to Adam. "What about you, Adam? What do you think?"

He paused, glanced at Hoff, then back at me. "If tomorrow we might die, why not eat, drink, and be merry? Remember, it's in the Torah."

"I'll think about it," I said. "Have any ideas about what to do? Where to go?"

They had lots of ideas. By the end, I'd decided maybe it

would be good—even expected—that I'd get away for a while. I nudged them toward some sort of sailing journey. Adam suggested girls from school to invite. Hoff joked about the girls he'd have to keep away.

I played along as best I could, hoping the escapade could help distract everyone from what I really wanted. Everyone except me. Naomi wasn't leaving my mind any time soon.

The third day of *shiva* brought more surprises.

"You don't look sad." Those were Brie's first words. Chris's wife came by herself soon after dawn. She still looked like a supermodel, despite her seven kids and her plain black dress.

I met her eyes but didn't respond. I'd been enjoying my cappuccino and scone in the morning's golden light. I'd been enjoying being alone.

She sat down across from me and crossed her legs. She spoke with a distant smile. "I thought a boy who lost his father would be hanging his head, unable to eat."

"It's hard," I said, "but we all grieve in our own way."

She sat quietly with me, until eventually her big blue eyes began to moisten. Was she going to cry? "When did you really lose him?" she asked.

"What do you mean?"

"You lost him a while ago," she said, "I can see that now. I know how it feels. Daddy died five years ago, but he really left me a decade earlier, when he lost my mom." She paused. "You've already mourned for your father, haven't you?"

That made sense in a way. She'd come closer to the truth than all the visitors before her. "I guess you could say that," I admitted.

She nodded, as the first tear rolled down her smooth cheek.

"What's wrong?" I asked.

The tears kept falling, but her back was straight, her body still. "They took Chris, Elijah."

"I heard that. What happened?"

"You haven't seen?"

I shook my head. I felt bad. I'd almost forgotten about Chris after learning about my Dad. I was surprised Moses and Rachel hadn't said more about him.

"Here, better if you watch it." Her slender arm reached out to me, and she tapped her wrist against my temple. The most secure way to transfer data. "Go ahead," she suggested, "play it now."

I gestured for V to open the new file. I closed my eyes as a video began, transporting me to a different place. A seat in a crowd, in a row near the front.

Chris stood before me, looking every bit the mega-church pastor. We were in a stadium filled with thousands. He was on a huge stage, speaking and swaying and pulling the crowd into his message—things like *love everyone, love and peace and toleration.* Nothing strayed from what the government required of the religious leaders.

Chris was mid-sentence when a group of armed men rushed the stage. Without a word of warning, one of them slammed the butt of a gun into Chris's head. He went down limply and the men began dragging him away. There was nothing ceremonious about it. The crowd looked even more shocked than I felt. Then the screen went black.

"What did he do?" I asked, as my eyes opened.

"You know what he did," she said. "You saw it in the Cathedral—leading the real believers underground, teaching the Bible, serving the order."

"But nothing he said was against the law."

"Not in that sermon," Brie said. "He saved the real messages for the underground services, and he invited anyone who seemed to yearn for more. The problem is, he got caught."

"How?"

"Don Cristo." She swallowed as if poison were going down her throat. "The UN, the ISA, their networks are everywhere. The world has no more secrets."

I thought of the Captain, then of Naomi. Would her secret location stay secret? It made my stomach wrench. "They don't know everything," I said. "There are still things that are hidden."

"Yes, like my children. We sent them somewhere safe not long ago."

"Is everyone in the order going into hiding?"

"No, some of us fight." She paused, then put her hand on my shoulder. "You have to help Chris," she said. "Promise me."

"What can I do?"

She leaned forward, her poised face inches from mine. Her voice dropped to the softest of whispers. "I know who visited you yesterday. I know you've lost her for now, so you must know how I feel."

I nodded and began to open my mouth to speak. She put a finger over my lips, silencing me.

"Tell no one of this." She put her hands to the sides of my head. V registered something...different. "Keep it disconnected from the system. Do you understand?"

"No. What do you mean?" Brie's hands pressed against my temples. V registered the signal again. My body tensed. I gripped the arms of the chair tighter. "What are you doing?"

"Sync memory upload," she commanded.

What? Information flooded my mind, but not like the ISA-7 upload, not like my sync with Naomi. Brie had just *installed* memories. I could *remember* her memories, even without accessing my precept.

"Were you in ISA-7?" I stammered, rising to my feet.

She stood with me. "You'll see," she said, her voice strong. "Desperate times. Tell me when you learn more. I gave you instructions on how to contact me." She hugged me, then turned to leave.

My eyes escorted her to the door, while my mind took in the volumes of data.

There was pain. Suffering.

The images from her past flashed before me. Through the blur of *her* tears, I saw her father standing over her with his fists clenched. He moved to strike.

I fled from the memory before he hit her.

"Brie," I called after her.

She paused in the doorway.

"I had no idea," I said. She seemed so normal, so composed. How could anyone have guessed?

She glanced over her shoulder and nodded. "I have a healer who is bigger than those memories, but there's a reason why we were made to keep our memories to ourselves. I wish there was some other way, but we have little time left in this fight. I can't tell you more. It's too risky. You're being watched. Please, use what's in there to help Chris and to help yourself. Find your way to the edge of what's missing, and there you'll find what you need."

"Okay," I said, totally lost. "I will."

"Goodbye, Elijah." She left the room, but her memories stayed in my mind.

I waded into them. I *remembered* her alcoholic father. Her abused mother. I remembered being a scared little blonde girl with bruises on my body. There were counseling sessions. There were drugs. Then there was a friend who took me to a church. There was light. There were more counseling sessions. There were victories. Scholarships, classes, degrees. I *remembered* seeing a message inviting me to a fellowship with the International Security Agency—only, the name *Brie Madeleine* was at the top. Then the memories skipped forward to Chris and the children. There was joy. The bruises were gone from my skin, but I wore scars in my soul. Brie's skin, Brie's soul.

The memories stopped there. She hadn't given me everything. If her past was a canvas, it was like someone had gouged out parts of the painting—leaving all the context but taking the centerpieces. What had she held back? I explored her memories further, but after a while the effort exhausted me.

As I pulled my mind back into the parlor, I realized my hands were shaking. My whole body was shaking.

It was dark outside. Hours had passed.

Brie's lifetime had passed.

This was more than unnerving. It was bipolar. Could I stay sane with another person's memories inside me?

I felt broken. I needed a break.

28

I went to my bed and told V to bring up basketball highlights. I closed my eyes to watch them. The Knicks had won their playoff game in overtime last night. They were moving on to Round 2.

Would New Yorkers expect me to go to a game? It would be a sign of solidarity and support for our city. I told V to get four courtside tickets for the home game next week.

V didn't respond.

"V?" I asked.

Nothing.

"Precept status?"

I tried to focus, delving into my files. They were still there. I could still see the basketball highlights, but V was gone. Maybe the precept just needed a reboot.

"System re—"

"*Stop.*" It was a man's familiar voice in my ears, the way V's should have been. "I wouldn't do that, Elijah Roeh Goldsmith."

I jumped to my feet. My body was shaking again.

It was Don. In my precept.

"*Relax,*" he soothed, "I just want to talk to you."

"How did you—?" My voice sounded weak to my own ears. My eyes searched around the room, but of course he wasn't there. I shook my head violently, as if I could shake him out.

He laughed warmly. "It's okay," he said. "I won't hurt you. This is one benefit of your father's investment in the Omega Project.

"What are you talking about?" I demanded.

"You wanted to know about that right? How I knew him? Your precept has been running a lot of interesting searches, looking under stones better left unturned."

"You've been monitoring me."

"No need to act surprised, Elijah. Even friends keep an eye on each other."

"We're not friends."

"Not yet."

His words sent chills down my spine. I had to get away. What if he needed my home's network for this hack? I sprinted out of my room. I ran to the elevator and took it straight to the roof of the building. The night air was warm. The moon was high over the city's buildings. It was delightfully silent.

"Still here," Don whispered in my mind.

"Get out!" I shouted, gripping my head. "System reboot! Shutdown!"

"It won't work, Elijah."

"SHUTDOWN, SHUTDOWN, SHUTDOWN!"

"Easy now, take a deep breath. I told you I wouldn't hurt you. I visit only to extend an important invitation."

An invitation? I slumped down to sit on the roof, breathing heavily. "I'm listening."

"Thank you," he said. "First, let me save you and your precept some time: your father and I met a few years ago and we immediately struck a chord. He was a great man. A man of immense force. You should be proud to be his son. I see much of him in you."

"You don't know me." I thought of my Mom. I felt certain Don knew nothing of her, and so he couldn't know me. My Dad had drifted so far after she died.

"What I know is not relevant now," Don said, his voice composed. "Your father and I agreed that people needed something different, something better for their lives. He told me your mom wouldn't have died if she'd had a precept. The doctors couldn't save her, but technology could have."

"That's not true." But I had to admit it was possible.

"Your father believed it. That's what led him to me in the first place. We both knew it was no good letting humans have jobs machines could do, but what's the world to do with all those unemployed people? That's what the Omega Project is for. Your father believed in it, and he trusted me. I think you will, too."

Part of me was intrigued, but I knew better than to prolong this. The more he talked, the more I started to believe his words. That was a bad sign. "You mentioned an invitation," I said. "Why not just send me a message?"

Don responded with laughter. The sound was musical—so infectious it almost made me want to laugh with him. "You are special, Elijah. I don't talk to just anyone like this. I am inviting you and the fifty richest in the world to an exclusive meeting with me in Geneva. You'll see it in the press in a few weeks. But I'm telling you first, because I have one offer that's only for you."

I laid all the way back, staring up at the night sky. It glowed orange in the city's light. "I'm still listening," I said. "Do I have any other choice?"

"That's a deeper question than you know. Here's the offer. When you come to Geneva, if you bring the woman clothed with the sun, I'll make you the second most powerful man in the world."

Naomi? The image of the dragon popped into my head. I remembered how it had killed her on Patmos, and how it had looked at Don in Rome. I remembered my dream, and Don's fury when she wasn't in that little stone cottage. No way I was bringing Naomi to him. But could he do that? Make me the second most powerful man in the world? What did that even mean?

"I won't hurt her," Don continued. "I just want the child. After that, she'll be all yours. I can make her yours. Think about it, Elijah. Give me what I want, and I'll give you whatever you want. See you in Geneva."

I didn't answer, and he didn't say anything else. I laid there listening to the city. The sounds of taxis and people stumbling out of bars.

"What happened?" I eventually muttered.

"Temporary signal interference," answered V's cheerful voice. "But your order is received and processing for second-round Knicks tickets."

"V, shut down," I said.

"Shutting down," V replied. Then she was gone.

But not everything was the same. Brie's memories were still in my mind, as if they were my own. What had she done to me? And what was I going to do about Don's invitation? Was that why ISA-7 wanted me back? More questions and no more answers, despite the voices in my head.

29

Access. Everyone wanted access.

ISA-7 did not appreciate losing my precept's connection. The day after Brie and Don paid their visits, Wade Brown came by. He pleaded with me to connect my precept again. He asked my why I'd disconnected. He warned of the dangers of isolating myself.

I wasn't going to tell him about Don. I told him instead that I just needed a break, that all the information was too much. He did not argue with me, but he kept asking questions. He explained that the Captain and Sven had found a way to keep precepts connected through a safer link, wholly off the UN grid. I sank deeper into my leather chair and stared around absently, like any mourning son would. He eventually relented and said he was sorry for pressing me. One more visitor down.

After Wade left, more people came—more family, more classmates, more employees, and the chief executive officer of my father's company. Everyone asked me how I was doing. What a stupid question. *Seriously? How am I doing?* Well, my Dad was dead. Both parents, actually. The girl I loved was pregnant and lost in a desert somewhere, and now apparently she wanted me to stay away. If all that wasn't bad enough, maybe we could chat about how the President of the UN—the freakin' devil if you'd believe it—had invaded my mind and left his voice echoing there.

So, of course, I told everyone what I was supposed to tell them: "I'm doing okay."

The absurdity of the lie might have made me laugh, but as days five and six passed and the stream of visitors became a blur, I was feeling worse and worse. I started wondering if this was what depression felt like.

The sixth night, when I had a rare stretch of waking hours alone, I curled up in my leather chair and read an entire book. What else was I supposed to do without a precept? It was *The Catcher in the Rye*, a yellow-edged hardcover from my father's library. It was on the reading list for my English class. Hoff had told me the book was good. And it was. If Holden Caulfield were around, I'd invite him to come with Hoff and Adam and me on the sailing trip.

In the middle of the seventh and final day of *shiva*, the rabbi came again in the late afternoon. Instead of sitting with me, he stood by my side. Then he paced for a while and stood by my other side. We didn't talk much as time passed.

The sun went down. The parlor's gold leaf walls glittered in the fading light. The room's chandelier looked like a little exploded sun. The old rabbi, with his pale skin and black robes, loomed over me like a grim reaper. His body rocked this way and that. And so it went until it was dark outside.

The rabbi finally sat in the chair across from me. He looked tired. I figured I did, too.

"Am I done?" I asked. "I've mourned a lot."

He studied me but didn't answer. The old man had proved he was willing to waste a lot of time on me.

I decided to be blunt: "I think this was the worst week of my life…even worse than after my Mom died."

"I know, son." He was nodding somberly. "I've witnessed pain like this over a thousand lives, so I also know life can grow even from ashes. Now, can you tell me what you want?"

I had fewer guesses than when he'd asked a week ago. Then I'd wanted Naomi, but now I had to stay away. Then I'd been desperate to find her, but now I feared that finding her would lead Don straight to her. Then I'd had my memories, now I had Brie's as well. *So what do I want?* I turned the question around. "What do you want, rabbi?"

"That's easy," he smiled, "I crave the glory of God. Do you want that, too?"

I shrugged. "I don't know."

"I think you do know. Your problem is you're scared to admit it, and scared to commit."

"Why don't you go ahead and give me your advice?"

"Your faith is not about the girl you love."

My mouth fell open. "What?" How could he know about Naomi?

"The girl, son." He reached over the table and poked his gnarled finger at my heart. "When both of a child's parents die, the child becomes lost. But a child who has already cleaved to another is not lost. You've cleaved, son. Tell the girl you love her, get on with it, but it can't change your soul."

"What do you mean?"

He held up his two pointer fingers and drew a line in the air between them. "This is you and the girl, okay?"

"Okay."

Then he moved one of the fingers up above, and drew the lines of a triangle. "But you need to focus on this line." He moved his finger from one of the lower points to the higher one. "The link between you and God."

"I keep hearing that, in one form or another. But I need to know what to do."

"We all need that." The rabbi dipped his head, like a gracious acknowledgment. "Money can't buy wisdom, Elijah. You have to earn it—knock on God's door every day, beg for it, work and scrape for it. Then, when you get a little piece of wisdom, study it and love it and live it. The market for wisdom is scarce. Be thankful for what you get."

"Thanks, rabbi."

"What's her name?" he asked. "I won't tell anyone."

"Naomi. Naomi Parish."

"Good." His tired eyes twinkled in the chandelier's light. "I'll pray for you two. But your path has to go through God. He's not a detour."

"Okay... goodnight, rabbi."

"Goodnight, Elijah. The *shiva* is over. *Hamakom y'nachem etkhem b'tokh sha'ar avelei tziyon v'yrushalayim.*"

As he slowly ambled out, I remembered again what the last words meant: *The mourners of Zion and Jerusalem.* My Mom and Dad had taught me that, and now it brought tears to my eyes.

30

I went to my bed and laid down, without changing clothes, brushing my teeth, or taking a pill.

My eyes were heavy, but my thoughts drifted, light as feathers, to Naomi. I fingered the cross on her necklace. Was she thinking of me now? Was it really better *not* to search for her? I had a feeling that whatever I knew, Don could know, too. I feared how his silky invitation tempted me. Something about the man, the devil, was hard to resist. If God was as great as the rabbi and the order said, why wasn't he at least as appealing as Don? Maybe getting away from everything was safest for Naomi, and for me.

My mind began flipping and churning around strange places—the signs of sleep and lucid dreams. I was at school, then on a tropical island, then in a crystal building.

Eventually my Mom paid a visit. I knew it was a dream,

but I saw her clear as day. In some ways, she felt even more real than my visitors from the week.

We were walking beside each other through swamp and forest. The water around us was black. Trees grew out of it reluctantly. Their elaborate roots spread wide before plunging into the water, like a child's toes testing a frigid pool before taking a plunge.

Under our feet was a raised wooden walkway. Its surface was moss-covered and decaying. Each step of my heavy rubber boots made the thin platform creak and groan. Ahead, the path curled and weaved through the trees. It seemed endless.

My Mom's hand gripped mine tight. I looked at her, but she kept her eyes ahead. She wouldn't look at me. I saw only her profile, half hidden under dark curls.

"You're off the path, Elijah." She sounded sad.

"What path?"

"This one, the right one, the one above the muck and mire of the world. Your feet are getting wet. The reeds are slowing you down. The more you slow, the more likely you are to stop."

"This path doesn't feel safe."

"It's harder to follow than ever before."

"Let's go another way," I said. "I have boots."

"Boots are like wealth." She glanced down at my feet. "They can't stop you from sinking if you step into the deep. Then the boots become like an anchor holding you down. You would drown."

"Okay," I swallowed. "Where does the path lead?"

She kept walking and looking ahead. There was a purpose in her steps. "To the great white throne."

"What's that?"

"Do you still know so little, my son?"

"What am I supposed to do? Tell me," I pleaded, "and I'll do it."

"Life is never that simple. This is my path. You have yours. Stay on it, and maybe we'll end at the same place. Leave the path, and you'll die."

"Like Dad?" I did not hide my frustration. I wanted clarity, not metaphors.

"That is yet to be seen," said her emotionless voice.

"Why did you show me that he would die?" I asked.

"A warning to protect you."

"Protect me from what? I wasn't in New York when the wave hit."

"His death had nothing to do with the wave." Her voice broke slightly. "It began long before that."

"How long? What do you mean?"

"I was not sent to speak of this."

"Of what?"

"No, Elijah," she whispered.

We came to a split in the wooden platform. She pointed to the path leading left. "We part here."

"But I want to stay with you."

"You're not ready."

Her words were like a punch to the gut.

"Mom, I need your help."

She stopped and looked at me for the first time. She

took my face in her hands. Her eyes were full of love and grief. It made my throat clench.

"You have long been given to wander," she said. "You have squandered your gifts, and so you will continue." Her voice grew firm. "But when you see you are no longer worthy to be called his son, when you say, *treat me as one of your servants*, then you will be ready to return. Your true father's arms will be open wide, and he will say, *my son was dead, and is alive again; he was lost, and is found*." She released my face. "Goodbye, Elijah."

"Wait!" I begged. "What does that mean? Can't you tell me which path to take? I want to go the right way."

"You can't go the right way until you *know* the right way. Some things you must learn for yourself. When you do find the way, *she* will be waiting for you." She turned to walk down the path to the right.

I moved to follow but the branches of trees swung together before me, forming an organic wall.

"Who is waiting?" I shouted after her, peeping through a thin gap in the wall.

I heard my Mom's words drift over the swamp like a fresh breeze: "The woman clothed with the sun."

The words echoed in my head until the boards at my feet cracked. The sound was terrifying.

I charged toward the path to the left—the only path open for me. I tried to leap for it, but it was too late. As I pressed my foot down to jump, the platform broke.

The black water swallowed me, boots and all.

31

After my week of mourning, it was a relief to leave New York and return to my school in Massachusetts. Maybe it was wrong to go back as if nothing had happened since Rome. But the order—and perhaps Naomi herself— had stolen my goal of finding her. ISA-7 didn't seem like much help anymore. I didn't dare turn my precept back on or try sleeping again without my pills. Don's meeting in Geneva was coming. In the meantime, maybe God would show up and I'd "see the light" or "find the path" or whatever else.

Part of me wondered what would happen if I never found Naomi. I wouldn't let myself believe it, but what if? And what if the world kept on going? I wouldn't just live in a hole. I'd go to Princeton, I'd make the world a better place. I had a fortune to spend. But first I had to graduate.

So I went back to school.

My dorm room was tiny and poor compared to our Fifth Avenue penthouse, but it felt more like home. I had a twin bed, a desk, and a shared bathroom down the hall. I ate meals with people I knew. It was simpler, with simpler expectations.

I'd missed more than a month of the semester. The school's headmaster, without even asking where I'd been, had granted an exception for me. He just said he was sorry for my loss, and that the school had the deepest gratitude to my father for his years of support. I knew they wouldn't turn away their richest student ever. But, to graduate, I still had to pass exams.

That meant I had to cram.

From dawn to midnight, I lived in a corner of the library. Without V, I had to rely on the school's old-style tablets for my lessons and studies. I watched all the lectures I'd missed. I read book after book and even caught up on the homework. After five days, I took my first exam—English—and passed. I nailed the question about Holden Caulfield. I took my next exam two days later: precept coding. I aced it. ISA had picked me for a reason.

On the tenth day since I'd returned, I stumbled out of my last exam. I'd done everything required to graduate. Adam and Hoff were waiting for me when I walked out.

"Congratulations!" Adam said.

"Now you can do whatever you want," Hoff announced. "There's going to be a huge party tonight. We're here to help you get started."

"A party?" I asked, rubbing my eyes. "I'm exhausted."

"It's at the castle," Adam said, as if that was all I needed to know. "Everyone's going to be there. They'll be expecting you!"

"Yeah," Hoff added. "You've been MIA for weeks. People have all kinds of theories about you."

"Theories? Like what?" I asked.

"Some of them say you're a spy," Adam suggested. "Like an international double-agent."

"Ha," I laughed, "what else?"

"Let's see," Hoff mused. "You disappear for a month without telling anyone, and then you show up at a train station in New York right after your father dies. And the guy who's with you works for the International Security Agency." He drew a line with his finger in the air. "Even I can connect those dots."

I tried to laugh it off. "I told you I was in Rome when the earthquake hit. You know it took me a long time to make it back after that disaster."

"I know," Adam said. "But people always ask questions. You're a popular topic these days, that's all."

"So why not make the most of it?" Hoff asked. "Why not live it up? Come with us to the party. Finish with a bang!"

That's how I ended up at "the castle." It was a couple miles from our school. An alumnus who'd made a fortune growing kidneys had built the place a decade ago. Once a year, a few days before graduation, he invited all the seniors from the boarding schools in the area for a party.

"*The* party," Hoff clarified, as we walked up to the castle. There was a huge pool, a full band on stage, and a bar of champagne and cocktails. It seemed like a thousand frenzied seniors swarmed over the enormous space.

I mostly stayed on the balcony overlooking the pool and the fun. Adam and Hoff took turns bringing drinks. Lots of people came up to say hi. They said things like, *Sorry about your dad*, and *What are you doing after graduation?*

"Thanks," I'd say. "Travel the world, then Princeton."

We'd toast together, "Congratulations!"

The bubbles tickled my throat going down, and I mused about how these kinds of things might have mattered to me once. Inspiring awe in classmates, earning their respect, or at least their envy. But maybe it wasn't me, I had to admit, it was probably just the money.

True to his word, Hoff helped beat off the girls. He let the pretty ones hang around. A blonde girl named Veronica sat beside me and made me laugh. After a while, Adam told a group around us about our sailing journey. He made up plans as he went. Some of them wanted to come.

"That's okay with you, right Eli?" Hoff asked.

"Sure. I'll buy a bigger boat."

Our group grew as the evening wore on. We laughed more. We drank more. I forgot about ISA and my dreams. The band's bass rhythm took over the party. It thumped and the guests danced and bounced around the castle. At some point, a group of us dove into the pool. The water looked nothing like a black swamp. It glittered under the castle lights as it played on my numb skin. The air was electric. The world spun around me in chaotic glee. I didn't remember leaving or falling asleep.

When I woke up in my dorm room, my jeans and shoes were still on. The sun was bright on my bed. So was Veronica. How had she ended up here? I felt disgusting, my mind like a shaken jar of cotton-balls. I stood to head out for fresh air.

"You're leaving?" Veronica asked, as I opened the room's creaky old door. She was leaning up on her elbow. She was wearing one of my shirts.

"Yeah, I need some air. Have fun last night?"

"It was amazing!" she said. "Best party of the year. Hoff and I had to drag you to bed. You were hilarious—didn't want to leave the pool. You kept shouting, *It's my black water!*" Veronica laughed. "Remember?"

I stared at her blankly. *What else had I said?*

"Anyway," she continued, "we managed to get you back, and you fell right asleep. Hope you don't mind, I borrowed one of your shirts and crashed here. Hoff said you wouldn't care. It would've been a long walk back."

I shook my head, mad at Hoff but relieved that's how the night had ended. "It's fine," I told her. "You can keep the shirt."

"Thanks!" She swung her feet to the floor. "So I guess we'll be flying out in a few days for our trip, right?"

"Yeah."

"Can't wait!" Her bright smile made me think of Naomi, only shallower.

I felt desperate to get out. "I have to go," I said.

"Okay." She waved goodbye. "See you on Sunday?"

"Hoff is coordinating everything. He'll let you know where we'll meet."

"Sounds good. Bye Eli!"

My head spun and throbbed as I walked out. If this was what everyone expected of me, I might have a problem.

Thankfully, I graduated two days later.

32

The day after graduation, seven of us took my jet straight from Massachusetts to Brazil. We'd settled on a week sailing around a virgin archipelago off Brazil's northeast coast, known as Fernando de Noronha.

A limo picked us up when we landed, taking us toward the ocean. I saw the boat before I saw the harbor. It seemed bigger than the harbor itself, with a metallic mast and white sail reaching high into the sky. At Hoff's suggestion, I'd bought this brand new sixty-foot catamaran with a vintage cedar interior. From the pictures, it looked epic, so that's what I named it: *Epic*. It was even more impressive in person.

As we stepped out of the car, a man rushed to us along the dock. He was like a bronzed Brazilian god, barefoot and barechest. Long dreads were pulled back behind his head, and he wore bright green tropical shorts.

"Ho' there! Goldsmith party?" His accent was foreign and relaxed.

"You're the captain?" I asked.

He turned to me. "None other, mon." His dreads bounced as he bowed his head. "Call me Ronaldo. This ya crew?"

I nodded. "I'm Elijah." I pointed to the others one by one. "This is Hoff, Adam, Veronica, Liz, Penelope, Adley, Bea, and Madison." Hoff had insisted on the two-girls-to-one-guy ratio.

"Welcome, friends," Ronaldo smiled, "you a fine-lookin' bunch, but ya boat has already stolen my heart. She's a thing of beauty. Good times awaitin'. We still leavin' for Fernando today?"

"That's the plan," Hoff said. "I've heard it's the best destination in the hemisphere for secluded beaches, clear water, and fresh fish?"

Ronaldo laughed and held his muscled arms out wide, as if measuring a fish. "Finest yellowfin ya ever taste."

He led us onboard and showed each of us to our quarters. He prepared to set sail after that. Within an hour, we were cruising the open seas. Land soon drifted out of sight. While Ronaldo worked the boat, the rest of us drank piña coladas and laid out on the deck.

"I like this guy," Hoff was saying about Ronaldo. "Where'd you find him?"

"Funny story," I said. "With only a few days' notice, there weren't a lot of options. A friend I met in DC had sailed with Ronaldo before." I didn't mention it was Brie, or that I *remembered* that she and Chris had spent a week sailing with him. That trip was one of the holes in her memory, so I'd poked around the memory's edges as much as I could. No leads, except Ronaldo. "Turns out," I continued, "he doesn't have any listed contact information, so you have to know someone who knows him. That's how we got him." Or so I guessed. After I'd given Bruce the name, he took care of the logistics.

"Well done," said Hoff. "Always pays to know someone."

"That's why we're keeping you company, Eli," Adam joked. "Someone has to keep you from paying for the wrong things."

I smiled at the group around me. "Money couldn't buy any finer company."

The girls laughed. They were like stripes of a rainbow, each with a bikini in a different neon color. I let my eyes close. I felt the ocean breeze and remembered Naomi's face. As much as I tried to distract myself, I missed her.

After a while Ronaldo brought another round of drinks.

"Stay and have one with us," Hoff said.

"Nah mon, I don't touch the stuff. Who's going to keep this ship going straight?"

"Your loss." Hoff sighed and took a sip. "But nice work...it's delicious."

Ronaldo tipped his head. "Keep enjoyin' the ride." He turned to me. "Ain't no wound a lil' ocean salt can't cure."

And so went the sailing. We made it to Fernando de Noronha that day, with *Epic* slicing through waves faster than the dolphins leaping from the water at our sides. Hoff's skin had burned like a lobster after he fell asleep on the hull. I assigned Penelope to watch after him. It was clear enough she wanted to.

The first island where we stopped was perfect for escaping all the things that are easy to escape. But not thoughts, not memories. The bars of those cages are strong around a mind.

The next day, when we all drank too much and slept on the beach, Ronaldo planted umbrellas in the sand beside us. He also built a fire and cooked fresh yellowfin tuna. We woke and ate under the stars, with the sound of lapping waves.

The second day we explored the island. It was empty except for lizards and birds. Hoff and Penelope stayed behind. The other girls were fine company. They followed Adam and me around and laughed at our jokes. It was a blur of rum and skin and sun.

We found an outcrop of twenty-foot cliffs dropping into the water. I dove off first. I scraped up my back pretty bad on the coral. Nothing too serious, but the girls took turns rubbing on aloe.

By the third day I'd mostly stopped thinking about my family, Don, ISA, or anything else of consequence. The only exception was Naomi. I still thought about her as often as I breathed. Veronica and the other girls only made it worse. Sure, they looked great. They were fun to drink and dance with. But they were empty of substance—weightless compared to Naomi. It seemed like the further I ran, the heavier she was in my soul, and the worse her words hurt: *please don't try to find me.*

I did not remember falling asleep any of the nights. I kept V turned off, so I had no record of what happened except for the group's hazy memory. All I knew was: wake up, pour a bloody mary, and dive into the water. By noon, my head would stop throbbing and start grooving to Ronaldo's steel drum music. Then it was fresh fish, rum, and *Epic* until I woke up again.

33

By the fifth day, I was bored and annoyed. Hoff was spending all his time with Penelope. Adam cared only about the girls. It seemed like they'd given up on me.

Maybe they were afraid. I'd heard them whispering about things I said in my sleep. Apparently the dream pills had limits. I said things I couldn't remember. This morning Veronica had asked me about Naomi and the dragon. I wondered what it would be like if the group left me alone.

I'd asked Ronaldo to prepare the biggest feast yet. Now, as the sun dropped below the horizon, he was cooking a pot of lobster on a roaring fire on a secluded beach. I was drinking by myself while I watched him work. The others were swimming and laughing by the shore. *Epic* gleamed behind them, in the cove.

"Ya missin' the fun," Ronaldo said.

"Fun?" I kicked at the sand, burying my feet under the fine white powder. "This was supposed to be an escape. Now I just want an escape from them."

"They's tried to cheer you up, mon."

"Not hard enough."

"Mon, you got it bad. Can't see what ya got till ya lost it. I figure that's the way most of us do."

"Just watch," I said, "I'll be better off without them."

"I'll watch, but I've warned you, mon."

"I'm in charge here."

"As far's a man in charge, I guess that's right."

We were quiet then. I finished my drink and poured another. A full moon rose over the water. It lit a silvery path to the horizon.

Eventually Ronaldo looked out to the others. "Lobster's ready!" he shouted.

The group of them staggered toward us.

"You should have come!" Hoff said to me.

"The water's perfect!" Veronica laughed, her chest heaving and sparkling in the moonlight. "After we eat, you've gotta come. Someone's gotta show Adam how to keep his hands to himself."

They all laughed as if it were some inside joke. Veronica grabbed my hand, swaying this way and that, trying to pull me to my feet.

I yanked my hand free. "What if there isn't a next time?"

"Come on, Eli!" Adam rubbed his hand in my hair. "Lighten up, buddy. We're just having a laugh."

"That's all you guys want to do. Have a laugh."

"Aren't we here to have fun?" Hoff asked. "You got a better idea?"

"Yeah." I sprang to my feet. "You can all leave, go home."

"Come off it!" Hoff said, grinning drunkenly.

"I'm serious."

"Yeah, we can see that," Adam said, his voice rising. "One minute you're all fun, then next you're all dark and stormy. Get over yourself!"

I stepped forward, into Adam's face. "You think I invited you so you could just take whatever you wanted?"

Veronica stepped between us, facing me. "Guys, it's okay, take it easy. Eli, what's wrong?"

"What's *wrong*?" I tried to move around her but slipped in the sand and fell into her and Adam. The three of us went crashing down.

Next thing I knew, Adam and I were going at it. We rolled in the sand, shoving and kicking. I managed to pin him down and pulled back my fist to knock him out.

Then something pulled me off, my arms and legs flailing in fury. "Let me go!" I shouted.

"Nah, mon, I allow no fightin' among my crew, no matter what's the reason."

Ronaldo's burly arms gave me no quarter. My body sagged and he let me go. The world spun too fast under my feet. I willed myself to stand straight as I squared off against Adam again.

"I'm leaving," Adam threatened.

"Fine. Go ahead. Pack up tonight." I wiped my mouth. There was blood on my hand. I looked around at the group. They were staring at me as if I was crazy. "Ronaldo, make arrangements for a helicopter to fly them back at dawn."

Veronica stepped forward. "But—"

"All of you!" I shouted. Then I stormed off, without a clue where I was going.

34

I gazed up at the dragon. He was on the mountain's peak again. I'd seen him there before, with the baby in his mouth. Now his mouth was empty, except for razor teeth and a serpent's tongue. He blinked at me in contempt, as if he had no use for me.

His giant wings unfurled and flapped. The wind almost knocked me back as he took flight. His long body soared like an eagle away from me, toward flashing lights in the distance.

Not just lights. Bombs. Explosions.

I knew I could not stop the dragon. I could not stop the bombs. I could only run. Run and hide.

I turned the other way down the mountain and sprinted. I leapt over rocks and bounded toward the vast plain below. Half way down my foot caught against the root of a gnarled little tree. I tripped head over feet. I tumbled down, my body out of control. I fell and fell, reaching and searching for something to stop me.

There was nothing but the sense of falling.

After what felt like an eternity, I slammed onto the bottom. It was a flat plain, the earth cracked with dryness. I laid on my back, my body scraped and bruised, knowing this pain would take time to heal.

I breathed deeply and opened my eyes.

I was under a palm tree. I must have forgotten my dream pill and everything else before falling asleep.

My head was throbbing. My mouth was parched. The bright morning sun was painful in my eyes. My only solace was the sound—gentle lapping waves, singing tropical birds, and a soft melody on a ukulele.

Ronaldo was sitting on the shore, strumming the strings and gazing out over the perfect blue water. *Epic* was still anchored in the cove. There were no other signs of activity.

I was tempted to turn on my precept for the first time since Don had hacked into it. V would be good company. She'd confirm that all the others were gone. She'd give me reports on more disasters around the world, on people with real suffering. There was nothing like a dose of true pain and loss to cure the whining of the privileged.

But I resisted. Turning on my precept would mean access. I would not risk another visit from Don. I could not bear any more messages from the real world. Not yet.

I rose slowly to my feet and walked to Ronaldo. He

didn't budge as I sat down beside him. The song he was singing sounded familiar.

"*Riches I heed not, nor man's empty praise,*
Thou mine Inheritance, now and always…"

By the end, I'd remembered that Naomi sang the same song when she took me to her order's meeting underneath the cathedral in Washington. The memory was a world away.

"They're gone, aren't they?" I asked.

"Yeah, mon." He continued plucking quietly on his strings. "They caught another ride, like ya told 'em to."

"It's all a little fuzzy, whatever happened last night. What did they say about me this morning?"

"You really want to know?"

"Yeah, but maybe after I've had a drink. Maybe a mimosa this morning?"

He reached into a bag by his other side. He held out a bottle of water. "Try this."

"Fine, thanks." I took a long drink. "What did they say?"

"They worried about ya. They say ya still messed up since ya lost ya dad. Some say worse, too. Like the money's finally gone to ya head, or ya crazy from the start. We all hear ya sleep talk. Heavy stuff, mon."

"I'm glad they're gone," I said. "I didn't need them."

"The friends or the visions?"

His question made me laugh a little. "Neither, I guess."

"I believe ya need both, mon. A good name, a friend— they better than silver and gold. And visions? I know something of what ya seen, mon. It's more important than a good name and a friend."

"How would you know? What do you think I've seen?"

He turned to me. His dark eyes were clear and kind on his weathered face. "Think it was coincidence that led ya to pick me as ya captain?"

It was not coincidence. It was Brie's memory. "Who are you?" I asked.

"I told ya, mon. I'm Ronaldo. My grandpa was the world's best football player."

"What was his name?"

"Ronaldo."

"Never heard of him. Did he play in the NFL?"

"What's the NFL, mon? He played in the World Cup."

"Oh, you mean soccer?"

Ronaldo laughed and shook his head. "Americans still think the world turns around ya. Look, I was rich because my grandpa's feet were golden. I could've lived like this," he motioned to the boat, then to me, "trying to find meaning in the bottom of bottles and other shiny things."

His words were a punch to the gut. Was I doing what I'd accused my father of doing? I felt sick to my stomach. "So what did you do instead?" I managed to ask.

"Way I see it, mon, when ya wealth doubles, ya soul cuts in half. That's why I gave all mine away."

"Your soul?"

He let out a barrel-chested laugh. "Ya funny, mon. I wrote a big check to orphans in Rio. I walked away from the fame and the riches to serve a better master."

"By sailing the open seas as a captain for hire?"

"We all use our gifts, mon. How else ya think the Lord gonna connect me with you?"

"The Lord?" I asked, connecting the dots. Brie had led me to this man.

"None other than Jesus Cristo, mon."

I glanced at his thumb. He wore the translucent ring, like Bart, Chris, and the others. How had I missed it? *Too much rum...* "You're in the order, aren't you?"

Ronaldo smiled, his bright white teeth gleaming in the sun. "They all said ya smart, kid. Glad to see ya wits returnin'."

My heart leapt. "Do you know where Naomi is?"

"Hiding, from everybody," he answered. He tapped his finger against my forehead. "I figure ya know better than anyone."

"How should I know?"

He shrugged. "You the seer, not me."

Another surge of sickness hit me. I leaned over and spilled my insides onto the sand. I hurled out everything, lobster bits and all. It didn't make me feel any better.

"It's alright, mon." Ronaldo handed me a towel from his bag. "Sometimes ya gotta be brought low, fess up the bad to make room for the good."

"I've had dreams about that," I said, remembering my Mom's words about the wandering son.

"No worries, mon. We'll fix ya up."

35

Ronaldo and I talked a lot in the following days. We talked while we fished in the morning, while we caught lobsters and cooked them over a fire, and as the sun went down. I drank only water. I slept without dreams. The days passed simply and steadily, like my time in the desert—only without Naomi.

The best thing about Ronaldo was that he gave straight answers. I never sensed him dodging a question, unlike the other leaders of the order I'd met. He was one of the two leaders for South America. It was still hard to believe, given I'd never seen the guy wearing shoes or a shirt.

He confirmed what I'd heard from Moses and Rachel about Naomi: she was safe with Jacques. Ronaldo explained that Naomi had been in Casablanca when Jacques sent the message. But Jacques, Camille, and Naomi had fled soon after the message for a new hiding spot. Now Ronaldo didn't know where they were. The order believed it was safer for Jacques alone to know. I still had my doubts, but I also still had Naomi's necklace as a constant reminder. She wanted me to stay away. So I'd left it at that.

Ronaldo and I were grilling tuna one night when I brought up another question that had been burning inside me. "Who is the woman clothed with the sun?"

He looked up from the grill. "Mon, ain't ya got any easy questions?"

I shook my head and smiled. "Nope."

"Well, ya know where to start with a question like that."

"You'd say the Bible. I'd rather run a search in my precept, but it's turned off. Besides, I have a feeling there's no clear answer."

"Clearest answer ya can find is in scripture."

"Okay, so what's it say? Who's the woman clothed with the sun?"

"Here's what the word says." He began to recite from memory: "*Now a great sign appeared in heaven: a woman clothed with the sun, with the moon under her feet, and on her head a garland of twelve stars. Then being with child, she cried out in labor and in pain to give birth. And another sign appeared in heaven: behold, a great, fiery red dragon having seven heads and ten horns, and seven diadems on his heads. His tail drew a third of the stars of heaven and threw them to the earth. And the dragon stood before the woman who was ready to give birth, to devour her child as soon as it was born.*

And her child was caught up to God and his throne. Then the woman fled into the wilderness, where she has a place prepared by God, that they should feed her there one thousand two hundred and sixty days." Ronaldo paused. "Got it, mon?"

"Um...no." It sounded like some surreal fantasy or metaphor to me. "What's it supposed to mean?"

"Here's the rest." He seemed to have the book memorized. "After a war breaks out in heaven, this dragon goes after the woman. Then the word says, *'And the dragon was enraged with the woman, and he went to make war with the rest of her offspring, who keep the commandments of God and have the testimony of Jesus Christ.'*"

"So the woman is Naomi," I said, "and Don and his dragon are trying to kill the order?"

"Ya got the last part right. We think the enemy is tryin' to kill all twelve leaders. Only eight of us are still alive. I figure Don thinks he'll wipe us all out before this ends. He went for Bart and John first, 'cuz they had the strongest gift of prophecy."

"You have different gifts?"

"We all do, mon. You know the gifts of the spirit?"

I shook my head.

"Prophecy is one of them. Bet ya can guess why the devil wanted to take out Bart and John. God gave them glimpses of the future. They were our eyes."

"What about the rest of you?"

"Oh, we all got something," Ronaldo answered. "Apollos had knowledge. Vicente has it, too. Gregory had speakin' in tongues; same for Mehmet." *Tongues?* I wondered, but Ronaldo spoke on. "Neo and Zhang Tao are the teachers. Jacques and Emeka have wisdom. Chris is a pastor and administrator."

Makese sense, I thought, remembering Jacques's frequent nuggets of advice and Chris's convincing smile. "And you?"

Ronaldo shrugged. "Why you think God led you to me? My prayers can work a healin' in a man."

"Healing?"

"Ya, mon. I fix ya up." He pointed at my chest. "I pray ya get better, inside and out, and the Lord listen."

I guessed my gift was prophecy, too. But why weren't Don and the dragon still trying to kill me? I thought of something else Ronaldo had said. *The dragon was enraged with the woman.* "The woman you mentioned in that verse, the one who had a baby, is that supposed to be Naomi?"

Ronaldo shook his head and flipped the tuna on the grill. "Didn't Bart tell ya, mon? John's visions in this book, they mostly for people in his day, warnin' about the Romans and the fall of Jerusalem. We livin' at the end, when the dragon's unbound. Only ONE child's been born to rule the nations and be caught up to God. Ya know who that is?"

"I know who you think it is—Jesus."

He nodded.

"But what about the woman?" I asked. "Is that Mary?"

"Maybe, mon, but maybe it's the church. Some think it's Israel. No one in the order thinks it's Naomi."

"Why not?" If I was going to tell anyone, it might as

well be Ronaldo. The issue felt lighter, more open among deserted, tropical islands. "You know Naomi's pregnant. Don thinks she's the woman clothed with the sun."

Ronaldo hesitated. "About that, mon, we a bit divided." He paused again. "Ya sure ya ain't the daddy?"

I couldn't hold back a laugh. "Yeah, I'm sure."

"So why would Don think she clothed with the sun?" Ronaldo asked.

"Maybe he's the father."

Ronaldo turned slowly away from the grill and studied me. "Now ya soundin' crazy." He looked back at the grill. "Let's eat first. I need to think about ya words."

We ate on *Epic*, with our feet dangling over the clear aquamarine water. Halfway through the tuna, Ronaldo brought it up again. "So ya say the devil himself think he the father. Ya dreams show ya that, mon?"

"I've seen some hints," I said. "In one dream, Don said, *She has my child*. He also touched her in a weird way in Rome. Then, a few weeks ago, he hacked into my precept. He told me that if I bring him the woman clothed with the sun, he would make me the second most powerful man in the world." I paused, taking in Ronaldo's surprised look. "So what if Don is the father?"

He shuddered and said softly, "Ya question ain't no easy one. See, the word don't have many clues about what he'll do when he's unbound for a little while. Some say it's war. Some say chaos. I fear it's worse. Ya know why God threw Satan out of heaven, mon?"

"No," I said through a mouthful of food.

"He was the best of the angels. Lucifer, the angel of light. Problem is, sometimes the best can't handle bein' second-best. Lucifer wanted it all. The honor. The glory. The praise. But that's not how God made it. Only *He's* worthy. So Lucifer rebelled. War broke out in heaven, and Michael led the loyal angels to victory. Now, mon, if Don has Lucifer's spirit in him, what ya think he'd do if he were unbound on earth?"

"I guess he'd try to one-up God somehow. Maybe take what God did and do the same, twisting it?"

"Well said, mon. *He shall exalt himself and magnify himself above every god.*" Ronaldo gazed out over the water. "So maybe Don wants to make his *own* woman clothed with the sun. He'd find a good, innocent, and beautiful girl like Naomi. He'd make her pregnant, make it look like a miracle. He might even modify the DNA, do something to pick the gender and enhance the boy. Then she'd have his son, and he'd raise that lad to rule the world."

Strangely, that sounded like the most reasonable theory yet. "But what about the dragon?" I asked. "You know, it killed Naomi on Patmos before a man brought her back to life. Wouldn't it be on the same side as Don?"

Ronaldo's normally cool gaze lit up like a fire. "I heard about this, mon, about her dyin' and coming back. That's a miracle, and you was *there*. Chris and Jacques say ya wouldn't talk about it. Who brought her back, mon?"

"I didn't say because I don't know. Maybe an angel.

Maybe Jesus. But what about the dragon?"

Ronaldo did not look satisfied with my answer. "Ya know God has three parts, right?"

I shook my head no. Naomi had mentioned it, but I'd kind of tuned it out.

"It's the trinity, mon. Three in one. Father, Son, and Holy Spirit. The Son, Jesus, he healed when he walked on this earth. And ya think maybe ya saw him? Ya saw him healin' Naomi? Brought her back to life?"

"I don't know. How am I supposed to know? He didn't say his name."

"What did he say?"

"He told me he would defeat the dragon, and that I would learn his name. Then he told the dragon to stop, and it did."

Ronaldo clapped his hands. "Praise the Lord! Ain't nobody else stoppin' the devil. The Son of Man be comin' in full glory soon."

"If that means the dragon is defeated and Naomi is healed, I'm cool with that."

"Mon, ya gotta be more than *cool* with that. It's all that matters. Ya gotta *believe* that. Ya gotta *yearn* for that. Ya gotta give ya allegiance to the true God. Otherwise him comin' back won't do ya no good. Without him, ya goin' to the same burnin' pit as that dragon...and forever, mon."

His rhythmic words made me shiver.

"The Lord say anything else to ya?" Ronaldo asked.

I shook my head. "Don't think so."

"Think harder." He stared at me, waiting.

I went back through the memory, and one other thing came to mind. It hadn't made any sense at the time. It still didn't, but I told Ronaldo anyway: "He also said, *You are the second Elijah to come*."

Ronaldo's mouth fell open. "Now I heard it all, mon." He paused. "Listen to these words: *Behold, I will send you Elijah the prophet before the great and awesome day of the Lord comes*."

"What does that mean?"

Ronaldo shrugged. "Ask Malachi."

"Who's that?"

"I'll let ya borrow my Bible. You can read about it."

"Okay, thanks." Part of Ronaldo's little speech had left me confused. *Why hadn't I seen the dragon since Patmos?* "You mentioned the dragon and a burning pit. What's that about?"

Ronaldo hung his head, staring down at the water. He spoke low and quiet, "Mon, that's a mystery in the worst way. Ya remember what I said about the Trinity? Well, some think Satan's somethin' like that. Maybe the dragon is like Father, the true essence of evil and chaos in physical form. Maybe Don has the dark one's spirit in him. And maybe," Ronaldo hesitated, "mon, I don't want to say it, but maybe Naomi has the son in her."

I shook my head, but I knew he might be right. "Even if the baby is somehow Don's, it's human."

"I hope ya right, mon," Ronaldo sighed. "All I know is don't underestimate Satan. The Lord don't name just anybody an adversary."

"But—"

Ronaldo held up his hand and locked his eyes on mine. "More important, *never* underestimate the Lord. No matter how twisted and evil the dark one, our God is stronger. If ya wanna talk more about Jesus, I got lots to say. But I'm done guessin' about Satan. You the seer, mon. Why don't you take a look at the Good Book? Tell me what you see."

"Alright," I said.

And that's what I did, that night and the following days. I felt like I was starting to have the right questions— the kind that could wash off the black water from my dream. I was finding my way to the path my Mom had showed me.

37

The days turned into weeks. Ronaldo and I grilled our last burgers on July 4, in honor of Independence Day. My birthday, and Naomi's, came and went. Our boat's canned food supplies ran low. We mostly lived off whatever we caught. Lobster wasn't special anymore.

I finished the whole New Testament. I admitted to Ronaldo there was more to it than I'd thought. The story was fascinating, not that I believed every word. I went through Revelation at least four times. Several parts kept eating at me.

"What about these locusts with lions' teeth and scorpions' tails," I asked Ronaldo one day, while we were spearfishing in a clear, shallow cove. I remembered Bart had mentioned the armored insects. They sounded ridiculous. "It says *they had as king over them the angel of the* *bottomless pit, whose name in Hebrew is Abaddon...*is that supposed to be Don?"

"Not so clear, right?" Ronaldo said. "Some say the locusts represent armies from history. Maybe they already came, we just didn't know it. I doubt that, mon. Some say the locusts symbolize a spiritual plague of the last days. Others say they an army of demons to come, led by Satan. A few think the locusts are just what they sound like." Ronaldo stepped smoothly onto a rock and studied the water at his feet. "What ya think, seer?"

"No clue. Maybe symbolic."

Ronaldo laughed. "Ya, mon. Ain't no easy answers. Don't believe anybody who tells ya otherwise." He suddenly froze, then hurled a spear into the water. "Got one!"

And so it went. The wild visions in the book continued to drive my imagination. When I read and reread the verses about a beast with ten horns, I couldn't shake the memory of my dream with the dragon and the satellite, how they rose up from the water and merged, and how dark the world became after that.

The more I considered the words, the more certain I became about what I had to do. These were mysteries, and for whatever reason, I had some gift for seeing what others couldn't. I had to accept Don's invitation. I couldn't just stay on a boat in paradise. I had to go there. I had to help the world. I couldn't let it remain blind.

One morning in early August, I made up my mind to go to the meeting in Geneva. But first, I would pay a visit to Washington. The Captain had said ISA-7 was monitoring Don. I would learn what I could from him, and maybe reconnect with Patrick. I couldn't just waltz into Geneva knowing nothing. They could help me prepare.

I turned on my precept to arrange the travel. V came on like a lighthouse in my mind. There were messages and stories, all about...*THE MISSING ELIJAH GOLDSMITH.* I ignored them, because they weren't from Naomi or anyone in the order. I told V to send a helicopter and prepare my jet on the mainland for my return. I also told her to message Wade Brown with my arrival location and time.

"Message sent," V announced happily. "Helicopter arrival in thirty-seven minutes." I'd almost missed her voice, and her precision.

As I left my quarters for a last breath of tropical air, Ronaldo was standing outside the door.

"Ya leavin'," he said. It wasn't a question.

I nodded. "I'm going to Washington, then to Geneva."

"To the devil?"

"I've seen things, and I can't just ignore them. What if my vision can help?"

"Mon, I think ya healed. Now, ya ain't got it all figured out. None of us do, but I think ya ready."

"Thank you," I said, "for everything. And I'm sorry, but I have to go alone."

"Ya, I know." He smiled, motioning to his bare feet. "Big cities don't like people who don't wear shoes."

I smiled back. "Where will you go?"

"My work here is done," he answered. "I'm headin' back to the Holy City. The order is gathering."

"Jerusalem?"

He nodded. "You and me, we gonna meet again."

"I hope so." I paused. "You stitched up a lot of wounds, Ronaldo."

He shook his head. "The Lord did that, mon, and he ain't done with you yet."

Not long after that, we said our goodbyes and I flew off in a chopper. I found myself hoping he was right that we'd meet again. Hoping he wouldn't be Don's next target.

38

V guided me through the news on the flight to Washington. It seemed like there were hundreds of stories about me. Rumors and lies, or at least half-truths. Some said I'd disappeared with a harem of girls. They called me an international playboy. It hurt when I thought of Naomi seeing this.

One story profiled Veronica. She refused to say where I was hiding, but confirmed that I'd sailed away to a tropical paradise. She alluded to her complicated *relationship* with me, and how she hoped I'd come back soon. But she also alluded to *another girl*. She said her name was Naomi, and that I talked about her in my sleep. No one had met her. One report said Naomi was a virtual girlfriend. It almost made me laugh.

More recently, the news focused on Don's invitation of

the richest to Geneva. The big mystery was whether I'd show up. Four days prior, Don had answered a question about me specifically in a press briefing. He'd said, "Of course my friend Eli will come! My ties to his family run deep."

By the time my plane landed, I knew what to expect from the reporters. Dozens of them crowded outside my plane, as if I were a celebrity. Maybe I looked the part, with my aviator glasses and Brazilian bronze tan. Ronaldo would have been proud, if only I'd been barefoot.

I decided to say nothing. Let the mystery build.

I walked out the plane's door. Wade Brown cleared a path between the reporters to the black limo.

"Goldsmith!" they shouted. "Goldsmith!"

It was déjà vu.

"Where have you been?" asked one of them.

"Are you going to Geneva?" asked another.

The questions filled the air faster than even my precept-fueled mind could process them: *What is your connection to the ISA? How does it feel to have graduated? Who is Naomi? How does Naomi feel about Veronica? How far back do you go with Don Cristo? What are you going to do with your fortune?*

I remembered one of Ronaldo's sayings: "When ya fame and fortune double, ya soul's cut in half." I'd have to avoid that, and the reporters.

I reached the limo and ducked in. Wade followed after.

"Nice tan," he said, as the car raced away. "Invite me next time?"

"If there is a next time."

The Washington Monument was gleaming white across the Potomac, like a mast. A beautiful late summer day, as if nothing were wrong with the world. It seemed some cities were unscathed by the disasters. DC's shield still held.

"The Captain is waiting for you," Wade said.

"Is he in a good mood?"

"About the same as always." Wade's voice dropped to a whisper. "Turn your precept off?"

"Precept shutdown." As V faded, I asked, "Why? You think Don is listening?"

"Not now, but he could hack into your system again."

"You know about that?"

"We figured it out. We're not sure how much data he got last time, or what he told you. But I also want your precept off because I'm going to tell you something the Captain might not." He paused, taking a deep breath. "You need to know how thin we are stretched, Eli. The Captain won't say it, but things are looking bad. We lost three more agents last week. There are only seven agents left in ISA-7, and we're counting you."

"Seven?" I'd figured there were dozens, if not hundreds.

"We are watched closely," Wade continued. "The ISA, our parent organization, hasn't funded us since Don came into power. Our budget is down to almost nothing. We can't afford to train another class, not safely anyway. But we still have some secrets. Like the Captain and your class. We've done everything we can to make ISA think your group is really just a bunch of student fellows."

Wade glanced out the window, then back at me. Our car had arrived at the Pentagon.

"I've served ISA-7 most of my life," he said. "I've never seen things this bad. The truth is, I'm scared. First the disasters, and now all these lost agents—y'all are like my kids. It's one thing to lose a few here and there in the drone wars. This feels different. Like someone's handing them over, double-crossing. We always knew the UN had capacity for great power. With that can come good as well as bad. ISA-7 was one of the checks on that power. Without us, and under President Cristo, I fear the UN has bad things on the horizon."

"Agreed. That's one of the reasons I'm here."

"I'm glad you are. The Captain took it pretty hard when you didn't come back after the funeral." The way he said it made me think he'd taken it hard, too.

"I'm here now. What about Patrick and Aisha? Have you heard from them?"

He nodded. "They're on a mission in the Middle East. I don't know more than that. The Captain does, but he's grown more secretive."

More secretive? That seemed impossible.

Wade pushed the button to open his door. "Let's go. The Captain is waiting."

I followed him into the building. People in the halls stopped when I walked by to stare at me. Apparently the news about me was mainstream.

Wade led me up to the second floor to a hall of boring looking doors. He pointed to one of them. "The Captain's in there."

"Really?" It looked nothing like the Captain's room in the bowels of the building, or the training room at the top.

Wade nodded. "You'll be leaving straight from here, so this is goodbye." He held out his hand.

Leaving? Going where? I thought, as I shook his hand.

Before I could ask, Wade pressed his palm to the panel beside the door. As it opened, Wade smiled at me, seeming genuinely happy. Maybe I was later than expected, but he'd predicted it right: I came back to ISA-7.

30

The Captain was standing inside in a plain business suit and tie. He looked like he'd lost twenty pounds.

"Come in," he ordered.

I stepped in and the door slid shut behind me. The office reminded me of Bart's—dusty and antique, without a hint of technology. There was even a stack of papers on one corner of a desk, beside a plain black box. The window behind the desk was open. It looked out over a small courtyard. A fresh breeze stirred the room's dust.

I sneezed.

"Gesundheit," the Captain said. "Sit." He motioned to one of the chairs. We sat across from each other, leaving the chair behind the desk empty. "Precept off?" he asked.

I nodded.

"You've kept me waiting," he said. "Now the day has

finally come. President Cristo's invitation hit the press last week. Is that why you're back? You want my help in Geneva?"

He'd gone straight to the point, so I did the same: "Yes. I want to be prepared going in."

The Captain leaned forward in his chair and grinned at me. "We're very different, Elijah, but I think we can come to an agreement. If my hunches are right, you also want to find Naomi so you can protect her from Cristo, yes?"

"He must not find her." I kept a straight face, even as the Captain's words brought back the pain of Naomi wanting me to stay away. This was not about her. This is about what *I* needed to do.

"And you don't care that much about the politics or the religion, do you?"

"Stopping Don is my priority right now."

"On a first name basis with the President?" the Captain asked. "You see, I don't care about the religious crap, but the politics is in my bones. There's only one thing I want, and you're my best chance for getting it."

"What's that?"

"The same thing you want."

"If you'll prepare me to face Don, we can work from there."

"Shhh," he whispered, holding his finger over his lips.

He picked up a piece of paper and a pen from the desk. This was getting weird. I'd never seen the Captain avoid technology. He wrote something short and held the paper in front of me.

The tiny scrawled words said: *To kill DC.*

Whoa, bold. "But you're talking about Don Cr—"

"Don't say it!" he breathed out.

He pulled out a lighter and lit the paper on fire. He dropped it in a half-full trashcan and smoke drifted up into the room.

"I can scrub your precept, make it safe from him. I can get you a clean, secure link, free from Don's meddling. All I ask in return is that you help me get close in Geneva. He's watching for me. I need a cover. Got it?"

My first instinct was to run away from this as fast as I could. But getting rid of Don, without risking my own neck? That seemed worth working with the Captain, even if I didn't trust him.

"Okay," I said.

He held out his hand. "Welcome to ISA-7."

I looked down at it. I coughed. The smoke was starting to sting my eyes. "So I don't have to take the test?"

"You already did. In January. Your score was tied for the highest ever, even higher than mine."

What? I failed to hide my shock.

The Captain spoke on, "You and Naomi—we've never seen anyone with the capacity to sync the way you two can. Good job. It's in the record books."

"But you failed me?"

"I figured you learned why from your father."

Not entirely, I thought. My father had said nothing about how I actually did on the test. But it was clear he had wanted me out of ISA, and he always got what he wanted.

"I thought it had to do with my visions."

"Oh, you're crazy," the Captain said. "But your mind is exceptional. We would have let you in," he shrugged, "if not for your father's offer. We might have shut down without his funding. Ironic, right? The same money that bought you that enhanced brain bought your way out of using it for us."

I took a deep breath. This wasn't about the test, or about my father. This was about Don. "If money buys anything, how much to buy an ISA-7 plane?"

"Smart boy. But those aren't for sale. You know what I want. You help me get there, and you can have the plane and whatever else you want from ISA-7."

"If I agree, what's next?"

He reached over to the black box on the desk. He tapped it and pulled out a long string. "You ready to go?"

"I guess so. Where are we going?"

He placed the loose end of the string in the trashcan where paper still smoldered. The string lit like a fuse.

"We run," he whispered, "and in case anyone asks, I died in here. No backing out now. Got it?"

Before I could answer, the fire alarm went off.

The Captain pulled on a broad-rimmed hat and handed me a similar one. His hat covered the circuits on the side of his head. "Keep your head down."

I followed after him as he hurried out. We paced quickly down the Pentagon's main hall.

We'd walked a hundred yards when...*boom!*

The room where we'd been exploded in flames.

40

Pandemonium erupted in the Pentagon. The Captain and I joined hundreds of office workers racing out of the building. Everyone's eyes were on exit signs, but the Captain and I kept our heads down for good measure.

Once we were outside, the Captain walked briskly with the masses streaming out of the building's main entrance. As he led me across the vast parking lot, I considered turning and running. He'd acted so fast, so unexpected. Now the ISA surely had a record of me with him. He was right, there was no turning back now.

We'd crossed the parking lot and reached a thin strip of grass by a highway when he turned to me. "We're waiting for Sven," he shouted, over the rising sound of sirens. "He'll reconnect our precepts to a safer system. Here's our ride."

An old red pickup truck stopped in front of us. A glance back showed no one outside the Pentagon paying us any attention. Emergency vehicles were filling the parking lot between the building and us.

"Hurry, get in," the Captain said as he opened the passenger-side door.

Sven was behind the steering wheel.

I jumped in and slid to the middle of the seat.

"Hey Eli!" Sven said. "Like our ride? It's the Captain's."

"I thought we were trying to avoid attention. How old is this thing?"

"Fifty-nine years old," the Captain boasted, closing the door. "It was made the year I was born. It was almost the last year they made a truck without a computer system. Runs exclusively on gas. We might get some attention, but not for the reasons we're worried about."

As I was puzzling over why the Captain would own a truck, much less one this old, Sven accelerated down the highway. Trees swept by on either side, and the Potomac River flowed in a rocky valley to our right. We were heading west, out of the city.

"Where are we going?" I asked.

"I don't know," the Captain said.

"You're kidding, right?" I'd assumed we were heading to some secret ISA-7 base. "You just blew up part of the Pentagon, and now you don't have an escape plan?"

"Sven picked us up. That was the plan. If I'd known where we're going, ISA would have been able to track us down. Besides, I knew you'd come up with a place. You've got the fortune. Where can we hide for a week, before we go to Geneva? There's a lot you need to learn."

"What kind of place are you looking for?"

"Something extremely remote, but still in the United States. Sven has arranged a plane. Anywhere out west?"

"Let me think." *Where to go?* We needed somewhere hidden. Without V's help, for some reason I thought of Brie. She'd said her children were in hiding. I plunged into her most recent memories. I saw her kids—seven of them—through her tearful eyes. I remembered how adorable they were. They were hugging me and saying goodbye. Mountains were in the background. I *remembered*: Montana. Then my own memories came back. My father owned a ranch in Montana. It seemed like my best chance of reconnecting with the order. Why not try? "How about Montana?" I suggested.

"Have you ever been there?" the Captain asked.

"No, but my father bought land there just last year. He told me the market for cattle would be tight this year. The ranch has cows roaming its ten thousand acres."

"Perfect. You know the coordinates?"

"My precept has the information."

"Don't connect it until we're further away. Sven, you can get us to Montana undetected, right?"

"Of course, we're heading to our plane now. But I'll need the coordinates, and you'll have to cut out your tracker."

"I know," the Captain said, sounding grim. "Pull over

there."

He pointed to an exit for a scenic view. Sven took the exit and parked. It was a little loop off the highway, just large enough for twenty parking spots and a few picnic tables overlooking the Potomac River below. Only two other cars were there, and no one was in sight.

The Captain hopped out and sat at one of the tables. He pulled a long knife from his boot.

"What's he doing?" I asked.

"There's more to the Captain than you might think," Sven said. "Ask him when he comes back. You need to reboot your precept and write down the location in Montana. Then shut off your precept again. Here." He handed me a notepad and a pencil.

I did as he said. V showed me the coordinates and I wrote them down. I ignored the queue of messages and briefings and shut down V again.

"How long until we can reconnect?" I asked.

"I'll set up a link once we arrive," Sven said. "I bought a satellite last year. We'll use it. No one knows it's connected to me, and I'm on vacation this week."

"Vacation?"

"Yeah, the Captain took every precaution to keep our team from being followed. I usually take time off in a virtual world. So I'm logged in there, and my avatar is fighting dragons on auto-pilot. No one looking for me would raise an eyebrow about that."

"Interesting," I said, readying a quip about my virtual girlfriend. But then the Captain walked past us, blood streaking down his arm.

"Back in the truck," he grunted.

Sven and I climbed in. The Captain sat beside me again. He was holding gauze clamped over his forearm. His shirt sleeve had blood all over it.

"You cut out your tracker?" I asked, as Sven pulled back onto the highway.

"Not just my tracker." The Captain held up a nanochip and another tiny device he had smashed. I hadn't seen anything like it before. It was like a minuscule chrome centipede.

"What is it?" I asked.

He lowered his window and tossed the two pieces into the forest blurring by. "It's an early prototype of what every ISA agent gets these days."

I looked down at my own wrist. It had a standard data card, but not the centipede. "So I didn't get one because I failed the test?"

The Captain nodded with either a grimace or a smile on his face. It was hard to tell.

"What does it do?"

"It's a biometric reader," the Captain said.

"These bugs are a work of beauty," Sven added. "You can program it to bore into a person's body and do pretty much anything."

I shivered at the thought. The tiny dot on Naomi's stomach sprang to my mind. Could Don have used a bug to impregnate her?

"They're not available outside ISA," Sven continued.

"Every agent has to have one. They provide health and location data to the ISA's database. But these things have so much potential." His voice grew excited. "You could even control somebody through the bug. First you'd program it to crawl through an agent's body and into the mind. Then it links with the precept, where it can alter neural pathways. Imagine the power!"

"I don't have to imagine it," the Captain said. "I think Cristo's been sending stuff into our agents. He didn't try it with me. But now that I'm dead, I can't have my biometric data feeding into the system."

"So we can't be tracked now?" I asked.

"Right, but guess who can be?"

"All other ISA-7 agents?"

He nodded. "When Sven reconnects our precepts, I'll have him include their tracker coordinates."

"But—" Sven began.

"You can do it," the Captain interrupted. "Elijah, you'll be able to see exactly where they are. See, I'm giving you what I can, so you'll give me access to Cristo."

I wanted to learn Naomi's location, but how would it help? I couldn't go to her. And it did little to assuage my growing fear: was it really possible to help the Captain— while he tried to kill Don—without ending up dead myself?

41

"Here we are," Sven announced.

Apparently "here" was the old Central Intelligence Agency's building in Langley, Virginia. When the ISA took over intelligence thirty years ago, the government moved the Environmental Protection Agency to this spot.

"I thought we were trying to stay hidden," I said. It didn't make any sense to go into another government building, even if this one's spies were long gone and replaced by climate scientists.

"You'll see," Sven said, as we drove down the long entrance road. "Old properties like this have tricks up their sleeves. You know what they say, 'once a spy, always a spy.' I figure that applies to buildings, too."

We drove past the main building and parked outside a small warehouse. It faced the woods, and no one was in sight. We hopped out of the truck and Sven leaned his face in front of a scanner by the door. It lifted open and revealed a disc-shaped plane filling the space inside. The plane looked like the same one that had picked me up in Morocco a couple months ago.

"Nice work," the Captain said, as he inspected the plane.

"Aren't they going to notice if it's missing?" I asked.

"Not this one," Sven bragged. "I removed the tracker and gave it to Aisha and Patrick. They buried it near an airfield outside Tehran. Anyone looking will think they're still using it for their mission."

Aisha and Patrick. Was their mission still trying to stop Don? Naomi had wanted me to find Patrick. "What are they doing in Iran?" I asked.

"We have an alliance with the Iranian leader," the Captain said dismissively.

The Mahdi. "What kind of alliance?"

"The only kind that matters—taking down our shared enemy. We'll be in contact with them soon."

Sven pressed a button on the bottom of the plane, and a ladder dropped to the floor. "All aboard!"

I glanced back, out of the hangar. They had to have cameras everywhere around here. "Won't someone notice us leaving?" I asked. "You said yourself there are only a couple of these planes left."

"A few might notice," the Captain answered, "but they can't catch us and can't track us." He began to climb the ladder. "Come on, time's wasting."

We boarded the plane and went to the cockpit. As the warehouse's ceiling slid open, it revealed bright blue sky through the windshield. I tried to shake off the memories of Bart and the dragon. Where was the dragon now? It was almost as if the creature had forgotten about me. Not that I was complaining.

A few moments later the Captain fired up the engine. We shot up into the air like a rocket. Someone definitely had to notice, but maybe the Captain was right. No alarms went off in the complex below.

"It's a little over two thousand miles," Sven explained, once we were airborne and zooming through the sky. "It should take about an hour. Hey, I saw a lake near your father's land. Know anything about it? We need a place to park this."

I shook my head. "I've never been there. All the info is on my precept, but you're the only one with a precept connected."

"So I am." Sven grinned. "Makes you kind of depend on me, huh?"

Sven talked on about the plane's technology for a while. The Captain sat quietly, staring out the dash. It was not long before we were lowering over the lake in Montana. The Captain landed it in shallow water near the shore, just like its sister ship had in Patmos. This time no reporter, or anyone else, was around to welcome us.

42

The Captain led Sven and me to the back of the plane, where a ramp had opened and extended onto the shore. A green military truck was waiting on the ramp.

"You brought this?" I asked.

The Captain rubbed his hand along the bar across the vehicle's open top. "It's normal stock for the plane, but Sven stripped it. Now it has the best tires and engine of today, without an ounce of working circuitry."

We loaded in, and the Captain drove onto shore.

"Wait here," Sven said. As the Captain stopped the vehicle, Sven gestured toward the plane. It shut its doors like a clam, drifted away from shore, and then sank underwater. "No one will find it until we return."

"Well done." The Captain sounded almost happy as he drove away. Maybe he liked the fresh air. The view over golden plains to immense mountains to the west probably helped, too. No wonder my father had wanted land out here.

As we barreled through the open country, I felt a million miles away from yesterday. It felt harder to steer my path without Ronaldo around; he'd been like my rudder while adrift at sea.

"They're also precept holdouts." Sven's words caught my attention. He'd been telling the Captain what he'd learned about the couple that maintained my father's ranch. My ranch. "The government's list of holdouts is getting shorter, but cities are still the focus. Remote places like this"—Sven motioned around us—"are last in line for mandatory precept sweeps. I figure it'll be done within a couple years. Despite lacking precepts, though, these two have logged some unusual activity."

"What do you mean?" I asked.

"Their supply orders," Sven answered. "They've gotten way more food than two people could eat in a year."

"Maybe they're stockpiling for a disaster?"

"Maybe," the Captain said, doubtful. "We just need a few days to set up for our mission. No matter what these people are hiding, it's safer here than in DC."

The Captain went on to explain that, once we arrived, he would pretend to be my personal assistant. Sven would be a consultant from one of my new tech startups. I'd be myself, the inherited landowner coming on a whim to see his ranch.

The sun was an orange ball hovering over the

mountaintops when we first saw the herd of cows. A man on a horse waved and rode toward us. As we got closer, he took off his cowboy hat. I'd never seen anything like it, except in clips from old movies.

"Hey there, strangers," the cowboy greeted us with a half smile. "What brings you out here?" The man had bright blue eyes, blonde hair to his shoulders, and a wide jaw.

"To see some beautiful country," the Captain answered, climbing out of the vehicle.

The cowboy swung off his horse and began pulling off his worn leather gloves. "You've come to the right place." He held out his hand to the Captain. "I'm Tristan Baines."

The Captain shook his hand. "I'm Prescott Walker. You can call me Scott." And just like that, I learned the man's name, or at least a name he called himself. "I'm the assistant for Mr. Goldsmith." He turned and bowed his head slightly to me, like a herald announcing my arrival.

I stepped forward and held out my hand. "I'm Elijah Goldsmith. I own this land."

Tristan shook my hand and spit out a dark liquid at the ground. It landed a couple inches from my feet. "Goldsmith, eh? Last I'd heard, some fella named Jones owned it."

"My father bought it last year."

"So doesn't your father own it?" Tristan's hand drifted to a gun at his side and rested easy on the holster.

"He's dead."

"So it goes," Tristan said. "The land changes hands, but

it stays under my feet. I figure the herd has more claim to it than any of us. They're the ones chewing the cud." He spit another wad of dark juice on the ground.

"You know that stuff will kill you," Sven chimed in. "How do you get tobacco out here anyway?"

"I grow it." Tristan sounded amused. "And you are?"

The Swede adjusted his glasses. "Sven Thorsson. I'm a technology consultant."

"Consultants…" Tristan sneered. "You know, Sven, out here lots of things will kill you. Most kill fast, too. A bear'll finish you in a minute, and bitter cold will shut you down in a day. I like things that take years to kill. Like time and tobacco."

"Elijah just wanted to come check out the place," the Captain intervened. "We'll lay low for a few days and get some rest."

"No better place than here," Tristan said. "We've got room in the barn."

"Does the barn have electricity?" Sven asked.

Tristan let out a little laugh. "It's the twenty-first century, ain't it?"

43

"You hungry?" Tristan asked as he swung down from his horse. "We're having stew tonight."

We'd agreed to follow him, which meant slow going as the sun set behind the wall of mountains to the west. Now, just before dark, we'd reached a cluster of small buildings.

Tristan first showed us the barn, where he unsaddled and fed his horse. Seven other horses were inside, but at least a dozen stalls were empty. The back of the barn had lighting and a work bench. Tristan probably used it for fixing horseshoes, but Sven told us it would suffice for a telecommunications base. He'd brought enough gear to hack into ISA.

Next Tristan led us to the cabin beside the barn. The home was made of huge timbers, wider than my arm was long. There was a pot cooking on a wood-burning stove.

The pipe reached up two stories to poke out of the steeply vaulted ceiling above. The cabin couldn't have had more than five rooms, but it felt grand all the same. The smell of roasted meat made my stomach growl.

"Mara?" Tristan called.

A woman emerged from a room in the back. Her eyes opened wide in surprise. She looked like a true native, with high cheekbones, dark wide-set eyes, and straight black hair down to her waist.

"Guests?" she asked, striding toward Tristan. "You could have warned me." She put her hands on his cheeks and smiled up into his eyes.

He bent forward and kissed her. "Thought you'd like a surprise."

She laughed and turned to us. "You must forgive him," she said. "He spends most of his days with the herd, so he can be a little rough with people. I'm Maralah. In my people's tongue, it means born during an earthquake. But please, call me Mara."

"I'm Scott," said the Captain, tipping his hat toward Mara. He kept it on his head, though. I realized Tristan had not yet seen the circuits there. "We're from out of town."

"I can see that," Mara said. "Well, welcome to Blackfeet lands. And who are you?" She looked at me.

"I'm Elijah Goldsmith. My father bought this ranch, but he died a couple months ago, so it passed to me."

"Elijah." She stepped forward and clasped my hand. Her touch was warm. "I'm sorry for your loss. We will mourn with you. It's good that you're here. We will share in this land's beauty. It can heal sorrows, especially in this season."

"Thank you, Mara." I found myself smiling. I sensed something in this woman that reminded me of Naomi.

"And I'm Sven!" the Swede chimed in, as if feeling ignored.

"Nice to meet you all," Mara replied, motioning to the table. "Please, sit. Luckily, I've made a large batch of stew." She moved over to the pot and began filling bowls.

"You know what I like about herding cattle?" Tristan asked, as we took our seats.

I shook my head. "What?"

"Plenty of meat. We eat well."

Mara brought the food to the table.

"Hat's off at dinner," Tristan said to the Captain.

"I'd rather not."

"Then you can leave."

The Captain opened his mouth but stopped short of speaking. He reached up slowly and took off the hat. The metal circuits on the side of his shaved head gleamed in the room's warm light.

"Satisfied?" he asked.

Mara's eyes opened wide, but Tristan nodded as if this was nothing unusual. "I'll bless the food," he said, bowing his head. "Lord, we welcome these guests in peace. Bless their visit, bless this meal, and bring healing to our world. Amen."

"Amen," Mara echoed.

The order? Someone in the order would say a prayer like

that, but why would they give it away? Perhaps Brie's memory had led me to them again.

What were we doing here?

We began eating. The Captain and Sven seemed focused on the food. Mara and I caught each other's eyes. She didn't look away.

"The stew is delicious," I said.

Mara smiled. "Thank you."

"What kind of meat?" Sven asked. "Deer?"

"Beef," Tristan answered.

"Right." Sven swallowed. "It's good. So…you shoot your own cows?"

Tristan shook his head and sighed.

"What?" Sven glanced at me. "Did I say something wrong?"

"You don't shoot a cow," the Captain said. "You slit its throat."

"Oh."

From there, we ate mostly in quiet. The Captain said nothing as he devoured the food, rigid as a soldier. The silence grew more and more uncomfortable.

After a while I broke the silence, "So, Mara, how long have you lived here?"

"All my life," she said proudly. "Tristan came ten years ago, after he finished school. He was going to work the ranch for a summer, but then he met me."

"Never went back." Tristan smiled at her. "Life's better here."

"Better?" asked Sven. "But you have no connection to

the world."

"Exactly," Tristan said.

"The land provides what we need," Mara added. "We have good work for our hands. We have books to pass the winter. We keep each other warm. What else could we want?"

"You could want to make the world better," the Captain answered. "It could use more honest people like you."

She glanced at him with plain skepticism. I felt the same doubt. The Captain I knew didn't talk like that.

"Tell them," Tristan encouraged Mara.

She shook her head. "It's a heavy story."

"Look at them," he said. "They're afraid. I bet they are running straight into this. They should know what they face." Tristan leaned back in his chair and folded his hands behind his head, gazing at us.

"What are you talking about?" I asked.

"Listen," Tristan said. "She'll tell you."

"The earth is dying, friends." Mara's somber eyes met mine. "Since my birth, the earth has groaned with the pains of death. Eight signs of my people have come, and only the ninth remains." Her voice grew deeper, as if imitating an old man. "*You will hear of a dwelling-place in the heavens, above the earth, that shall fall with a great crash.*" She raised her arms overhead and closed her eyes. "*These are the signs that great destruction is coming. The world shall rock to and fro. The white man will battle against other people in other lands—with those who possessed the first light of wisdom.*"

The room fell into quiet. I could hear Sven chewing loudly. After a moment, Mara opened her eyes again. She looked somehow smaller, meeker.

"What is this supposed to mean?" the Captain asked, shifting in his seat. "Why are you telling us this?"

Mara's eyes bored into me. "Perhaps Elijah knows. The signs of it are in his eyes. The earth cracks and groans and prepares for destruction."

My mind went to Don, to the Vatican and to the dragon. "There have been earthquakes," I said, "just as there have always been."

She smiled at me. "This is a safe place, Elijah. You need not fear while you are here. Tristan's God will protect you from these rising evils."

I kept my face blank. My body was tense.

"What does Eli have to do with this?" Sven asked.

"That's enough for now," Tristan said. "Mara, you can ask them more later. They've had a long day." He rose to his feet. "I'll take them to the beds in the barn."

"The barn!" Mara protested. "No, no, they will sleep in here, as guests in our home. I will make the beds on the loft."

Tristan hesitated, but then nodded. "They must keep their work in the barn." He looked to the Captain. "Understood?"

"Understood," the Captain answered.

"And um…I was wondering if we could tune your power, like all of it," Sven said.

"I figured," Tristan said. "We don't need it. How long

will you be here?"

"A week or two, at most," the Captain replied. "Sven may leave within a few days, if he can finish his work."

"Fine. Come on." Tristan led us up to the loft, where there were four bunks tucked under the eaves of the giant timber rafters.

I laid in my bunk and thought of Mara's words. *The signs of it are in his eyes.* What was that supposed to mean? I doubted it had anything to do with my precept lenses. I realized why Mara reminded me of Naomi. There was a depth to her.

As my mind drifted, thoughts of Naomi blanketed me. I fell into her depths, and into sleep.

44

I laid flat on my back on a stone slab. My arms were crossed over my chest. Naomi was beside me in the same position. Our bodies were close, but could not touch. I knew without trying that we could not move. We stared up into the sky, only it wasn't a sky. We were in a white space. No color existed around us.

"They must find each other." It was my mother's voice, distant and desperate.

"They must reunite." Was that Naomi's mother? Where were they? It almost sounded like they were in the stone underneath us.

"Not yet," said a man's unfamiliar voice. "For when they do, I will have returned to the earth to lead the first wave into battle."

The white space was quiet again. A shadow fell over

Naomi and me. It was a terrifying shadow. Only something brighter than the sun could cast a shadow like that. Then the shadow became a man, leaning over us.

"You're listening," he said, looking down at me. "Good." It was the same man's voice. The light was so bright behind him I could not see his face. I felt sure it was beautiful and terrifying, like the light. Something loomed behind him. Were they wings?

"He can hear," said my Mom. Her voice meek, coming from below.

The man nodded. "But can he see?"

"He can see," my Mom answered.

The man frowned and shook his head. "He *can* see, but he *won't*." He reached down and put his hand over my eyes. His touch was hot, almost burning.

I wanted to cringe back. The stone was unforgiving at my back. The hand was unforgiving on my face.

"He *will* see." It was the other woman, Naomi's mother.

"He will see," echoed Naomi. Her fingers touched mine. I still could not move, but I could feel the heat. Her touch was as hot as the man's.

"When he sees me," the man warned, "the war will soon begin. Until then, his vision darkens before it sees the light. His actions have consequences." The man lifted his hand. My eyes would not open.

"So be it," my Mom said.

"The world's taint is heavy." The man's voice was calm, and maybe sad. "The one my enemy calls 'clothed with the sun,' she must pray. I will fight as the dragon takes her child. Can she help lift the taint from the seer?"

No one answered. My eyes would not open.

"Can she lift it?" he repeated.

The question floated down like a pure white feather from the heavens. My closed eyes rocked back and forth with the feather until it landed on me.

My eyes blinked open. The thick trunks of giant pines were above me. I was in the cabin, somewhere in Montana, in the middle of the night.

"Elijah?" Mara's voice shocked me. She was sitting right by my side, watching me. "Will you come with me?"

I nodded.

"Come quietly."

She led me out of the cabin to an empty field away from the cluster of buildings. There was a stone jutting from the ground, at a good height for sitting. She sat without a word, and I joined her.

We were quiet for a long time. The chill of early fall was in the night air. The sky was vast, as big as it had been in the desert. The moon, full and shining, was nothing to the stars. Any one of them could have been the source of the feather that had fallen on me in my dream. I shook my head, trying to shake the surreal thought away. Stars were distant suns. They were nothing more than blazing planets adrift in space.

"You're right to question dreams," Mara said.

"Dreams?"

"I heard you talking in your sleep."

"Okay." *How much had she heard?*

"Dreams reflect truths known by our souls but hidden by our minds. You should question dreams because some might never come to be. They are not truths at all. They are future alternatives, sometimes dark alternatives."

"Yeah, I've seen that."

"What do you mean?"

I shrugged. "Most of mine seem to come true."

"Who's Naomi?" Mara asked.

So I'd said her name. "A friend," I answered.

"You said she's the woman clothed with the sun."

I turned to find Mara studying me. The enemy of the man in my dream had said that, not me. "What else did I say?"

"You said many things. You whispered them in terror. A boy with those kinds of dreams should be careful."

"What else did I say?"

"You said a name: Abaddon. You spoke of an unborn baby. You said it would be born but taken away."

"Who would take it? What did I say about Abaddon?"

"I don't know." She looked away into the night. "But this I do know, Elijah, your dreams matter."

"What do you think it means," I asked, "the woman clothed with the sun?"

She was silent for a while, then said, "It sounds like a woman for the end of times. My people know the time is coming soon. I have studied the words of Tristan's God. They are shrouded in mystery, but they speak of this woman. It is a great sign when she appears, clothed with the sun, with the moon under her feet, and on her head a crown of twelve stars. She will cry out in agony and give birth to a male child."

Ronaldo had recited the same lines. "Are you in the order?" I ventured.

"What order?" Her innocent eyes were calm and sincere.

"Never mind. You mentioned Tristan's God. Don't you share his beliefs?"

She sighed, as if I'd touched a sore point. "We share many things, including his God. But I've never been able to give up the old ways—the ways of my people. Tristan sees one spirit of the Messiah. I see many spirits." She paused. "The difference does not affect our love, though Tristan's friends think it should."

"Which friends?"

"I can't say." She turned to me again. "You said Naomi was called the woman clothed with the sun."

"It was a dream. Maybe just a metaphor."

"Why do you think that?"

I pointed up at the glowing silver orb in the sky. "Have you ever seen a woman with the moon under her feet? Or with a crown of twelve stars?"

Mara smiled. "I can't tell you the meaning of dreams. But maybe I can help you catch them."

"Catch them?"

"Here." She pressed something into my hand.

I held it up. It was the size of a small plate, with a woven web in the center. A wooden cross and a large white feather hung from the bottom.

"It's a dreamcatcher," she said. "The nightmares pass through the holes. The good dreams are trapped in the web and slide down the feather into your sleep."

"Thank you." The feather looked just like the one from my dream. "What about the cross?"

"Tristan told me I had to add it if I gave this to you."

It seemed like an odd mix. "You really believe it works?"

"I do. Hang it above you when you sleep."

"Thanks, I'll give it a try." It was no sleeping pill, but it was better than nothing.

45

"Why is Don gathering the wealthy?" I asked.

The Captain and I had been talking through the morning. Sven was unusually quiet and working on reconnecting our precepts. Neither of them had mentioned anything about the night, or even about the dreamcatcher that was now hanging above my bunk.

"I don't know as much as I'd like," the Captain answered, "but surely he plans to ask for money. His headquarters, telecommunication systems, and drone forces have cost a fortune. There's only so much he can get from the UN member countries. These disasters must have stretched his finances thin."

"That sounds right." Though I felt sure there was more to it. "So I'll be there as myself. Who will you be, Scott?"

"I'll be your servant. Same name."

"You think that'll work?"

"Cristo might figure it out, but that's only the first step. When the real moment comes, I won't be in this skin." He ran his fingers along the side of his bald head. "Sven is preparing your precept with a preloaded connection to one of the other rich leaders—the one I'll be using."

"Using?" I thought of Charles, and shuddered. "Tell me you're not going to kill one of them."

"No, this is different. I've done it once before." He blinked slowly, like someone stuffing away a bad memory. "I'll use your precept as a bridge between my precept and the other person's. My body will go into a coma-like state while I take over the other body like it's a drone. This requires my full mental capacity. Sven says it will work."

I rubbed my eyes in disbelief. This was almost as bad as Don, taking over someone's body by hacking into their precept. When my eyes opened, the Captain was studying me calmly. "What happens if I don't come back?" I asked. "Or if I shut off my precept?"

"It would be like when a drone is shot down. I might eject and return to my body, but I also might go into shock. I might die." He was just reciting the facts. "It's worth the risk."

"What happens to the other person?"

"She should be fine," the Captain said.

"*She?*"

He nodded. He'd let that slip on purpose.

"Whose body are you going to take?"

"I've said enough."

"There are twenty-one women out of the fifty. Once my precept is back, I'll research them all. I want to know which one it is. And if anything goes wrong, don't you want me to be able to do something, whether it's helping you or running?"

He mulled my words. "You'll know."

"How?"

"Trust me, you'll know." The boulder had crossed his arms over his chest.

"So if you won't tell me, why do you even need me?"

"I told you, your precept will be my bridge. Sven says it's necessary. You'll also help me get into Geneva smoothly. Don rules that city like a tyrant. There is more surveillance there than anywhere else in the world. If the system detects a new person who is not on official business, Don's guards will move heaven and earth to figure out who it is, who it *really* is."

"You'll be a new person even if you're with me."

"Yes, but I will be official. Sven is uploading the identity into my precept now. Remember, I am Prescott Walker, your new assistant."

"Did you kill the real Prescott Walker?"

I wasn't kidding, but the Captain laughed like I'd said the funniest thing in the world. It took a few moments for him to compose himself.

"Are you growing cynical, Eli?" His smile gave way to his normal hard stare. "We're just borrowing Prescott's digital identity. I don't need his body."

"Why not?"

"Let me tell you a story," the Captain began, like a father lecturing a child. "Prescott lost his job as a tailor fifteen years ago. The android that replaced him does much finer work. Poor Prescott, though, he's been living on the government dime ever since. The UN's basic income gives him enough money to pay for a bunk in Brooklyn and a connection to the virtual world of his choice. He still enters the real world to eat and piss, but that's about it. So, you think anybody knows what Prescott looks like?"

"He looks just like you," responded Sven. He'd been quiet for a long time, and now he looked exhausted. "It's finished."

"Excellent!" The Captain sprang out of his chair. "Let's connect it."

"Sorry," Sven stopped him. "Can't do that yet. We'll need to connect you both simultaneously. It'll look more natural that way—like you both rebooted your precepts with the same trip information at the same time, the way someone normally would with his assistant. I also need to install my latest hacking code. You and Eli are about the only two agents gifted enough to use it."

"Fine." The Captain sat again. "How long will this take?"

"I'll have it done before dinner. It takes longer without our normal backup system," he explained. "And trust me, you want me to take every precaution to ensure the link with my satellite is tight. If it's not, the UN's algorithms will sniff you out in minutes."

"You're adding the other agents' trackers, right?" I

asked.

Sven shrugged. "That's the deal."

"Come on." The Captain stood and motioned for me to follow. "I need to stretch my legs, and what I'm going to tell you next about Cristo's plans warrants some fresh air."

We walked outside almost ten minutes before the Captain spoke again. "It's nice out here, being disconnected, don't you think?"

"I'm surprised you like it," I said. "It's a little too wide open for my taste." In New York, all I had to worry about was the block I could see in front of me. "Besides, what about what you said to Tristan, about how he should want to make the world better?"

"I meant it," the Captain answered. "People like him can enjoy this frontier freedom only because we fight for it in the places that matter. The future lives in cities."

"You think anyone would actually bother Mara and Tristan out here? Does it matter to them who has power in the world?"

"Tristan and Mara might sneak through their quaint

lives without trouble, but it never lasts. Peace and freedom endure only with security. They have security out here thanks to your ownership and non-interference with these lands. They have security thanks to our government protecting the nation's borders. And they *had* security under the UN's strong web of international order. That's what I'm fighting to protect."

Fair enough, I thought, but why not try to "sneak" through life the way Tristan and Mara did? It had never been my way. Maybe I'd changed. With the world spiraling down, wouldn't I be happier settling with Naomi in some hidden and safe place? Would she accept that? These were not questions for the Captain. I thought of a question that was: "So, why are you afraid of Don Cristo?"

"Afraid?" the Captain scoffed. "I don't fear him, but only what he plans to do. For years the levers of power have been consolidating. A single man, in the right position, can now speak to every person in the world at the same time. With enough computing power, he can monitor each movement, each communication, and even each thought. Can you imagine that?" The Captain stopped walking and met my eyes. "No man should have that much influence over the world, unless he can be trusted with it."

He was right, except I doubted any man could be trusted with that kind of power. Much less Don. "How did the world let this happen?"

The Captain held up his hand like a puppet master. "Cristo has been playing the world's leaders for years. His steps were measured at first. Incremental, imperceptible altruism—nothing to raise an eyebrow at, especially with these recent disasters and drone wars. Who could object to the UN helping? As soon as Cristo sells pieces of his power for fortunes like yours, I believe he will proclaim world control. Even the major powers that have long limited the UN's reach will cave, because their people have grown loyal to Cristo, putting their hopes in his promises. You think Americans have an appetite for war against UN drones led by a man they worship?"

I shook my head. The Captain sounded spot on, but without a key piece of the puzzle: Don had the devil's spirit inside him. "You think killing Don will stop this? Won't someone else come along in his place?"

The Captain's face twisted into a half smile. "We'll cross that bridge when we come to it." He turned toward the buildings. "Come on, let's head back and get connected. Once our precepts are on, no more talk of Cristo. Even with Sven's protected link, it's too risky."

He took a few steps but then looked back.

I had not followed him. Something made me hesitate. Had I said something to make him cut off the conversation?

"Are we on the same page?" he asked.

I nodded with a straight face. We'd never be on the same page, but at least our next steps were aligned: securing our precept links and reaching Don.

"Good," the Captain said. "I knew I could count on you."

47

The next few days, I got the sense that Tristan was watching me. In the morning, while I ate Mara's oatmeal. In the afternoon, when I walked from the barn to the cabin. At night, while I sat alone and reviewed reports with V. Tristan's glance never stayed too long. He looked away a moment before it would've been suspicious.

It was suspicious.

Now it was the third night, after dinner, and all of us were sitting around the fireplace.

"Ever been hunting?" Tristan asked me. He happened to be cleaning a shotgun.

"For animals?" I replied.

He nodded, his cool eyes following his hand as it slid up and down the gun's barrel, polishing.

"No," I said. I'd never shot an animal, unless Jezebel

counted. Not a pleasant memory.

"Wanna join me tomorrow for a hunt?"

He didn't look up from his gun cleaning as I considered his request. I wanted to learn more, to figure out what he was hiding. It could be good to get out of the camp—away from the Captain and Sven—for a while. So I said, "Okay."

The Captain spoke up then. "What time?" He seemed to have given up the ruse of me being in charge. Maybe Tristan and Mara seemed harmless enough to him, especially since they lacked precepts.

Tristan met the Captain's gaze. For a moment I wondered if they were sizing each other up, as if ready to come to blows. But all Tristan said was, "We'll leave an hour before dawn. Back the next morning, with an elk if this kid doesn't scare 'em away."

"Fine," the Captain said, turning to me. "Be here early the day after next. Sven's leaving that morning, but he needs to run a final security sweep on our precepts."

And that's how I found myself on a mountain ridge the next morning, overlooking a herd of elk in a valley below. The air was thin. I was catching my breath after the harrowing ride on horseback up and over half a dozen other ridges, each growing in height and steepness. In just a few hours, we'd made it far from the sight of the cabin.

"Shoot like I told you," Tristan whispered beside me. "Set your stance, steady your arm, and watch the bullet all the way through the scope mark, right into the elk's heart."

"I know how to shoot," I said, though I'd never held

an older rifle like this.

"You know to hide things, boy. Like what you're hiding from the Captain." He spat tobacco juice on the ground. Guess it was never too early in the day for cancer, or for surprising questions.

"That's what most people do," I said. "Hide things."

"Do most people also finger crosses in their pocket?"

My breath froze. I let go of Naomi's necklace and slowly took my hand out of my pocket. He was right. I'd been gripping it a lot lately, whenever I thought of her. A mistake. But what was Tristan's point?

The elk herd began stirring down below. "Want me to take the shot or not?"

"Take it." He raised his rifle, too. We were kneeling beside each other, like two soldiers facing a vast and nameless enemy.

I picked my elk. He was the biggest of the herd, near the front, with an immense rack of antlers. The alpha elk moved slowly, confident, as if expecting obedience from the herd behind him.

"Take the shot," Tristan said again. "You'll get no better chance. Hit the heart."

I took a deep breath, set the scope's crosshairs right above the elk's front shoulder, and pulled the trigger.

BANG.

BANG. Tristan fired an instant after I did.

The herd erupted into action, like a calm pool of water rippling after a stone is hurled into it. My eyes followed my elk, the alpha. He bounded frantically, limping with every leap. My heart sank at his pain. Maybe I'd missed; maybe he'd survive.

Another elk not far behind collapsed. Tristan's shot, I figured.

Soon the herd had stampeded out of sight, my elk included. We had destroyed their serene morning.

"You missed the heart." Tristan rose to his feet and stepped down the other side of the ridge, to the three horses tied just below us. "Let's go see how long he suffered."

We mounted our horses and rode along a thin path down into the valley. Halfway there, my precept's signal was lost. It could still happen in very remote areas, but it made me nervous. Not much I could do about it.

We found Tristan's elk motionless on the ground. Its huge round eyes stared vacantly at the sky. Its antlers looked new, never to reach impressive heights.

"Yours went that way." Tristan pointed to a trail of blood. There were two parallel lines along the ground.

"Why two lines?" I asked.

"You probably shot clean through his throat. He'll bleed out both sides until he falls." Tristan snapped his head up toward the opposite ridge. I followed his eyes and thought I glimpsed a figure ducking out of sight.

"What is it?" I suddenly felt very deep into these

mountains, and very far from help.

"Friends," Tristan answered. Then he put his fist over his mouth as if to amplify the sound. "*Hoo! Hoo! Hoo!*" he called in quick succession, like a night owl's cry.

"What's going on?" I studied the ridge above.

"Here." He pulled out a giant knife and motioned with it to the fallen elk's side. "Hold the body steady while I clean it."

I stood my ground. "Who are they?"

He pointed the tip of the knife at me. "I told you—friends. You'll see. Now, hold it steady. Understood?"

I looked along the blade's sharp edge. It's not like I could run, and I felt sure I'd rather fight a bear than Tristan. So I did as he said. I leaned over and pressed my hands against the elk's still-warm fur. "Like this?"

He nodded. "Hold it firm."

I put all my weight against it, and he started carving into the animal. I watched in mesmerized horror as he sliced around its neck, reached inside the throat, and twisted and cut with the calm of a master surgeon. None of it prepared me for his sudden jerk, yanking at something inside the elk.

"Off now," he grunted, his arm buried deep in the carcass.

I stepped back. He yanked again. Then again, and this time he pulled a mass of bloody, slippery organs clean out of the elk's body.

I looked away in disgust, as my stomach churned. That's when I saw them around us. Five men fanning out maybe fifty feet away. They looked way too normal to be in the middle of nowhere like this.

"Good," Tristan said, still bent over the elk. "He's ready for carving and the feast now." He looked up at me, then past me, and his bearded face spread into a smile. "Ho there!" he said, as they approached.

"Brother Tristan," one of the men said. "Who's this green lad?" He sounded friendly. I couldn't tell if he was referring to my inexperience or the color of my face after Tristan's gory work. Probably both.

"This is Elijah Roeh Goldsmith," Tristan answered. "He's the new owner of these lands, and he's proof of our Lord's hand at work."

"Not that I need more proof, but that's mighty fine to hear." The man drew closer and held out his hand to me. "Nice to meet you, Elijah. I'm Thomas Turner."

I shook his hand, studying his gentle face.

"I want him to see your town," Tristan said. "We'll need to haul this elk out to the ranch, but there's a bigger one a few hundred yards out of the valley." He pointed after the blood trail. "Elijah got him. Perfect for a feast." He almost sounded proud.

"Well done," Thomas said. "Don't you worry, we'll take care of getting the elk back to our place." As if such a worry would cross my mind. "Come on, it's just over this ridge."

I don't know what I expected. Maybe a bunch of radicals, living off the grid. And that was close to the truth. As we rode over the ridge, I saw a cluster of buildings in the center of the next valley. It was like a small mountain mining town, without a mine. Each tiny building had solar panels on its roof. Greenhouses were scattered throughout. There were few other signs of the modern world. No vehicles. No street lights.

I probably should have been afraid. Instead, I felt at ease as we approached. The few who greeted us were nothing but normal. Their clothes were plain and worn, like any group of Midwestern farmers. Everyone smiled as if this were the happiest day on earth.

"Hey Tristan!" yelled a pack of kids running down the main dirt street between the buildings.

He lifted one of the little boys, who laughed and laughed as he rode on Tristan's shoulders. He looked just like Chris's little blond boy, with shorter hair. Kids that age always looked the same to me.

At the end of the main street was a bleach-white church with a bleach-white cross on top of its steeple. I felt an urge to double-check Tristan's thumb. No ring was there. But then a man waved ahead, and sure as day he had the ring, marking him a leader in the order.

"Tristan!" the man said, stepping toward us from the church. He had dark brown skin and black hair shaved close. He was huge, built like a linebacker. "Who's your friend?"

Tristan bowed his head slightly. "This is Elijah Goldsmith." He looked to me. "Elijah, this is Neo. He's one of the order's leaders, from the Pacific islands."

"Not just any island. Java, man." Neo gave Tristan a

friendly shove in the shoulder. "But hey, no complaints from me. You're still a miracle worker."

Tristan shrugged and pointed two fingers into the sky. "All the praise to God. A few days ago Elijah and two others showed up on my land. *His* land, actually. His dad bought it last year, but he died in the New York flood."

Oh no. My dad's purchase of this land suddenly made sense. "I have to warn you," I said. "I think President Cristo wanted my father to buy this land. He must know you're here. It's not safe."

"Nowhere is safe," Neo said. "Many more will die before this cat-and-mouse hunt is over. We make of these last days what we can." He paused. "But thank you for the warning. We've long prayed for you, Elijah. Ronaldo updated the order on your journey. Another miracle that was, you finding him."

I nodded along, thinking, *Not a miracle. Brie.*

"Now you come to us," Neo continued. "We know of your dreams, and of your growing wisdom. What message do you bring?"

Where to start? If he was looking for some divine guidance, I didn't have anything to offer. A crowd had gathered around us. Most of them were either children or geriatric. "I'm going to Geneva in a week, at President Cristo's request."

"Bold plan," Tristan grunted.

"You don't sound ready," Neo added.

"Why not?"

"Because you make it sound like you can do this on

your own." Neo looked out over the crowd. He shouted out a question: "How do we face the devil?"

The children answered together. "Resist the devil, and he will flee from us!" they finished with a shout.

"Good, good." Neo turned back to me. "We resist the devil, we don't run straight to him."

"I have to go to Don," I said. "I've seen it."

"Hmm, interesting." Neo glanced to the crowd. "Kids, you run along and play. Everyone else, help prepare for the feast. It will be dark soon." He turned back to the smaller group around me. "Come, Elijah, Tristan, Thomas, let's talk inside."

49

Neo led us into the church. It was a simple wooden box with pews and a podium in the front. Neo stopped near the middle. "What did you see?" he asked. "Did God tell you to go to Geneva?"

No. But then I remembered my dreams from New York and the desert. "Maybe," I said. "In one dream, the dragon I saw swallowed a satellite and gave Don Cristo control over the world. I think I'm supposed to fight against that. In another dream, I led Don to a remote place. He thought I led him to Naomi, but she was not there. This made him furious, and that was my role."

"Anything else?" Neo was studying me. Behind his eyes lurked an edge. It reminded me of Bart, in a good way.

"You knew Bart?" I asked.

Neo nodded somberly. "He was the best of us."

"Bart told me to trust my dreams, to act on them," I said. "I have to go to Geneva. What else am I supposed to do? Your order told me to stay away from Naomi. She agreed. That doesn't mean I can sit and watch from the sidelines."

"Fair enough," Neo said. "Naomi is still safe."

"With Jacques?" I asked.

He nodded.

"How do you know?"

"Because we haven't heard anything to the contrary."

"You trust Jacques that much?"

"With everything," Neo said.

"Where is she?"

Thomas answered, "She's safe."

"And how would *you* know?" I pressed.

"I have a precept," Thomas said. "I would be the one to receive a message from the order if something went wrong. There's been no message since the last one from Jacques. Our network spreads wide. We would know."

"Fine," I said, "but don't you risk this whole town by using a precept?"

"He doesn't use it in town," Neo said.

"You don't have to be using it to put yourself at risk."

"No one told you about the rings?"

I shook my head, failing to hide my curiosity.

"The order's leaders all have them," Neo explained. "They're jamming devices that release electromagnetic pulses, like little solar flares. When activated, no precept or any other digital signal can function within a few hundred feet. We have to be careful about using them in cities to avoid detection. Out here it's no problem. I keep mine activated all the time."

"That's amazing," I said. "How did you get it?"

"You should know," Tristan answered. "It's ISA-7 technology."

"How do you know about ISA-7?"

"The order's connections are deep. I'd heard of a man with a circuit board on his head, then you brought him to my home. Then the skinny guy set up a satellite system in my barn." Tristan smiled. "Kind of obvious."

"Right," I said. "I was never fully trained as an agent, so I don't know all their technology. But even if ISA-7 had this, that doesn't explain how the order got it."

"You think it's a coincidence that Naomi and Patrick were in your ISA-7 orientation?" Neo asked.

"Not anymore."

"We've learned a lot through our people's work in ISA, and especially ISA-7. Mainly we've learned how little of this technology we can trust."

I thought of Brie, and her memories in my head. "So what's next?" I asked.

"You're going to Geneva." Neo clasped my shoulder. "You're going to follow your calling. In the meantime, we might as well feast and pray for you. You're going to need it, because the plans of man often do not come to be."

50

The town's "feast" was in a long, narrow building with a concrete floor and a metal roof. A series of plain, bench-lined tables stretched the hall's length. When we entered, the sound of children hit me like a waterfall's roar. Their talking, laughing, and babbling reverberated off the smooth surfaces. They shuttled around with the controlled chaos of an ant farm. I figured there had to be a few hundred of them.

Neo left us and drifted into the crowd, with kids clustering around him. Tristan and Thomas led me toward the food at one end of the hall.

As I followed, an old woman grabbed my arm and stopped me. Her wrinkled face and body looked frail, as if she'd topple over if I breathed on her. But her grip was strong. Her eyes were like faded grey steel.

"You look like my grandson," she said.

"Okay?" I tried to pull my arm away.

She squeezed tighter. "See now, he was a good boy. Died five years ago. His dad wouldn't take a precept, so they killed 'em."

"Both of them?"

She nodded. "His dad wouldn't take a precept, so——."

Thomas appeared beside the woman and put his hand on her shoulder. "That's enough, Ma. Let our guest come and get his food."

She unclenched her bony fist from my arm. "Nice to meet you. Elijah, right?"

I nodded as Thomas guided me past her.

"Don't mind her," Thomas said. "She's an amazing woman, but her mind is departing from us. She turned one hundred twenty-nine a couple weeks ago."

"That's too bad," I said. "I'm guessing she has no precept to keep her mind fresh?"

"Right," Thomas answered. "Out here, we care for those who can't care for themselves. They do just fine without precepts." He stopped in front of the table of food. "Your elk," he grinned. "Dig in."

Thomas walked off, and Tristan pointed to a table where I could join him. I began filling my plate. The elk had been shredded. There were potatoes and broccoli to go with it. Plain as the food, it looked delicious. My stomach was growling.

The old woman was standing there, staring at me again with her pale eyes. "Hey, Elijah?"

"Yes?"

"You look like my grandson."

I nodded.

"He was a good boy. Died five years ago. His dad wouldn't take a precept, so—"

"I know," I said. "You told me, and I'm very sorry to hear about your loss."

She gave me a toothless smile. "You're a good boy. Don't let anybody tell you otherwise."

"Thanks," I said, confused.

"It's just—" she hesitated.

"What?"

"Not everyone has an angel follow him to the edge of town. That's quite an escort."

"An angel?"

She shook her finger in my face. "Don't play dumb with me, boy. You look like my grandson. He died five years—"

"I know," I said. "I'm sorry. Look, we better eat before the food gets cold."

She turned and, as she began to shuffle off, said, "Sweet dreams, Elijah."

I shook my head and headed to Tristan. If there had been an angel, I would have noticed. I was the one who saw the dragon, after all. Poor lady. It was wrong to make a woman that old live on without a precept.

I found Tristan's table near the center of the room. About ten kids were sitting with him, ages anywhere from five to fifteen. No other adults had joined them. Ronaldo's words came to me, about the leaders of the order having different gifts. He'd said Neo was a teacher.

"Is this a school?" I asked Tristan, as I sat on the far end of the table from him. It was the only open spot.

Tristan opened his mouth to answer, but one of the kids answered first. "Sure is!" said a girl. She seemed about twelve years old, maybe Japanese. "We're Christ's Neo School. Get it?"

I shook my head.

"*Neo*," she giggled, "like *New*!"

"Christ's New School," agreed a dark-skinned boy, with a thick African accent. He was about the same age as the girl, but at least my height. "Neo saved us."

"From what?" I asked.

"Different things," the boy answered. "For me, it was starvation." He held out his rail thin arms.

"How long ago?"

"Two months," he said. "We eat like kings here. I've gained fifteen pounds."

The Japanese girl spoke again. "My parents wouldn't take precepts when the government swept our town. The agents lined them up and shot them. They took five of us kids, but Neo and his men broke us out. He saved us, brought us here." She put a finger to her temple. "I miss my parents, but at least my mind's free. No precept."

"Same here," said a younger red-haired girl with an airy Russian accent. She smiled at Tristan. "It took me a long time to get better. Mara helped. She taught me about the land in this country. The mountains and the stars. Why isn't Mara here with you?"

"She couldn't come," Tristan said, his voice tight.

"But you say that every time!" the girl complained.

"Not everyone likes it when she visits," Tristan said.

"Like Neo?" the girl asked knowingly.

Tristan shrugged, but didn't answer.

"My mom said Mara isn't saved," said a squeaky voice. It was the youngest boy at the table. He couldn't have been older than six.

"No one can know that," Tristan responded.

"My mom said we shouldn't listen to Mara. She said she's—"

"Stop." Tristan stared at the boy. "You like riding on my shoulders? You like it when I bring you gifts?"

The boy nodded, his flaxen blond hair bobbing, his blue eyes innocent.

"Then I suggest you say nice things about Mara."

"Okay, Tristan. Sorry!" the boy replied. He turned to me.

"What's your name?" I asked him.

"Everybody calls me Toph. Rhymes with loaf. It's short for Christopher."

"And your last name?"

"Max," the boy said.

His answer was like a key unlocking Brie's memory. I dove into the information Brie had given me, ignoring the kids' continued chatting around me. I remembered Toph's first birthday party, and how he'd smeared the cake's white icing all over his face. I remembered the first time he'd ridden a bike. I remembered how much Brie loved him.

"Eli," Tristan was saying. "Eli!"

"Sorry, what?" I pulled out of the memories, then I noticed Neo standing by my shoulder. The children at the table were gazing up at him with admiration and respect in their eyes.

"You finished eating?" Neo asked.

I nodded.

"It was quite an elk you took down. Sure you don't want to hang around and hunt with us instead of going to Geneva? You could help teach some of our students."

"Sorry," I said. "I have to go. But I'm impressed by what you've done here." I motioned to the kids. "I heard how you saved many of them."

"Thank you," Neo said. "This is one of dozens of the order's schools. The UN's persecution has left many children orphaned. There are UN centers for them, but they install precepts subject to President Cristo's control. We save every child we can." He messed with the hair of the tall African boy sitting beside me. The boy smiled up at him, like a son at his dad. I wondered if I'd ever looked at my Dad like that.

"*Hey-o!*" Neo shouted. "Everyone gather around. Time to lay hands on Elijah. Gather round!"

The room sprang into motion. The kids around me all pressed close and put their hands on me. Others filed in behind them, all reaching for me. I fought back a wave of claustrophobia.

"Lord," Neo prayed out, his voice echoing through the

dining hall. "We thank you for this young man. We thank you for his gift of vision. Give him the armor of God. Let him fight for you in the last battle. Help him submit to you. Help him resist the devil, and make the devil flee from him." Neo paused. "Amen?"

"AMEN," the children chanted back.

The hands all over me relented, except for Neo's. He was clasping my shoulder, studying me. "You ready to confess the Lord?" he asked.

"Ah, sorry, no—" I stammered.

"Take your time," Tristan interrupted. "God works at a pace, and in ways we can't understand."

Neo's gaze swiveled to Tristan. "Only a clear confession of Christ can save a soul."

"Only Christ can save a soul," Tristan replied. "It doesn't matter what we think."

Neo blinked slowly. "Another time, friend."

Tristan nodded.

Neo looked around at the others. "What time is it?"

"Worship time!" several children shouted.

"Let's go," Neo invited, pulling me along.

He led the sprawling group out to a blazing bonfire. Tristan had found a guitar and started playing. The kids began to sing. Everyone sounded happy.

I studied the flames as the music filled the night air. I thought of Naomi, and of Mara. Did Naomi have to defend me the way Tristan defended Mara? This seemed like no easy thing for these people. I suddenly felt gratitude for the beautiful girl with the honey skin. For the first time since her message telling me to stay away, she felt closer.

The fire had burned down to bright red coals by the time Tristan led me away to a plain house with our beds. I was asleep in seconds.

The dream came after that—the one with Don and the stone cottage. It was exactly the same. The man in the cottage. Don's fury at me, because Naomi wasn't there. But something new happened: as Don held me up by my throat, squeezing, someone attacked him.

51

Tristan woke me before dawn to leave the order's makeshift town. The trip back was uneventful and gorgeous as the sun rose over the ridges. We arrived at the cabin early, as the Captain had demanded.

"Eli got an elk," Tristan said when we walked in.

The Captain looked up from his oatmeal breakfast. "Nice work."

"How'd you get it out of the mountains?" Sven asked.

"We quartered it and divided the weight among the horses." Tristan turned to Mara. "All well here?"

She greeted Tristan with a kiss. "All's well. I'm glad you're back safely." She smiled at me. "Aren't the mountains beautiful?"

I nodded. "It's a rugged terrain. I learned a lot about surviving off the grid."

"You won't need that anytime soon," the Captain said. "We're going to the heart of the grid, and we're leaving in three days. The meeting in Geneva is only a week away."

He didn't ask anything about my trip with Tristan. Maybe he still thought Tristan was a simpleton without a precept. He should have known better.

Later that day Sven ran the final security sweep of our precepts. Before he left, he finally lived up to his word and implanted the other agents' locations.

I immediately checked Naomi's.

Jerusalem.

I had her exact coordinates and her heartbeat. *But what about my dream?* I suddenly wondered if I could trust the signal. How hard would it be to remove a tracker? The Captain had done it. Either way, I would live by Naomi's wishes. I would not try to find her. For now.

I spent the following days with the Captain, going through video briefings and reports. I tried to ignore the constant media reports and rumors about me. I didn't dare search for Naomi, Neo, or anything about the order. Too suspicious. Instead, I learned everything I could about the UN, Geneva, and Don. I already knew most of it, so I soon turned to the other invitees to the meeting. Like me, each of them had mountains of public news and files to study.

Whenever I wasn't reviewing precept reports, I left the Captain and joined Tristan and Mara for long walks. Mara talked about light things with depth. Every flower, every breeze was a wonder to her. She was like a wisp floating along the crust of the earth, untouched by the darkness she believed weighed it down. Tristan was mostly quiet, but I'd seen how he'd defended Mara before Neo. I'd seen how the children loved him. He and Mara didn't need precepts to excel. They kind of began to feel like family.

Three nights later, we were still eating elk meat. The Captain confirmed after dinner that we were leaving at dawn the next day. After a night of fitful sleep, I found myself standing beside our vehicle as the sun rose. My things were packed, including the dreamcatcher.

Tristan and Mara stood with us.

"I have enjoyed our talks," Mara said to me.

"Me too," I said. "I'll miss you both."

"When you showed up," Tristan said, "I had my doubts about you. I thought you were just like the landowners before you, absent and empty. But you're not like them. This land will welcome you back. And so will we."

"Thank you," I said. "I will come back to visit again." And I would bring Naomi, if I could. Tristan gave me a handshake and a wink. Mara pulled me into her arms and hugged me tight.

"Very well," the Captain coughed, turning to climb into the vehicle. "Thank you for hosting us. You'll say nothing of our visit here. Understood?"

Tristan nodded with a slanted grin. The Captain started the engine, and I climbed in beside him. Tristan and Mara waved as we drove off. Leaving them felt like leaving a sanctuary. I was getting used to the order.

The Captain and I rode in quiet back to the plane. It

emerged from the lake as Sven had said it would.

When we landed in Geneva early the next morning, Tristan and Mara and peace felt as far away from me as Naomi. I had entered Don's domain.

Neo's words came to me: *Resist the devil, and he will flee from you.* Easier said than done.

52

My suite had four rooms and a private deck overlooking Lake Geneva. The Captain was sitting across from me in the suite's living room, staring into space with a look of concentration. Nothing like a precept to kill conversation.

"I'm heading out for dinner," I said.

The Captain blinked and shook his head as if to return to our place and time. "Where are you going?"

"Some French place my family's butler picked."

"You can't go alone."

"Why not?"

"You'll be watched."

"Of course I'll be watched, but so what? I'm a guest of honor in this city, and I can take care of myself. It's safer than going with you. The more distance between us, the better."

"Fine," he grunted, "but keep an eye out for traps. If Cristo finds out you're linked to my plans, you'll be tied to my fate. You don't want that, do you?"

"No, but do you expect me to go into this meeting blind? I barely know more than public knowledge."

The Captain shook his head. "I know it's frustrating, but these are our terms. You've complied so far. We're almost there." A rare tone of pleading was in his voice.

"You really think you can do this?"

"Yes. After I finish my mission, you'll be free to do whatever, without anyone standing in your way."

But what if you fail? He had the ISA-7 agents' locations in his precept, including Naomi's. Couldn't Don track her down if he captured the Captain?

"Promise me something," I said. "You will delete every bit of data about the other agents before you make your move. Agreed?"

The Captain was quiet for a moment. "You are right about that. Agreed."

That was progress. I pressed on. "And tell me what the others in ISA-7 are doing. What about Patrick and Aisha in Iran?"

"I will tell you more," he said. "Or rather, Patrick will. We're going to meet with him tomorrow morning."

"Where?"

"In a secure place Sven has constructed."

"What does Patrick have to do with our mission?"

"It's all connected," the Captain explained, "that's why

I've protected you from the information. As soon as you start to be sucked in, you won't be able to stay ignorant. You'll learn more tomorrow, trust me."

Great. Trust the Captain. "Fine. I'm heading out."

"Be alert." He stared back into space, absorbed in his precept again.

I left the room and made my way out of the hotel. Geneva was gorgeous in the gloaming. The city had grown rapidly since Don had come to power, but it still felt small beside the huge lake in the broad valley between the Alps. I found the restaurant in the heart of the city. It was called *Les Halles*. Bruce's message had said my dad always came here when he visited Geneva on business. It made sense as soon as I walked in: white tablecloths, formal wait staff, and total absence of technology. Just my Dad's ironic dining style.

"Mr. Goldsmith," said the greeter with a bow. "Welcome. We are honored you have chosen *Les Halles*. Come," he gestured for me to follow, "we've reserved your table."

It was in the corner, overlooking the city. An old man in a white tux came to me as soon as I sat. "Welcome, Mr. Goldsmith." He held a pencil and paper in his pale, withered hands. "What would you like tonight?"

"Whatever the chef recommends."

I turned to a series of new reports V had prepared. She began flashing the words. The first report was about rumors of a recent meeting between the two leaders of the United States and China. Apparently it had happened in

Geneva earlier this day. Knowledgeable sources speculated they were aligning against Iran.

I was moving to the second report when something tapped my shoulder. It was the old waiter.

"Yes?" I asked.

The wrinkles by his eyes folded like origami as he blinked. "Your father used to order the same way," he said with a tinge of sadness. "He always said our chef made the best meal in Switzerland."

"You knew him?"

The old man nodded. "Your father was a good man. I am grieved by the loss." He bowed and walked off.

I went back to my reports. A different person brought my appetizer. The plate was gold-edged porcelain with a line of escargot. I dug into the food and more reports. I'd reviewed seven of them and had taken my last bite when the old man came back and stood beside me.

"Here." He held out a small, fancy-looking box. "This is for you."

I took it. "Why?"

"Your father gave it to me. I think he would have wanted you to have it."

"What makes you think that?"

"When he first started coming here," the man explained, "maybe twenty years ago, he and I talked about being fathers. He was about my son's age, you see. My son and I didn't always get along, especially after my wife died. One morning after a fight, my son was just gone. I did not hear from him for years. Then one morning, a few days before I happened to first meet your father, my son sent me a note. The note said I had a grandson, but he was dying. My grandson had cancer, and my son could not afford to pay for the cure. It was very expensive back then. Your father, after he ordered his lunch, must have sensed that something was wrong. He asked me about it, so I told him. He, well—" the man pulled out a white handkerchief and wiped at his eyes— "he transferred a huge sum of money to my account, right then and there. Then he took off his watch and gave me that, too. It was a marvelous watch. He said my family should keep it as a memory of him. Well, I went to my son, and we used the money to save my grandson. He's about your age now. Your father saved his life. I kept the watch hidden over the years. I'm not sure why. But now I know. It's for you."

"Thanks," I said, totally caught off guard by the story. "My father just gave it to you, right off his wrist?"

"Sure did. Like I said, he was a good man. He visited every time he came to Geneva. He always talked about you. He was so proud of you."

My breath froze in disbelief. "He never said that kind of thing to me," I said, fighting back a surge of emotions. I met the man's eyes. "Please, would you like to join me?"

The old man shook his head. "It can be a hard thing for fathers. Sometimes we can't say what we feel. When feelings overwhelm a man, he might stuff them down in places where they shrivel and die. But that doesn't mean he never felt them."

I ran my fingers over the watch. "I appreciate you

giving this back, and your words."

"No, thank *you*, Master Goldsmith. Your father saved my grandson, and he helped bring me back together with my boy. I'm eternally grateful for that."

The man bowed and walked away.

As I finished my dinner alone, I might have missed my father more than any time since he'd died. He would have been proud to see me here. But was that a good thing? Something Don had said came to me. He'd hacked into my precept and called my father a great man. *A man of immense force. You should be proud to be his son. I see much of him in you.*

53

The Captain looked almost giddy as we sat across from each other in the suite. "The room is as secure as it can be," he said. "We're so close. I can *feel* the power. It pulls me like a magnet pulls a knife."

"You sure our connections to Patrick are safe?" I asked. Maybe it was exciting for the Captain to be close to his objective. It was exciting for me the way a horror movie is exciting. My hair stood up on my neck as if Don's eyes were on my back.

"Sven's network is isolated, encrypted, and wholly unworthy of notice. He uses it for games. We'll be safe there. Are you ready?"

The Captain had explained that we'd connect to Sven's virtual world. Patrick was waiting to meet us there. Aisha was standing guard by his body somewhere in Tehran. The

Captain still hadn't told me what they were doing there.

"Here you go." The Captain handed me a headset. It was a mobile version of what we'd used in ISA-7 orientation. Plugging it into my precept would allow a complete immersion in Sven's world.

"Great." I put on the headset. "Let's go." I leaned back in the chair, gave instructions to V, and was transported away.

Pounding techno music flooded my mind. I was in a dark room full of dancing people. It was a concert, or a rave, or something like that. Welcome to Sven's world.

"Can you hear me?" shouted someone beside me, barely audible over the thumping bass. It was an average-looking guy—brown hair and brown eyes—except he had piercings all over his face. "It's me, Patrick."

Sven had a funny sense of humor. I looked down and saw tattoos covering my bare arms. My shirt was black leather. "Where's the Captain?" I asked.

"Here," chirped a girlish voice. "Follow me."

Patrick and I looked at each other and shared a smile. Sven had put the Captain into a tiny woman with bleach blonde hair, wearing a tight black leather dress. Something about her tugged at my memory, but it was hard to tell through her eye makeup—the blackest I'd ever seen.

We followed the woman to another room in the back of the bar. The room was small with a card table in the middle. "Sit," said the Captain in the woman's voice.

We did, staring at him or her. I could not wipe the smirk off my face.

"There's a price to dealing with Sven's fantasy world," the woman said grimly, in just the Captain's tone. "Ignore it. We have little time before we risk detection in Geneva. What have you learned, Patrick?"

The piercing-covered guy's smile faded. "This has expanded beyond just the wealthy. Don has gathered the most important people in the world. He is planning three steps. First, he'll have the religious leaders confess their teachings support him. They will declare loyalty to Don and his creed. Chris Max is one of them."

"I know this," said the woman, leaning forward with her elbows on the table. "I've told you, Chris is a lost cause."

"You're so close," protested Patrick. "You have to try to break him free. If Don seizes the people's faith, their hearts will follow."

"I care little for the people's faith. Let them declare for Cristo. What matters is power, which is why I will not move until he gathers the rich."

"You're already too late, Captain." The guy looked a lot angrier than Patrick could have—Patrick's mind channeled through a face with metal studs and chains decorating its frown. "We should have protected Chris and those like him from the start."

The blonde woman ignored the words. "First the religious leaders. Then what?"

"He will gather the rich."

"As we thought." The woman nodded to me. "You and forty-nine others. We've been unable to figure out how he'll do it, but we know he plans to promise or coerce his way into your bank accounts."

"Elijah is not ready for this," said Patrick. "He can't face Don."

"He's ready, but that doesn't matter. I'm the one who'll move next." The Captain somehow sounded even more threatening in this form. "Elijah and I have figured out a way to get me in the room. You know what will happen from there."

"I know what you *think* will happen, Captain. And you know I think it won't work. Do you have any idea how many attempts against him have failed?"

"Two hundred twenty-seven in the past year," the woman recited, unflinching.

"And you think you're different?"

The woman stared down the guy.

"Why not let him try?" I asked.

The guy's pierced brow lowered in anger. "Because we cannot afford to lose *you*," he said. "You are—"

"He'll be safe," the woman interrupted. "We've arranged it so that he will have no connection to me in that gathering. Whether I succeed or fail, he walks away unharmed."

"You can't be sure of that. You are out of your depth."

"Boy, you have no idea of my depth."

"Look, both of you," I interjected, and they turned to me. "We're on the same team, right?"

Neither responded, other than to share skeptical glances at each other.

"It sounds like we're agreed on what will happen," I continued. "Don has his gathering with the religious leaders. Then he gathers the rich. The Captain tries to do his thing. If he succeeds, we're all happy, right?"

This time they both nodded. "He's not going to succeed," said Patrick.

"Okay, fine," I said. "But he thinks he will, and we agree he should try if he's willing to take the risk?"

The guy nodded reluctantly.

"If he doesn't succeed, I'll try to get out of Geneva fast. Once I'm out, I'll connect with you, Patrick. But what's next? What's the third step?"

"Cristo intends to gather the world's political leaders," said the woman. "The final step is his outright power grab. He will stage a vote by the world's people. Direct democracy of the worst sort. By then they'll have little choice but to support him. He'll declare dominion over everyone and everything."

"But the nations will not allow that," added Patrick's voice. "Aisha and I have nearly finished our work. The Iranian leader will lead the first strike, but more will follow. Don and everything within a hundred miles of Geneva will be destroyed. The bombs will fall like raindrops."

My mouth fell open. It made sense. No wonder the Captain was so desperate. "So the Captain must succeed," I breathed out.

"He can't. Not against Don."

The blonde woman slammed her hands on the table and glared at us. "*I will.* Just don't get in my way."

54

The next afternoon I sat on the suite's deck, gazing out over Lake Geneva, taking a break from reports. The Captain was inside. I was about to head in for a snack when my vision went black. Total blankness. An instant later, my precept's screen took over my lenses. It showed the text: "Live Broadcast from the President of the United Nations."

"People of the world," Don announced. "Welcome to the World's Cathedral!" He was alone on a vast, empty stage, wearing a trim charcoal suit and a blood red tie. I hadn't seen him live in weeks. His perfect face commanded my attention.

"This place represents a new beginning for the faith of mankind." Don's black hair brushed his shoulders as he swept his arms forward. My view suddenly panned out, revealing a cavernous room packed with thousands. "It is the fulfillment, the completion, of generations of progress. Today you will hear from our greatest religious leaders, but before you do, watch and see the story of the Cathedral's construction. It required not an ounce of human sweat. We have built in one year what would have taken our ancestors a lifetime. Witness the future."

An immense screen appeared behind Don. The view was fixed on the almost-human face of a giant android. The robot turned and lifted a steel beam the size of a redwood. It hoisted the beam overhead and then slammed it straight down into the ground. Another robot began hammering the beam into the ground, while the first lifted another beam. The view zoomed out, revealing an army of androids in all shapes and sizes, working and building like a horde of ants.

The video accelerated. Days passed in seconds. The androids were relentless, working through every night, hauling steel and dirt, pouring concrete, and twisting pipes and wires through the structure. The rush of activity almost took my breath away.

Then the video slowed again, returning to its focus on the android where it started. The robot had something huge strapped to its back as it scaled up the scaffolding on the almost-finished cathedral. It reached the top and lifted the item from its back. It planted it precisely at the pinnacle of the cathedral: a twisting and coiling sculpture, abstract, but its identity clear.

It was the dragon.

"*This* is our future, the culmination of man!" Don said, as the video zoomed back to him. No object or ornament shared his spotlight. The cathedral was like a blank canvas presenting Don alone. "Some have resisted the help of our greatest creations, fearing the androids would replace us. But, under my control, they will replace only the curse of work. I will use them to give every single human on this planet freedom, equality, and happiness. These are my free gifts to you, my people. All I ask is that you join me in our march to a greater world, a greater faith, and our highest destiny."

"As you know well," he continued, "the world has tried many faiths. The world has tried crusades and intolerance. And the world has faced pain and suffering as a result. Today we can have a fresh start. We can learn how to find peace together on this common ground. I offer myself as a representative of this peace, but only if you wish it. You may vote with your precept any time, showing your support for these leaders and for me."

A question appeared at the bottom of my view. It read: "*Do you put your faith in President Donatello Cristo?*" A single interactive button appeared after the question: *YES.* A number showed up in the bottom right of the screen. It was already in the billions, and rising fast. 2,045,666,972. 3,356,980,321. 4,000,000,000. As it grew, I pushed nothing. The question and the button stayed on my screen, as if taunting me.

"Let's hear from our first leader." Don pointed to a row of men and women in the front of the crowd. "The

Dalai Lama will share his wisdom."

A robed man with a shaved head stepped up to the stage. Don slid to the side. The monk bowed his head for a long moment. When he looked up, his expression was blank. "We all seek nirvana," he began. "The path to liberation and enlightenment is peace and meditation on Buddha's Four Noble Truths. We can see this in Don." He glanced to the other man on stage, and then back to the crowd. "His creed, his person, they coexist with ours. Join me in this alliance, and the world will be one."

And then the monk was done. As he returned to his seat, the cathedral's crowd applauded. The tally ticked higher: 5,458,901,666.

Something wasn't right. I knew the Dalai Lama was supposed to be stoic, but he'd said the words with surreal calm. How could he make such a request without the slightest passion? What was Don doing? I remembered another verse Ronaldo had told me: *He shall exalt himself and magnify himself above every god.*

Don held his arms wide for silence. "Be one with me, my Buddhist friends. For as long as space endures, and for as long as living beings remain, until then may I dispel the misery of the world." He looked down again to the row of leaders. "Next, the great Christian evangelist, Pastor Christopher Max!"

Chris rose and stepped onto stage. I'd expected bruises and prison rags. Instead he looked glorious in a white suit and blue tie. It seemed impossible. He almost stole the stage from Don as he waved and smiled into the screen.

"Brothers and sisters!" he greeted. "We have found our champion of the faith in Don. Like Jesus come again, Don is a model of peace and tolerance."

No way, I thought. No way Chris would say that. No way the order would believe that.

Chris continued, "We must give up our crusades of conversion and intolerance. I call for harmony with believers of all faiths. Let's unite as one body with Don. Prosperity and joy and heaven will then await!" Chris waved again and flashed his pearl-white smile as he glided happily off the stage. More people voted "yes." The number ticked past 8,000,000,000.

Had Don killed Chris and used his body, as he had with Charles? But could he do that and stand on stage at the same time? That would take more processing power than anyone I'd ever met. Ten times as much as I had in my head.

"As you all know and mourn," Don said, as he moved back to center stage, "the world lost the Pope during the earthquake in Rome. While the Catholic Church selects its new leader, their council of cardinals has assured us of their agreement: the people must ally with me, as the best hope for this age. You may confirm now, Cardinal Ramirez."

Don motioned to a red-robed man in the front row. He stood and, staying where he was, waved to the crowd and the screen. "Thank you, Cardinal. Let this be another sign of unity to come. Religion is *for* man! We will not let the gods rob us of its benefits. Next, the Khalifat Rasul Allah."

The Muslim leader took the stage and put on the same

kind of show as the others. So did a rabbi, a yogi, and at least a dozen other religious leaders who followed after.

By the end I was convinced of two things. First, Don was good, really good, at persuasion. The number had reached twelve billion—nearly 80% of the world. It was hard to believe that many people even had precepts. A man could do anything with that kind of popular support. Second, Don was good, really good, at manipulation. I figured there was no way he could've gotten away with killing all these religious leaders and using their bodies. So whatever he'd threatened, whatever he'd promised, I was more certain than ever that I'd be no match for him.

And we'd meet tomorrow.

55

I took one last look in the mirror. My own face was comforting. Whatever happened, I'd still be me. My partnership with the Captain had at least made my precept safe from anyone's control, thanks to Sven's satellite.

This gave me some hope as I left my suite for the meeting. I strolled to the shore of Lake Geneva. The UN headquarters was a towering skyscraper emerging from the water, with thin pedestrian bridges connecting it to land. Among the lower buildings in the rest of the city, and even the mountains around it, this tower loomed like a stairway to heaven.

After a long walk down one of the bridges, I reached a gate and two androids. One of them scanned my eyes. A green light blinked, and the gate opened.

My precept's connection was severed as soon as I

stepped inside. We entered a vast room with wide stairs going down toward the center like an inverted pyramid. I recognized it as the place where UN leaders met.

No one could move around the room without an android escort. One of the robots greeted me and guided me to an elevator along the outer edge. It stepped in with me. Moments later I was zooming up the building.

The elevator doors opened to a different world. The sleek, modern style of the UN building was gone. The walls looked like gold, separated by high windows with closed crimson curtains. The chandeliers shimmered like diamonds. An android held out a tray of champagne flutes. I took one as I stepped forward, but didn't dare take a sip.

Small groups stood clustered around the decadent room. A quick glance around revealed familiar faces from my research. These were the richest people in the world.

I approached the nearest group.

"Elijah Goldsmith," said a young man's voice. He stepped forward and held out his hand. "I'm Namib Patel."

"Nice to meet you," I said, though I knew his name the moment I saw him. He was the heir of an Indian media magnate, and the only one in this room even close to my age. He spent most of his fortune on private islands.

"I'm Travis," said another man. He looked twice as big as Namib, and he shook my hand twice as hard. Travis Stump was old oil money incarnate, from his boots to his belt buckle to his wide jaw. The report had said he was eighty-three years old. He looked fifty, tops. Money was the fountain of youth.

"Why do *you* think President Cristo invited us?" asked a slim Hispanic woman in the group. Isabel Flores. Solar power in Mexico. Never married, art collector. Nothing about her made me think she might be the Captain.

Five of them were staring at me, waiting for my answer. I recognized the other two as a Dutch philanthropist and a Russian banker. I smiled at the group. "He must want our money, right?"

Travis clapped me on the back and laughed. "Told y'all that's what it was."

"What if President Cristo wants to partner with us?" Namib suggested.

"Yes," said the Russian. Dimitri Ivanov. His lips curved into a slight smirk. "He wants power. He needs us. We have good position."

"I still don't think this is about money or power," said the Dutchman, as he took another glass from a passing android's tray. "The President has nobler goals." Hans van den Berg spoke with nearly as much charm as Don himself. He was the only son of the woman who had created the first precept school. The school that had taught billions.

"Ain't nothing noble about this," the oil man challenged. His drink was still full, like mine.

"You don't think equality is noble?" Hans asked. "The President wants a precept for everyone."

"And he wants beauty," said Isabel. "Have you seen any building as impressive as this one?" She swept her eyes around the room. "Have you seen the cities his machines have rebuilt after the disasters? They are magnificent.

Imagine what he could do with our full support."

"I'd rather not," said a new voice, as an Arab man in a white robe joined the group. Khalil El-Amin. "We should be uniting against President Cristo. He grows too powerful."

"His power has limits," Dimitri said.

"There are limits, but not from your country, not anymore." Khalil turned from Dimitri to Travis, then to me. "And not your country either. The Mahdi and our people alone hold him in check."

Dimitri scowled at Khalil. "Your forces cannot stand against the UN's."

"He's right," Isabel said. "I'd rather be on the President's side than yours."

"A poor choice." Khalil held his open palms out to the group. "Cristo speaks of freedom but leads you to chains." His hands clenched into fists. "My people offer discipline that leads to freedom." His hands opened again. "You see?"

"I'm surprised you showed up." Hans swirled his drink as he stared at Khalil. "Just stirring up trouble?"

Khalil shook his head. "I was curious. I come on behalf of my people to learn what the President plans. I come on my own to see which of you will fall for—"

His voice trailed off as applause rose on the opposite side of the room. Don had entered.

Every eye was glued to Don as he glided through the crowd. His black suit was immaculate as always. His face was calm, despite the flurry of activity around him. Androids rushed about, offering fresh drinks and setting plush chairs in a large semicircle.

"Welcome!" Don greeted, making his way to the center of the room. "Take your seats, please."

We did as he said. I found myself in the second closest chair to the elevator. I knew it was little help, but I'd take whatever comfort I could get.

"Thank you for coming," Don said to us. "Your presence in person is priceless. I assure you, you are safe here." He held out arms, graceful and inviting. "I suspect you already have, but go ahead and sweep the room. You'll detect not a bit of data or signal from outside. You're connected to my personal network here. No one in the world may look in on us. It is just you and me. Please," he bowed his head slightly, "question me if you feel it is necessary."

No one did, not even Khalil. We all watched Don, in awe and silence.

"You're an elite group," Don began. "You may be asking yourselves, *How much money does this man want from me? Or, what kind of partnership will this man require?* Let me be clear. I will ask nothing from you. You may leave any time, if you wish. But if you stay, you will hear my offer. An offer that comes only once, and only for you." He paused. "Would you like to hear it?"

Don's gaze drifted around the room and hovered on me. Something clicked in my mind. I *did* want to hear his offer. I found myself nodding, transfixed.

His face lit up with a smile. "Wonderful. All of you, look at this."

He gestured with his hand, and a three-dimensional image appeared beside him. It showed the biggest gathering of people I'd ever seen. There were thousands upon thousands, maybe millions in the streets, churning and stirring like tadpoles in a mud puddle. The image scanned out, showing the city of Geneva.

Then the image shifted. It was London. The view zoomed in on another crowd of people, just like the one before it. The image continued shifting to different groups, in Sao Paolo, Beijing, Bombay, Sydney, and more.

"The world is restless," Don said softly. "The people

are tired of the governing elite, the powerful and the rich. They are united by technology. Their precepts link and allow universal, transcendent support...*for me*. This is democracy in its highest form. I am the will of the people."

He snapped his fingers and the image disappeared.

"You see, friends," he confided, "people like us face a grave danger. Our very way of life is endangered, but I've found the way to save it. I have the opiate. The era of nations has passed. My technology can preserve what we have. You may even be enhanced as the world unites."

"Enhanced?" Travis's voice was jarring, as if pulling me out of a trance. "I already have all that I could want. What could you possibly give me?"

Don beamed in response, as if it was the best question anyone could ask him. "You are all wealthy enough to know that money can't buy everything, and also that it buys most things people say it can't—like love and happiness. But what I offer is unique, and only mine to give. Look."

An image appeared behind him. It was a map of the earth, with ten regions in ten different colors.

"Each of you, after you swear your allegiance to me, will have an opportunity to submit a sealed proposal. Tell me what you would give me. How much? When? Offer me your best. I will rank all the proposals and give unique powers accordingly. To the six best, I will give dominion to one of these regions, subject only to my distant oversight."

"What do you mean by *dominion*—" began Khalil, but Don raised his hand to cut him short.

"The other four regions are already allotted," he said.

"I will clear the way for your power if you seize this opportunity. Put your faith in me, make your offer. And even if you do not win a region, as long as you commit to a good offer, I will accept and extend your life in exchange."

"That's hogwash," Travis blurted out.

"Is it?" Don asked. "We already grow new organs for our bodies. Why not whole new bodies? The difficulty is transferring the mind, the soul. I've discovered a way to overcome that. It is not cheap, but I will give it to those loyal to me. You'll get no better return on your fortunes."

He stepped to a small table in the corner of the room nearest the door. "First, sign your allegiance. Share what you have with me, and I will share what I have with you. Then, my friends, we will celebrate. We have no better company than each other."

A few men and women rose from their seats and started lining up before Don.

"What if we don't sign?" Khalil's voice filled the room.

"I hoped you'd ask that," Don replied. His eyes bored into the robed man. "Just for you, Khalil, let me show you what will happen."

Don flicked his wrist, as if evoking a thought. Khalil's face went blank, as if he were viewing a precept video. A look of horror grew in his face. His eyes opened wide, his lips turned down and quivered.

He fell to his knees.

"*Stop!*" he pleaded. "I'll sign, please..."

Don flicked his wrist again and motioned for Khalil to come. The man stumbled forward as if he'd just awoken from a terrible nightmare. What had Don shown him?

Khalil reached the front of the line. Don pulled out a needle and pricked its sharp point into Khalil's finger. The man's hand shook violently as he pressed his finger and blood to a translucent paper on the desk. After Khalil finished, Don patted him on the back like an old friend and waved him out of the room.

The next men and women in line did the same. We stepped forward one by one. Nobody resisted, nobody asked another question. Maybe ambition and fear were all Don needed to keep us in order. Maybe we were awestruck, stunned into silence.

I had my own reasons, waiting near the end of the line. There were maybe ten people to go when the woman in front of me glanced back.

My breath caught. Her pale face, her bleach-blond hair, they were familiar. She was dressed entirely different, but it was the small woman from Sven's virtual world.

57

Another person signed in blood. Then another.

Seven people remained in front of the blonde woman in the plain black suit. Maybe five minutes until the Captain, in her body, would stand face-to-face with Don.

I tried to stay calm but my heart raced. This woman was going to try to kill Don. How? The androids had scanned us on the way in. The Captain couldn't have brought a weapon. Without a gun or a knife, how did the Captain expect to take Don down? Poison. It had to be poison. The woman wore rings on almost every finger, as she had in Sven's world. Maybe one was loaded with poison.

I remembered the report on this woman—Helena Eriksson. Her father had been the Swedish brain surgeon who patented the process of internal precept installation.

That process now equipped the masses, and it produced a fortune.

Helena reportedly lived as simply as a person could with so much wealth. Her modest home was in a small town north of the Arctic Circle. She gave away billions to save seals, penguins, and their habitats. Maybe the Captain had picked her for her mild personality. Don would least expect a surprise from someone like her. What had the Captain done to her?

"Xing Xing!" Don's voice jerked me back to the present. He spoke on in Mandarin. V translated it instantly and played the English in my mind. *A pleasure as always*, Don was saying. *I knew I could count on you.*

"Friends of the dragon unite, do we not?" replied the elegant Chinese woman facing Don. She wore a slim red dress and spoke flawless English.

She bowed her head as Don kissed her hand lightly. She then let Don prick her finger with the needle. She smeared the blood into a crude Chinese character on the page on the table. The page seemed to absorb the blood.

Don spoke again in Mandarin. *Give your father my best. A general's loyalty moves armies, or keeps them still, when needed. He shall have his region. Wouldn't you like one for yourself?*

"Indeed, I would," the woman said. She leaned close to Don and whispered just loud enough for my enhanced hearing. "Visit me again soon. I have more to share."

Don smiled and spoke one word. *Soon.*

She sauntered out of the room, and the Captain in Helena's body stepped up next.

"It is good to finally meet you, Madame Eriksson," Don said, looking her over. "I hope your proposal is more forthcoming than your presence. You are rather reclusive, too much so for a woman with your…gifts." His voice had gone deep and seductive. I remembered him using that voice when he'd spoken to Naomi in Rome. "Wouldn't you like a region with warmer winters?"

"I guess so," replied Helena's mousy voice. "The nights can be long north of the Arctic." She held out her hand stiffly, as if to shake Don's. "Nice to meet you, too, President Cristo."

Don looked down at her hand with an expression of doubt or surprise. Then he studied Helena's face. "There you are," he growled.

The woman moved fast as lightening. She sprang at Don, swiping her ringed fingers at his face.

Don slid away in a blur. As she turned to face him, he fired something from his wrist into her body.

She fell flat on her face.

Don turned on me.

Before I could react, a shadow seemed to pass and he was suddenly behind me, pressing something against my temple.

"Both of you can rest now." His tone was soft, gentle, alluring. "Ponder what you've attempted in your subconscious. I'll be waiting when you wake up."

I heard a click and felt a pinch. All went black.

58

"Welcome back, Elijah."

It was Don. His voice had the same delicate touch. "You're safe here. We've neutralized our enemy. Open your eyes and take a moment to relax."

My eyes blinked open. I was leaning back in a chair, looking up at a ceiling. There was a fresco that would have made Michelangelo proud, except that its fine lines formed Don with a child in his arms and a dragon soaring behind him. The backdrop showed dark, roiling clouds like I'd seen in Rome. My gaze followed elaborate woodwork down the wall. For some reason, I'd expected to see only Don in front of me. What I saw made my head spin.

I was in one of four chairs around a low glass table. The Captain's pale body lay on the table. His chest rose and fell with the breathing of deep sleep.

Beside me sat the blonde woman, Helena. She was chained to the chair, with a white cloth tied around her head and over her mouth. Every feature of her face was twisted in pure terror. Was the Captain still occupying her body?

Across from me, on the other side of the Captain's body, sat Don and Sven. They reclined in their chairs and smiled at me, content as two men enjoying lemonade on a summer day. Only their glasses were full of red liquid. Not blood. Things hadn't gotten quite that strange...yet. I was having trouble with reality.

"Something to drink?" Don asked me.

"Water?" came the word from my parched lips.

Don shook his head. "How about wine?" He picked up his glass and swirled it. "Sven and I just opened a fifty-year-old bottle of France's finest. Remember, this is a party."

"I'm not sure—"

Don held up his hand to stop me. He stood, poured a glass from an ancient-looking bottle, and brought it to me. "Don't worry, Eli. You don't mind me calling you Eli?"

I shook my head. He could call me butterfly princess if that meant I'd get out of here alive.

"Good." Don returned to his seat. "I think we'll be fine friends, Eli. Let's enjoy this moment. A toast!" He raised his glass. "To our budding partnership."

I raised my glass and drank. The wine tasted smooth.

"Nice, eh? There are far better pleasures to come." Don turned to Sven. "Want to explain this?" he asked, motioning to the Captain's body as if was a rotten egg.

"Sure, yes of course!" Sven said with feverish excitement in his eyes. "Look, Eli, I know this seems bad, and I'm so sorry you had to find out this way. But the Captain, well, he's been lying to you about two important things. First, he told you he was going to kill Don to save people from world government, to restore the nations' power, right?"

"He said something like that." The Captain's focus had been on the assassination, not the aftermath.

"The truth is," Sven continued, "he planned to seize power in Don's place. Only a handful in the world have the processing power in their brains to control the world's telecommunications and algorithms the way Don can." Awe poured out of Sven's tone. What did he mean by controlling an algorithm?

"You, of course, are one of those few," Don said. It was unclear whether that was a compliment or a threat.

"The Captain might have been able to do it," Sven said. "That's what he was planning on."

I met Sven's stare, keeping my mouth shut. Questions ran wild in my mind: *So what if the Captain had wanted power? Who wouldn't? Wouldn't I rather have the Captain than Don in this position?*

Sven spoke on, "The Captain was a betrayer. ISA's mission is to serve the UN and each nation, to protect the peace. The Captain had been making ISA-7 into his own task force for years. He tried to kill the President!" His zeal reminded me of Charles.

I turned to Don. "When did you kill Sven?" I asked.

Don smiled at me patiently. "For once your skeptical mind *over*-reaches. Sven just knows better than most what I can do for the world. He's one of the first to have a constant paradise in his mind, through his precept. Soon I'll give the same gift to everyone."

Sven was nodding. "It's amazing, Eli. You have to let Don connect you to his system. Truly amazing…" He pressed his eyes closed and sighed in pleasure. Then he looked at me again. "Seriously, it's me, Eli. The same Sven who flew you to Montana and reconnected your precept. That brings us to the second lie. The Captain knew we didn't have a connection to the other agents' trackers, so he made me upload a loop of old information we'd gathered. Whatever locations you saw, those were old, not real. He lied to your face about it. Don't believe me? Go ahead, ask the Captain yourself."

Sven gestured towards the woman. The cloth over her mouth fell away.

She gasped and stretched her jaw. "Help me, please," she begged.

"Where's Naomi?" Don asked calmly. "Tell us and you can return to your body and walk out."

The woman began to speak, but hesitated.

"No guessing," Don threatened. "I want the coordinates straight from her tracker."

"Okay," groaned the Captain in Helena's voice. "31.78 degrees north, 35.22 degrees east." The woman's eyebrows lifted expectantly, as if she were praying against all odds that the coordinates were right.

Don turned to me, his face blank. "Elijah, what are the coordinates of the tracker from your precept?"

I summoned V and asked for them. *Weird*—they were not what I remembered, but they were the same as what the Captain had said. I repeated them aloud.

"Marvelous," Don said. "That's right in the heart of old Jerusalem. The problem is"—he surged to his feet and flung the bottle of wine across the room, shattering it against the wall—"*she's not there!*"

He took a deep breath and fell back into the chair. "You see, we've been following that agent all along." He pointed at the woman accusingly. "She's not Naomi and you know it."

"Let me go," pleaded the woman's voice. Her eyes were fixed on the body on the table before us. "I'll do anything…"

"Are you sure you want that?" Don inquired. "I'm the only thing holding *them* back, you know."

The woman tilted her head down at the floor and whimpered in fear. All I saw was rich wooden parquet. She obviously saw something I could not. That was a change.

"Please, no!" she shouted. "*LET ME GO!*"

Don smiled at her. He leaned forward and held his hands out over the Captain's body. "Voilà! You may go."

The woman's body sagged and then went stiff as a corpse, just as the Captain's body surged into motion.

His pale blue eyes passed over me without recognition. His gaze went everywhere at once, frantic. He hugged himself, twisting and turning. He looked down and jumped, as if leaping away from something. Again I saw nothing on the floor, but I lifted my feet just in case.

"What is it?" I asked, but he ignored me.

The Captain's sights turned to one of the room's tall windows. He let out a huge breath, as if releasing the last of his resolve. Then he charged at the window and slammed his body into it like a freight train. He went down with a loud grunt. The window had a hairline crack.

The Captain rose and kicked his heavy boot into the wall of glass, over and over. The crack splintered and spread. Eventually he backed away.

He glanced back over his shoulder. Our eyes met for an instant. His face screamed for release. Should I try to stop him? Could I?

Before I made a move, he charged at the window again. Harder this time. He barreled through it and the glass shattered into a million pieces.

I rushed to the window and looked out…and down, way, way down. The Captain's body was like a fleck of dirt on the ground, hundreds of feet below.

59

"Ah, guilt," Don sighed, "sure can derail a man. Come, Eli, I'd like to show you something." He helped me to my feet. I stumbled after him in shock.

As we came to a door leading out of the room, Don told Sven to arrange for a press release about the Captain's suicide. He walked with me through the door and into a vast room. It reminded me of my father's office, though twice as big. The ceiling seemed four stories high, and there was a sweeping view of Geneva, the lake, and the surrounding mountains.

"It's all show," Don motioned dismissively around the room. "Every leader must have a show of authority, but also a real seat of power. I'm going to show you mine."

I nodded as if he made sense and followed him to a glass elevator in the back corner of the room. We rode it up to the floor above. The elevator doors slid open and revealed a bare, modern room at the very top of the building. The floors were black marble. The walls and ceiling were glass. A giant spire reached into the sky high above us. The base of the spire was suspended in mid-air in the center of the room. A thousand translucent fibers dangled from it to a bowl-shaped object at head height.

"Beautiful, isn't it?" Don sounded as proud as a father.

"Sure," I said. It reminded me of what the Captain had used in the room hidden underneath the Pentagon. The Captain. The unflappable man who was so scared he'd leapt out of a building.

"I'd tell you what it is and what it does, but why not just give it a try? Then you'll *know*."

"You want me to put it on my head?"

"Yes," he encouraged. "Why not?"

I could give him more than a few reasons, but couldn't it help to know what Don was capable of? I was alone here, with no idea how I'd find Naomi and the order again. But that's what I had to do, and when I did, this information could help.

I stepped forward to the device. Don lifted it and set it on my head gently.

I felt a thousand little pinches and nudges against my head. They were automated and fast, like a robot's fingers tickling my scalp. Then came a rush of blood, overwhelming my thoughts. I closed my eyes and tried to concentrate.

My mind felt like it did when scanning my precept's

database, communicating with V, but this was different. It was like the difference between swimming in a bathtub and in the middle of a stormy ocean with no land in sight. No, not an ocean. That was too simple. This was a universe. There were billions of pricks of light in the darkness.

Choose one, said Don's voice in my head.

I chose a prick of light. My mind was instantly inside it. Thoughts collided with mine. It was a woman. She was Noma Hussein, thirty-seven years old, in a room serving breakfast to three kids. They were in Jakarta. Her every life detail washed over me as I tried to grapple with the information. Her emotions were a raging current. She was torn, sad, lost. Her husband was dead. Oh, how she had loved him! Her despondence threatened to undo me.

Go ahead, said Don's voice in my mind. *Speak to her. Tell her she can have him back in a virtual world to come.*

I'm sorry for your loss, I thought. The woman's mind reacted as if grazed lightly by my fingers. She was attentive, scared. She knew I was there.

No, said Don's voice, *SPEAK to her.*

I spoke. "I know how you loved him."

She stopped cold, with a bowl in her hand. She looked frantically around the room. She stared up at the ceiling. But I was *in* her mind. The three kids were staring at her with confusion, with their mouths hanging open.

"It's okay," I said. "You will have him back, in a virtual world to come."

She stumbled to her knees. "Who are you?"

Enough, said Don, *it is time to leave her, come back.*

I forced my mind away from her. I slid out of her mind and soared away, back into the universe where she was just one pinprick of light.

Relax, soothed Don, *ejecting now.*

Suddenly I was back in the room atop the UN tower, on my knees. The woman from Jakarta was gone. The bowl was suspended above me. Everything was dim and bland. I looked at my hands. They looked like shadows of reality. Part of a world without color.

"This is the Omega Project," Don said. "It is the lever that will move the world into eternity."

My body was still trembling. I couldn't think straight. "This is how you spoke to me, through my precept?"

"Precisely," he said.

It was like being a god. "And you can reach anyone, anywhere, as long as their precept is connected?"

"Yes. I'm preparing the way for everyone to have instantly, abundantly, whatever he most desires."

"How?" If he could be inside anyone's head, then it was only a small step to create a world for the person there. Was that what he'd done for Sven? "Even virtual worlds have limits, right?"

Don nodded. "For now," he said, "but some powers are beyond the physical and mental realms."

"Spiritual?" I guessed, thinking of the dragon I'd seen and that no one had been able to explain.

"You'll see," Don assured me, "but first we must find Naomi."

"Why?" I tried to sound amenable. I had to find a way

out of this.

"I think you know," he said. "Her order has twisted many truths and told you many lies. Why do you think two of their leaders have joined me?"

Two of them? Someone other than Gregory? Don didn't let things like that slip. He wanted me to know.

"But the order is correct about one thing," he continued. "You are special, Eli. You can see what others cannot. The order says it's because God gave you this gift. Another lie. It's because of what your father and I did to enhance your precept and your very mind."

His shocking claim rattled me, but I clung to my Mom's distant words like a man hanging from a cliff: *You must learn to see the truth in your dreams. They will pursue you until you heed them. The word is living and active, piercing to the division of soul and of spirit.*

Don was studying me. "I can help you understand your dreams, if you'll tell me more of them."

I thought of Don screaming in fury when I'd led him to the cottage and Naomi wasn't there. No way I was telling him that, but maybe that's how this was going to work. I could play along, but Naomi would be safe if my dream was right.

"What is it, Eli?" His voice was soothing, encouraging. "You can tell me."

"I won't let you hurt her."

"Nor would I!" he protested. "And you know why. She carries my child."

"Yours?"

"The child is mine, and Naomi is yours. Isn't that what you want more than anything—*her*?"

"What does that matter?" There seemed to be no point in denying it. Don had used this system to enter my precept, just as I entered the mind of the woman in Jakarta. I had *felt* what she felt. He must have felt my loss and my pain about Naomi. He must have felt my love.

"My business is to give people whatever they want," Don explained. "And what you want is clear. Let's work together to find her."

"I'd rather do it on my own."

Don smiled and put his hand to his chin. "You know the proposal you will submit?"

"What proposal?"

"Like the others from our meeting, you will submit a sealed bid—a financial proposal. These will be the basis for my grants of power."

I nodded. I remembered, but between the Captain and the Omega Project, I'd hardly given the proposal a thought.

"You have a head start, Eli. The gift your father left in his will for me—I will count that. But you still don't have enough to win if the others offer everything. That's why you should include Naomi. Make her part of your proposal, bring her to me, and you will offer a value the others could never match."

Never, I thought. I would never expose Naomi to that danger, and Don must have seen it in my eyes.

"Once you win," he continued, "Naomi will be yours, and you will be more than safe. Both of you will have whatever you want. A tropical kingdom, a mountain hideaway, a place of highest honor by my side—you name it. The world will worship her as the mother of its ruler."

I opened my mouth, but Don stopped me with a finger against my lips.

"I know this is a lot," he said. "Stay with me, Eli, and you'll understand. I won't make you rush to a decision. Just stay here and consider my offer. Okay?"

I shook my head. *Not okay.*

"What would you go back to?" Don asked.

"I don't know," I said, surprised that it was true.

"You are safe here. Naomi can be safe, too."

A thought struck me: *Resist the devil, and he will flee from you.* "Would you protect us from the dragon?" I asked. "It already killed Naomi once."

Don looked surprised. "What are you talking about?"

"On Patmos."

"What about Patmos?"

"You know the dragon. I saw you with it in Rome. Soon after that, it attacked a group from the order, including Naomi and me. The thing went berserk, thrashing everyone in its path. It bashed into Naomi and knocked her into a boulder. She died."

"That's ridiculous," Don said. "She's alive."

"I saw it happen."

He shook his head, then sighed. "The dragon and I do not always align. Sometimes it can lose control. But on earth, it is subject to my will. It wouldn't hurt Naomi. And if what you said actually happened, about the dragon going berserk, it would have killed you, too."

"It would have," I said, "except a man came and saved us. He told the dragon to stop, and it did."

For the first time I'd ever seen, Don looked afraid and speechless. His black eyes studied mine.

"What else did this man say?"

Resist, I thought. "I don't remember."

"Don't play games with me." Anger flared in Don's voice and swept over his face. Then it was gone. "Oh, I'm just curious." He was charming and calm again. "We can talk more later. I think you'll understand once you see what I can give you—everything you've ever wanted."

60

When Don and I returned to his enormous office below, two people were waiting for us. One was a guy who looked maybe thirty. He had short dark hair and an inquisitive face. He wore white linen and a smile—like a man on vacation. His sleeves were rolled up to reveal arms like a bear's, covered in thick hair. I could've sworn I'd seen him before, but I couldn't remember where.

Beside him was a thin older woman with purple-colored hair and a vivid purple dress. She spoke first. "President Cristo, we have excellent news."

"My favorite kind," he said. "Beatriz, Alexi, this is Elijah Goldsmith. We've finally found our seer."

"It is an honor," Alexi said, holding out his hand. As we shook, he introduced himself as, "Alexander Markos, Oxford professor and the UN's chief political scientist."

He looked awfully young for those titles.

"Alexi and I met at Oxford," Don said. "He was my student when I advised graduates in international politics. I saw as much genius in him as he saw ambition in me." The two of them laughed together. It didn't seem funny to me.

"I hear your ISA scores rivaled mine," Alexi said to me. His mention of ISA brought the memory back: he'd been the UN liaison, in the room that first day of orientation with Wade. He'd been watching us, evaluating us. "It's about time I had someone I could team up with to outsmart President Cristo."

Don smiled at Alexi. "Good luck."

Alexi laughed. "You'll let me host Elijah?"

Don nodded. "Take him to Babylon, first thing, and let him know about your other guest."

"President Cristo," said the woman in purple with impatience. "We've come with news that you must hear at once."

"About the attack?" Don asked.

"Yes, we've learned the opposition leaders have their nuclear arsenal armed and ready."

"When are they going to fire?"

"After tomorrow's meeting."

"Then what are you worried about?"

"If the meeting does not go as planned, then..."

"It will go as planned," Don interrupted, turning to me. "Elijah has seen it, haven't you?"

"Seen what?"

"The dragon," he said, "with the ten horns. Tell us

what you saw."

Was anything in my head safe from him? "The dragon or whatever it is. The creature covered in swirling shadows, in one dream it had ten horns."

"Yes, and what happened?"

"The horns grew after the dragon swallowed a sphere with ten satellite antennae. But then the horns were absorbed in the shadow, and the shadow came to rest in a vast city."

"See!" Don said. "They'll all swear to me."

"You put too much faith in this boy," Beatriz said.

"You have a better idea?"

"Let my servants occupy their leaders," Beatriz suggested. "We'll *make* them comply."

"No!" Don shouted, furious. "I told you, they must come to me freely. Mankind cannot be forced into loving me. We must seduce them. Isn't that why you're here?"

"I have done my job," she defended. "Let the people visit Babylon and they'll have all the seduction they could ever want, and more."

"Good. Leave the politics to Alexi and the visions to Eli." Don grinned at me. "You're going to like Alexi's place, and Babylon's even better." He bowed his head to us. "Time for my next appointment. I'll see you at dinner. We're in Beijing tonight."

Alexi and Beatriz bowed. I didn't, and no one seemed to notice. Alexi guided me out. We walked through the office's giant doors.

In the next room, three stunning women were lounging

in the chairs where I'd sat with Don, Sven, and the Captain.

"Hello, Elijah," they said together. Their appearances suddenly shifted.

I froze. Each one looked like Jezebel, with smooth black skin taunting me to come closer, begging me to touch. Their mouths were an invitation.

"Come on," Alexi was saying, tugging at my arm. "They are just Don's assistants. They meet with him twice a day. Why are you just standing there?"

"But..."

He laughed. "I know, I know, Don has a thing for French models. They're a little too thin and pale for my taste."

"Pale?" Their skin smoldered like magma.

Alexi pulled me away. "Just wait, it's even better in Babylon."

61

Alexi led me outside the UN skyscraper and toward a group of disc-shaped planes. We boarded one and flew off, heading south.

He started talking about the weather and Geneva, and then he turned to politics. "If the world's peace were still resting on the balance of U.S. and Chinese power, wouldn't that be more dangerous than a peace balanced on a single man, on Don?"

I nodded, though he sounded insane. Did he really think I was on his side? "What if something happens to Don?"

"I worried about that, at first," Alexi said. "But I've seen attacks come at him from a thousand different directions. The man is invincible. Unfortunately, the equilibrium of power in the world is not. Imagine the danger when a third party grows and seeks to rival our two megapowers."

I nodded. *Keep him talking*, I thought. There was no way I was changing this man's mind, so I might as well learn what I could about his views and Don's plans.

"Today that new rival is Persia," he continued. "Iran has taken so much territory, with such religious zeal, that it threatens the peace Don has brokered. Their leader, Mahdi, must be dealt with. That's why we must act."

"What will you do?" I asked, thinking of Aisha and Patrick. Would they know where Naomi was hiding?

"The world's leaders will meet soon. We will give the Persians and everyone else a final chance to subject themselves to Don. If they don't, we will crush them, of course. You saw the video of Don's androids building the Cathedral?"

"Yes?"

"Just imagine what he could do with an army of those."

"How many are there?"

"Legions. But no need to worry. Don will use them wisely. And if you submit the kind of proposal you're capable of, you'll be ruling your own region, without a care for what happens in the Middle East."

I played along. "What if I win and pick that region?"

"The Middle East? Sorry, I'm afraid you can't. That one Don will rule directly. His seat will be Jerusalem. We're sliding a few more pawns into place. World peace and unity are coming."

"When?" With an army of drones and a satellite system

like Don's, I was starting to think in terms of days instead of months. If this would be the end, then I was running out of time. I had to find Naomi.

"Patience, my young friend. Have you been to Greece before?" He talked on about Greek food and politics, and soon the plane landed. We'd arrived at a palace overlooking the Aegean Sea.

Two androids greeted us at the entry. Their synthetic faces met ours evenly, with dark glass eyes glaring out of shiny white masks. They looked almost human, about the right size, but with four legs and four arms instead of two of each.

Alexi looked to one of them. "Prepare dinner. Something with fresh fish, ready by 7 pm." He turned to the other. "Set up the Babylon link now."

Both robots departed.

Alexi led me through the mansion, across marble floors and down halls lined with giant columns, to a veranda in the back. We were perched high above the deep blue water stretching to the horizon.

"This used to be a five-star hotel," Alexi said, gazing out over the ocean. "My parents worked in the kitchens. We lived in a little cement house forty minutes inland, by foot. We never had a car."

"It's yours now?" I asked.

He turned to me with sheer delight in his eyes. "All mine," he said. "When I first met Don at Oxford, we talked a lot about the inequities of workers serving the rich, and the irony of the workers protesting against a labor force of robots. As you know, many governments banned robots from most of the work humans do, so that people could keep their jobs. Don and I realized, though, that if we fully utilized robots, people wouldn't have to work. What do people do without work? Well, they would enjoy themselves. Don suggested the idea of Babylon. It's brilliant. I've spent my life ever since convincing the world's leaders to adopt our simple package of reform: let robots do the work, and let mankind have more fun."

"But robots like yours are still banned, right?" I thought of my family's butler. It wouldn't have been the same growing up without Bruce.

"They're banned for some tasks, but allowed for others. You tell me, why would we ban robots from taking people's jobs, when we let robots fight their wars?"

He seemed to be drawing me into debate, testing me. I needed to preserve my options. "People say it's because work is part of life, but war leads to death."

"And people are idiots. I hope you don't believe that. War can lead to glory and to power. Work is tedious and boring. Don is going to save people from the curse of labor on this earth. We finally have the technology to be free from work, and Don is the leader the world needs to make us all see that." He paused. "Come on. I'll show you Babylon. Then you'll understand."

We walked back into the mansion and upstairs, to a small room with white floors and walls. The only thing in it was a man-sized, egg-shaped capsule in the center.

"Lay down in it," Alexi instructed me.

"Why? What's it do?" I asked, trying to delay.

"It's very safe," he said. "Your precept will serve as a bridge between your mind and Babylon, using Don's global network. Soon people will be able to connect anywhere, anytime. And I assure you, once they've been to Babylon, they won't want to come back."

"So why's this capsule necessary?"

"Your body is just a distraction. We've built these chambers to take care of all your physical needs, so everyone can stay in Babylon as long as they'd like. Go ahead."

I walked to it but paused before lying down. "And how do I leave once I'm there?"

"All you have to do is to think or say, *Omega*. This time I'm just giving you a taste. I'll disconnect you in ten minutes." He grinned deviously. "It's very easy to lose track of time in there."

I nodded and stepped into the capsule. The base of it was like a padded bed. It felt as comfortable as a coffin. Nothing happened as I laid there.

"It's all ready," Alexi said. "Say *Omega* and you'll be there. If anything is not to your liking in Babylon, just think about what you want."

"Okay." Omega. The last letter in the Greek alphabet—the end. The word slipped out of my mouth with an ominous taste: "Omega."

I was suddenly standing with soft white sand under my bare toes. The bright blue of ocean and sky were before me, tranquil. Two palm trees were to my side, full of ripe coconuts. A hammock hung between them.

Behind me was my bedroom from our family's home in New York. It was just how I remembered it, except one wall was missing, so that it opened directly onto this beach. There was nothing unusual about it. Why wouldn't my favorite room open onto my favorite place? Why wouldn't Naomi be waiting on my bed, basking in the sun?

She sat up and looked at me in delight. She motioned with her finger for me to come. She'd never been so...so sensual.

As I stepped forward, I thought she must be an angel. I blinked and she had wings. The white feathers were brighter than light.

No, I didn't want wings. The wings were gone.

"I've been waiting for you, Elijah," she said, patting the bed. "Come, join me."

I sat beside her. The sheets were like satin under my hands. My body shivered with nervous excitement. I did not want to shiver like that. I stopped shivering. I wanted to touch her hair, her skin.

"Elijah," she beckoned.

I put my hand on her cheek. I traced her neck and shoulder with my finger. She closed her eyes and sighed with pleasure.

I wanted to hear her sing.

She started to sing, "*Be thou…*"

No, something in French. Her song flowed into different words, inviting and soaring:

"Des yeux qui font baisser les miens
Un rire qui se perd sur sa bouche
Voilà le portrait sans retouches…"

I closed my eyes and let her voice wash over me. I felt the sun warming my skin, the ocean breeze fresh in my lungs. After a while the song ended. I opened my eyes and met Naomi's smile. I wanted her.

"Kiss me," she said.

I leaned forward, but a faint part of me hesitated. *What was this?* This wasn't Naomi. Not the real Naomi.

I froze an inch from her lips.

Then her face transformed. One instant it was Naomi, the next it was Jezebel. Her onyx-scaled skin and blazing eyes were irresistible and intoxicating.

"I am whatever you want." She put her hand behind my head and pulled me closer. My mouth touched hers and heat coursed through my body. I tried to pull away, but I could not. I could not want anything else.

But I *wanted* to want something else.

I blinked and shifted.

Now I was standing alone on a huge stage. Thousands were gathered to hear me. I felt like a perfected version of myself, from my crisp suit to my strong posture to my smooth voice. It didn't matter what words I said. The people adored me.

I was magnificent. I was what they wanted.

"My people," I began. Their applause overwhelmed me. I held up my arms. They went quiet, attentive. "We are—"

But then I was gone, ripped off the stage. I opened my eyes and a panel slid open above me.

I was in the capsule.

I had left Babylon.

"Quite a place, isn't it?" Alexi's amused face peered down at me. "I won't ask you what happened there. What happens in Babylon stays in Babylon. But let me say, it only gets better than what you tasted. The more time you spend there, the more you can control your desires. The more you desire, the more pleasure you'll feel."

"Interesting," I said, as I climbed out of the egg-like chamber. I didn't feel pleasure anymore. I felt like I needed a hot shower to wash off the experience. "So how long can people stay in there?"

"Forever!" Alexi said. "Don sent the first permanent member to Babylon four years ago. The man has not said 'Omega' since then. His brain activity has shown constant titillation, and the androids have cared well for his body."

That sounded awful. "But it's not real," I said. "What's the point of the place?"

"Deep question, Eli." Alexi motioned for me to follow him. "Don will give every human what he or she most wants," he explained, as we walked down a hall through the mansion. "And he will keep the world safe. The point is, Don will save humanity *from itself.* And Babylon will become more and more real as more people join it. The place thrives on human energy." Alexi stopped in front of a door. "Can you imagine Babylon holding the entire world! Our minds, our desires—they'll be *satisfied.* It will be the most beautiful moment in history." He paused, probably seeing the skepticism and fear I could not keep from my face. "Don't you see how this could change the world?"

"Yes, of course," I said. "It's just interesting, that's all." It was interesting in the way that the Holocaust was interesting. Maybe they'd let people's bodies live, but they'd destroy their souls. Every soul on earth—swallowed, consumed, and pointed to Don. This had to be stopped.

"Oh good!" Alexi said. "I knew you'd understand." He opened the door in front of us. It was a suite with a four-pillar bed and a view over the Mediterranean. An android was waiting just inside. "This is your room for tonight."

"Thanks. Can I explore the place?"

"Certainly. It's all yours. My android will stay with you wherever you go. It will take care of your needs." He clasped his hands and bowed. "I'm afraid I must go now. You heard Don earlier. We have to be in Beijing tonight. Just preparations for tomorrow's meeting, you know. Don wanted me to tell you it's worth visiting the lower quarters. A friend of yours is there."

"Who?" The way he said "lower quarters" made me think of a prison.

"Don't know." He shrugged. "My androids will make sure your stay fits Don's wishes. They'll bring you back to the plane's take-off area tomorrow at noon. Don has invited you to the meeting in Geneva."

"What meeting?"

"The one I mentioned, with all the world's leaders. It will be the greatest event in political history. The nations and their people will stake their futures on Don's authority."

Oh, how wonderful, I thought. "Good to hear, Alexi. Enjoy Beijing."

"Enjoy your stay!" He spun and walked away, leaving me alone with the android.

As soon as Alexi was gone, I started thinking of ways out. If the android was going to follow me, then I had to find a way around it. Anywhere away from here would be better.

I stepped to the balcony outside, and the android followed close. Fresh air might help me think.

The mansion was truly a masterpiece, wrapping around a tight cove and clinging to the rocky cliffs over the bright blue sea far below. The waves crashed over spires of rocks at the base of the cliff. As I looked back up to the mansion, on the opposite side of the cove, I noticed several little caves in the cliff. Were those people inside? It looked like a series of small rooms, each with an open wall inviting a jump below. Maybe it was the "lower quarters" Alexi had mentioned.

I commanded V to zoom in. Most of the rooms held one person. They were all men. They wore dirty-looking clothes and long beards. They'd probably been holed up in there a long time.

One of the men sat with his legs dangling over the ledge. V registered a connection. She requested permission to speak.

"Go ahead," I said.

"That is Christopher Max," she announced cheerfully.

Impossible, I thought. He'd appeared on stage before the world yesterday. "More info," I requested.

"Your last recorded interaction was in April 2066," V said. "It was a brief encounter not far from here, aboard a plane flying west over the Mediterranean. Would you like more detail?"

"No." That was when I'd connected my precept for a few moments after Chris and Patrick rescued Naomi and me. It was before the attack and the crash that landed us in Morocco. "How did he get here?" I asked.

"Information not available," V answered.

Maybe this was all a set up—Don was the one who'd sent me to this palace, and he'd basically invited me to talk to "my friend," Chris. I had to try to get to him without everything being recorded. I remembered my promise to Brie, that I would do whatever I could to save him. I'd been keeping my distance from her memories, but maybe it was time to return. She'd told me, *find your way to the edge of what's missing, and then you'll find what you're looking for.* Did that mean Naomi?

I sized up the android. I'd learned a little about this model in ISA-7 training months ago. They'd made it for home assistance, but it could do so much more. The red lights deep within its eyes were in constant motion, while its body was completely still. Analytical but lifeless. It was half impressive, half freak. No wonder people had joined together against these things. Most nations had prohibited them and taxed them so much that only the richest could afford them. I remembered the campaign slogan: *Workers build. Robots destroy.* My father had thought it all nonsense. Apparently Don agreed with him.

I cleared my mind. Maybe I could hack this thing. The execution had to be flawless, because they were built to stop any attempts to mess with their coding. But my attempt was not *any* attempt. I'd scored the highest ever on the ISA-7 test. I had V, and a few hacking programs. Sven had installed one of them with my precept. Maybe the traitor could still help me.

"Sync," I told V.

The instant I felt the android's data streaming at me, I held my wrist to its head. Drawing from Sven's program, I channeled all of the android's data back into itself, but also coupled with all the data V could pull from the global system. I hoped the android's processor could not handle the inflow.

It couldn't. Its system started to shut down. The critical moment came just as it began to reboot.

"Freeze," I commanded.

The android stopped its reboot, while its coding was in

startup mode. Now came the hardest part. These machines were too complex to rely on a wireless connection. I had to establish a physical link, and the only tool was the data-chip in my wrist. It worked better for buying things in stores, but I could code it to do more. With another ISA-7 program, I linked the chip to V, so that I could sync with the android.

Then I pressed my finger hard into my wrist. I felt the edge of the chip under my skin and pushed it. My skin raised as the chip strained against the surface. I gave it another hard shove. *Pop!*

The chip slid out.

The blood wasn't as bad I'd feared. They made these chips close to the surface for a reason. I took the little square and pressed it to the android's shiny white head. Its nanofibers attached and clung like a magnet. And just like that, I had a robot to use. The Captain would have been proud.

I tied a cloth over my wrist, went to the bed, and laid down. I had to still my body to focus on moving the android. I closed my eyes and looked through its eyes. From its vantage, I studied my still body on the bed. Anyone who came in would just figure I was sleeping.

I dug into the android's data and found a map. There was no list of prisoners, but at least I could get to the right place. Off we went, through the door and down a hall. The view bobbed up and down as the android walked swiftly through the mansion. I was dizzy by the time it reached the hall of prison cells. Nothing had tried to stop us.

I sent the android to Chris' door. I made it enter the access code into the lock. Click. The door opened and we approached Chris. He was sitting with his legs hanging over the ledge, his body slumped over.

He glanced back but turned to face the sea again, as if an android entering the room was nothing unusual. He didn't budge from his spot.

I sent the android to him and sat it down by his side. He looked at me—at the android—with his brow lifted in question. His permanent smile was nowhere to be seen. There was only a scowl hiding under his thick beard.

As I'd guessed, this wasn't the man who appeared on stage at the UN. Maybe that hadn't been a man at all.

64

"Hey Chris. It's Elijah," I said through the android's androgynous voice.

Chris registered no surprise. He shook his head. "Prove it. I've had enough of these games. I'm not telling you people anything."

"Don had Alexi bring me here, to this mansion. I hacked into this android. I want to help you get out."

"Nice try." He waved me away. "You'll get nothing from me."

I thought of something only I would know. "Naomi brought me to your home for dinner once. You took me to your study. You showed me your collection of pictures from visions like mine."

Chris's mouth fell open. Then he gritted his teeth with determination and shook his head again. "No!" he yelled.

"What have you done to Elijah? Have you hacked into him, too? You're going to suffer for the evil you've done."

"It's me, Chris," I said again. "Brie came to me. She gave me a block of her memory. She said I should use it, and do whatever I could to save you."

He ignored me.

I searched Brie's memories for things only she and Chris would know. I found one. "The night you met Brie, you told her your favorite verse was Proverbs 31:10. It was a joke, and Brie got it. She laughed hard."

Chris closed his eyes and sighed. "And what was her favorite verse that night?"

"Philippians 4:6-7."

"The peace that passeth all understanding." Chris blinked his eyes open and studied the android. "If that's really you, Elijah, how did you possibly get access to an android here. You'd have to be inside the mansion."

"I am. Look across the cove, up to the other side of the mansion. I'm waving." I froze the android and pulled my mind back into my body. I walked to the balcony and waved, then returned to the bed and to the android's body.

Chris was smiling at me—at the robot. "I couldn't quite make out your face from this distance, but I'm convinced." He jumped to his feet. "What's the plan?"

"I've got an idea how to get out of here. I'll need your help."

His brow raised. "I'll do what I can, but I'm in rough shape." He motioned to his dirty prison garb. "What are you doing here, anyway?"

"It's a long story."

"So make it fast."

"The Captain, from ISA-7, he used me to get close to Don Cristo. He tried to kill him, but Don caught him. Next thing I know, Don invites me to his office and then sends me here with his advisor, Alexi."

"Why?" Chris chewed his nails and glanced around the room, as if confirming no one else was around. "What have you seen?"

"Lots of things. I think Don is using me to find Naomi. He thinks the child she carries is his."

"What!" He started pacing around. He peered over the ledge to the water far below. "That's impossible!"

"It'll all be okay." My voice sounded sedate coming from the android. "Please stand back from there. You're making me nervous." Visions of the Captain's leap returned.

He stepped toward the other side of the room, still pacing. "So he can't find Naomi. That's good. We still have that."

"You know where she is?"

He shook his head. "They'd have found her if so. But I know someone who does."

"Who?"

He smiled. "Why did my wife give you her memory?"

Good question, I thought. I sent V searching through my own memories. She found the conversation with Brie, in the parlor of my home in Manhattan. "Here's what she said: 'Please, use what's in there to help Chris and to help yourself. Find your way to the edge of what's missing, and then you'll find what you're looking for.'" I paused. "You know what that means?"

"As brilliant as ever!" Chris said, looking up to the ceiling. "God, thank you for this woman." His excited eyes met the android's. "Elijah, not even I can know what it means exactly, but Brie installed her memories so that I can help you find what matters."

"Great. How?"

"I trust she did not give you all her memories, right?"

"That's right. I have most of her childhood up until soon after you two met. Then it's sporadic."

"It probably involves me. She wanted me to help you. Start with the night I met her. I bet she left out a detail. Tell me everything from the memory."

I plunged into her block of data. "You were both going to a party. It was at a farmhouse on a summer night. Brie walked up to the table where the hosts had arranged jars of lemonade. You walked up beside her. Your eyes met. You smiled, but neither of you spoke for a moment. The sound of crickets was loud in the air."

"Wait, stop there. You heard crickets?"

"Yeah. Why does that matter?"

"We couldn't hear crickets over the music. What song was the band playing?"

"There is no music."

Chris laughed lightly. "There's your answer. The band was playing one of Brie's favorites. A remake of an old U2 song."

"I don't understand. How does that tell me what I'm looking for?"

"Here are the lyrics." He spoke on in sing-song voice:

> *"I want to go, to the foot of Mount Zion*
> *To the foot of He who made me see*
> *To the side of a hill blood was spilt*
> *We were filled with a love*
> *And we're going to be there again."*

Chris stopped and looked at the android expectantly.

"So...Jerusalem?" I guessed.

Chris nodded. "That's the name of the song."

My heart sank. So much for that clue. "But I know Naomi's not there," I said. "The Captain lied to me and gave me the coordinates of another agent in Jerusalem. It's not Naomi. Don already looked for her there."

"Don doesn't know everything," Chris said. "I don't know all of ISA's devices, but remember what Brie has given you. She must have her reasons." Chris paused and peered closely at the android's face. "Is this your data-chip?" He pointed somewhere above the android's eyes.

"Yes, why?"

"Let me take the chip with me. I'll push the android off the ledge here, into the sea. Maybe then you'll have a better chance of getting away."

As appealing as the idea sounded, part of me resisted. I remembered again my dream with Don outside the cottage. I had no doubt Don would find me if I tried to get away, and what if I needed to be with him at that cottage. What if I had to be there to distract him from Naomi?

"I'm not trying to get away," I said.

"You can't go back to Don," Chris insisted.

"I can't get away from him."

"Has he spoken to you through your precept?"

"Yes. And I know how he does it."

"You know much less than you think, Elijah. His powers are beyond technology. If he is speaking to you, he is corrupting you. There is no neutral ground in this battle."

"Everything I've seen with Don can be explained by technology."

"The baby?" Chris asked.

"I think Don used a nanobug like my tracker to impregnate her. It may be a clone."

Fear and doubt crossed Chris's face, but he did not argue with my point. "What about the dragon?"

"I've seen no sign of it in months," I said, figuring dreams didn't count. "Maybe it was a holograph. I think that's what Don used to make you appear on stage before the world."

"On stage?" Chris asked. "Well, nevermind that. I'll learn more about it later. What matters now is that you are being corrupted. What you saw attack us on that plane was real, and you know it."

"Fine," I admitted, "but maybe it's gone now."

Chris let out a laugh. "It's unbound, Elijah. It is just getting started. Its destruction is touching things you cannot see. No one said your sight would be constant. Have you ever considered that your soul has to be in a certain place for you to see what God is revealing to you?"

"No, I hadn't."

"Think about it. So, what is Don planning next?"

"Alexi said he's going to take over the world."

Chris shuddered. "A man can't do that alone. He has spiritual forces on his side. You will see the dragon again, and it will be worse."

"So don't you think I should stay close to Don, and try to stop him when I get the chance?"

"You can't," Chris said. "He will overpower you."

"That's not what one of the order's other leaders said."

"Who?"

"Neo. I met him. He said: *Resist the devil, and he will flee from you.*"

"This is true," Chris said, "but you left out the beginning. You also have to submit to God. Have you?"

"I'm getting closer."

Chris shook his head. "Close isn't good enough. You've got to go all in. Look, I won't pretend to know what you're supposed to do. I don't know why God picked you. You're the seer, not me. And you're right, Don will track you if you leave. But maybe I can get out of here undetected with your help. I must warn the order of what's happened."

"Okay," I said. "I can open the doors, but how do you plan to get back to the order from there?"

A bittersweet grin touched Chris's face. "You still don't believe, do you? Otherwise you'd know I'm not alone."

I looked around the empty cell. He'd been in this

prison long enough to go a little crazy. "You sure, Chris?"

"The Spirit, Elijah. It's with you, too, if you'd let yourself believe."

"I'm working on it. I've been kind of preoccupied. You ready to go?"

"Almost." He stepped to the android and held his hand over its head. With his eyes pressed tight, he prayed words so quietly even the android could not hear them. Then his voice rose, "God, bless Elijah, and may your angels find him and lift the scales from his sight." His eyes blinked open. "Now let's go. We'll see each other again soon enough, whether in this world or not."

"Thanks," I said. "Take care out there."

"You too."

I sent the android to open the door, and Chris walked out. He went calmly down the hall to the right, like an ordinary guest. He took a turn and was out of sight.

I tasked the android with getting some food and returning to my room. As it moved, I also wiped its memory of the conversation and the hacking. All it could know was that I'd asked for milk. Alexi would have no record of my visit with Chris.

I returned fully to my body and walked to the balcony. Chris's little prison room was empty.

The words of his sing-song lyrics came to me.

I want to go, to the foot of Mount Zion.

It felt right, like Naomi was there. But that wasn't my path. Not yet. There seemed to be more to Don than the order thought. I had to face the devil again.

65

Alexi talked politics on our return trip to Geneva. Lots of politics. Apparently the guy ate it for breakfast. He'd met every nation's leader. He knew their families, their favorite drinks. He picked off the easy ones to support Don, and he identified which were the hard ones. They were left for Beatriz and Don.

"Three of the major leaders have been tough as nails," he said, as we walked from the plane to the UN skyscraper. "And no wonder: China, the United States, and Iran have the most to lose when President Cristo prevails."

"Why?" I prodded.

"It starts with each nation's history. If you go back far enough, they've all had their eras of dynasty. That leaves nostalgia for power. They all think they should run the world, because they've done it before. Of course, the leaders have a lot to do with it, too. No man rises to the top of countries like those without a huge ego. Can you imagine these men bowing down to anyone?"

"I guess not."

"Oh, they will," Alexi continued, "but not easily. We sealed the deal with the Chinese Premier just last night. The U.S. President gave in a few weeks ago. We're still working on the Mahdi, which leads to another reason for resistance: religion. Most people in the U.S. and China can get behind President Cristo's great message of tolerance and peace, but not the Muslim fanatics. They've resisted us because of the power they've accumulated in the Middle East. The strength of their renewed Persian empire holds together nations that spent most of history in violent war. But that's not it. Every one of them believes—and I mean it, they truly believe—that they cannot exist if *their* god is not the *only* god. Absurd, right?"

"It would take a lot to believe that," I said. The Muslims sounded a lot like the order. Maybe Aisha wasn't all that different, except that her people's faith had a strong government sponsor.

We came to the UN tower's doors and were scanned. Alexi said, "What a privilege we have, to be here, to see history made in person. The President mentioned your dreams. Have you ever dreamed of such an honor?"

"Actually, no." Of all my dreams, none had anything to do with political leaders.

An android guided us to a platform extending over the edge of the enormous inverted pyramid. Alexi pointed me to a seat between Beatriz and him. From our vantage, we could see the entire crowd.

Thousands were seated on the stairs descending toward the pyramid's center. They were representatives from around the world, their flags announcing their countries. The power and influence of the countries increased as my gaze descended, until my sights landed on the elite near the bottom. On the lowest platform sat the rulers of the United States, China, and Iran.

The sound of drums flooded into the room, as if announcing a royal procession. But it was Don alone. He rose up through the floor at the bottom of the pit, in the center of us all. His face appeared through my precept, as it had when he'd spoken in the cathedral. He was probably sending this to the whole world. I figured no one with a precept had a choice.

"Welcome!" Don announced. "You are witnesses to the greatest day in history. You, the people, have put your faith in a new order, an order of peace. Now we, the leaders of the world, have recognized your collective will. Disunity has brought generations of war and death and suffering, but thanks to the foresight of our ancestors, this esteemed body has heralded over a century of unity. Let us thank our ancestors. Let us thank the United Nations!"

As the crowd applauded, my precept's view panned out and showed what I could just as easily see through my own eyes. I tried ordering V to turn off the video. I was shocked when it worked. Maybe, because I was in this room, Don had allowed it. With the screen gone, it felt like a veil lifted.

Far below, Don looked smaller.

The applause faded and Don's voice projected again with unshaking confidence. "Today we complete what the UN's founders started and what our technology has enabled. The nations' leaders have forged a new government under my leadership. This government can protect the peace that you, the people, have chosen. But as with faith, leaders will no longer dictate to you from on high. You may choose for yourself. As you freely put your faith in me, you may freely vote your support for a united government, a true United Nations. I set before you the question: do you approve our new order of peace, or would you keep your separate, conflicted nations?"

A hologram appeared in the center of the room, hovering above the crowd. It must have been what the world saw on precepts: two bars with numbers above them. One bar said "United Nations" and the other said "Separate Nations." Like the voting before, the UN bar jumped to a huge lead. The UN numbers ticked.

7,340,666,809.

10,989,243,110.

13,045,658,986.

In moments it was 14 billion to 2.5 billion. Percentages appeared: 85% for the UN; 15% against it.

The bars disappeared and the image of a dragon replaced it. It was *the* dragon—the same one from my dreams, from Rome, from Patmos. It perched on the UN tower's pinnacle, on the tip of the giant antennae. The ribbons of shadow and smoke encircling its long body began to extend. They draped and twisted around the building like tentacles.

Fear gripped my throat. People around me were applauding. Could they not see this?

"This is the Omega Project!" Don's voice boomed over the continuing applause. "A global system to link us all, to unite us. Now, I give you a taste of Babylon, of the world to come."

A flash blinked in my mind. Reality *shifted*.

My feet were in the sand. An ocean breeze caressed my hair and urged me toward the bed. It was my bed from home, and Naomi was in it. She beckoned with her finger, and I went to her.

"Kiss me, Elijah."

Our lips met in an explosion of delight.

But the flash blinked again, and she was gone.

I was back in the UN tower, on the platform above the pit where Don was at the center. I glanced around. Everyone's faces were flushed, excited.

"A taste of Babylon," Don said, like a dealer who'd given someone his first hit of a new drug. "Did you like it? I will give you only what you desire. Tell me now. Would you like to go back? Would you like to stay and enjoy whatever your heart most wants?"

V displayed an option. I tried to shut her down.

Nothing.

The words swarmed my vision: "Babylon: yes or no."

I shook my head frantically, but the words remained.

Yes or no.

"A few of you can't decide," Don said, his gaze scanning the crowd, his voice filling my mind. "I understand that. This is new. It is hard to believe. But imagine what you've wanted all your life."

Naomi. The image of her on my bed was imprinted on my mind's eye. I couldn't shake it. I couldn't *not* want it.

Yes or no.

"Now imagine having that, right now. Even as your desires change, so too will Babylon change, to give you what you want, what you *need*. Your world will be overflowing with happiness, unceasing and in every form. Vote yes to enter into this delight."

He paused. His eyes met mine. The translucent words—"yes or no"—hung between us.

"If you deny yourself happiness," he continued, "you are accepting a dim world of work and pain."

Don's hard stare made me understand. He would know if I voted no. He would make me suffer.

Naomi in Babylon. Yes or no.

No. The word surged up from my depths, bursting through the image of Naomi like the sun through mist. Don couldn't change reality. Naomi in Babylon was a lie. I wanted reality. I wanted truth, even if it meant death.

NO. I clicked it.

V showed the tally. Babylon: 94% yes, 6% no.

Don's smiling face filled my vision. His voice was an invitation: "All who voted yes, you see in your precept the portal to Babylon. Stay there as long as you like. We will take care of your needs, so you can enjoy whatever pleasures you desire. Please, try it."

There was no "portal" for me to try. My precept screen began to fade, allowing me to take in my surroundings. Alexi and Beatriz were no longer beside me.

I stood from my chair and began to back away from the pit. No one tried to stop me.

"Tyrant!" shouted a man somewhere in the room.

I searched the crowd for him. Almost everyone looked asleep—probably awake only in the virtual world. Among the sleeping mounds, a large black man was storming toward Don.

"Devil!" he bellowed out. "The true King will return. And you will be destroyed!"

"I hoped you'd come, Emeka," Don said, holding his ground. "Still denying yourself a precept and pleasure? That's one way to die, but no way to live."

"Prince of Lies!" The man had reached the lowest platform of the pit, just paces away from Don. He stopped and held out a cross. "You *will* be defeated," he shouted.

"Your order is down to five leaders," Don replied casually. "And now you give yourself to me?"

"I gladly give up my life if it serves the King."

"Good, good." Don smiled. "Let the holdouts see that the only destruction is for those who flee from what they desire, from what I give freely." Don motioned above, to the few still awake in the pit.

His eyes caught mine. They paused in surprise. Had he expected me to vote "yes"?

Emeka spoke again, pulling Don's gaze away. "Let them see Truth." The huge man stepped forward. "Let them see the resistance. Let them know that, no matter your lies, you will be thrown into the lake of fire." Another step. "In the name of Jes—"

His voice froze as Don raised his hand. A thread of shadow snaked into the room from the pure white ceiling above. Then it snapped down like a cracking whip onto Emeka's head. The touch was silent and quick as a tap, but the man collapsed immediately.

"Anyone else prefer death over pleasure?" Don mused. No one stirred. No one said a thing. Don's gaze turned to the leaders nearest to him. The only one who looked awake was under the flag of Iran.

"Mahdi?" Don's voice dripped with scorn.

The Iranian delegate rose to his feet. "I've come to witness your end, Dajjal."

Don sneered at him as the thread of shadow dipped again from the ceiling above. "The resistance will see what you're doing," Don said. "Then they will know you as a murderer. All of you, watch!"

V's screen took over my vision again. It showed rockets flying like bullets over mountains, with the UN skyscraper in the distance. Don's laughter filled my mind. "These bombs are no use against me. Mahdi, you will—"

Something ripped into the image and Don's words. I could see the UN room again. V was gone. I'd been yanked out of my precept's control. *How?*

A hand was on my shoulder.

"Time to go, Elijah," whispered a familiar voice.

"Patrick?" I turned to him, and there he stood, looking strong and determined as always.

"Come on!" He charged toward the doors. I stepped after him, but paused at the sound of gunfire. I glanced back into the pit. Dozens of men who had been motionless, as if lost in Babylon, were rising up. They began drawing guns, firing at Don, as tentacles of shadow swirled around him. Was I the only one who saw the shadow?

"Now!" Patrick insisted, pulling at me. "If you stay, you'll die. I'm taking you to Naomi."

I ran after him.

We sprinted out of the building and onto one of the thin bridges over the lake. Halfway down the bridge, a disc-shaped plane was hovering over the water.

Patrick stopped in front of it. "We ride only a short way," he said, between heavy breaths. "Then we take the pod. The pact ends here."

A porthole on top of the plane opened. Aisha's head popped out.

"All clear," she said. "Let's go."

We leapt onto the plane and climbed inside.

67

A dozen Arab-looking men encircled us as we dropped into the cockpit. I recognized one of them. Mahdi, the leader of Iran. How had he gotten out?

"Elijah, this is our leader," Aisha said, "the Guided One, the Twelfth Imam, Muhammad al-Mahdi." She and the others bowed, then rose again as the plane soared into the air.

The man nodded, as if acknowledging the praise. His presence was commanding and smooth, not unlike Don's. "All the faithful bow." He stared at me. "I am the Ruler of Iran, the united kingdoms of Persia. Soon I will reign over all the world in justice and righteousness."

"It is an honor to meet you," I said, with as much formality as I could muster.

"And you, Elijah Roeh Goldsmith. Aisha has said

much of you."

It wasn't clear that was a good thing. "How did you get out of there?" I asked. "The shadow, it was so close."

"Shadow?" he asked. *So not even this 'Guided One' had seen it....* "There is no shadow in my presence," he continued. "Evil may not stand against me. I have returned to lead the holy war. My reign will be a caliphate that follows the Prophet. This has long been planned. As my holograph and our *mujahideen* distract Dajjal, our weapons will strike. The day of judgment is at hand."

Through the plane's wide window, I could see the rockets streaming over the mountains, forming puffy white lines straight to Geneva. I also saw something like black threads swirling out from the UN headquarters to meet them. I knew those threads. They were the shadow from the dragon. The lines of white and black looked on track to meet somewhere over the Alps.

"This is my seventh year of reign," the Mahdi continued. "All of it leads to this moment. Isa will return, and we will rid the world of Dajjal and his followers. Watch."

The room grew silent. We continued to soar higher. If the Mahdi could have seen the black lines, he might not have sounded so sure. There was nothing to be done about it now. Just over the ridge of mountains circling the valley of Geneva, just far enough from the city's reach, the black streams met the white.

I cringed, but the midair explosion started in slow motion. At first, there was no gray. Just black and white, swirling and exploding and struggling, as if every opposite force collided in that moment.

Then came the flash, like an exploding sun. A mushroom cloud billowed up and filled the sky. It took me only a moment to realize our plane was not rising fast enough to escape the cloud's reach.

"Go!" Patrick yelled, dashing to the cockpit's controls.

Aisha was already there, her face concentrated. A moment later the plane surged up like a popped cork. The sudden motion almost knocked me off my feet. The cloud, Geneva, and the world seemed to be left behind.

"So Dajjal would rather die in the great war." The Mahdi stood calmly, gazing out at the cloud. "We will raise the black flag in Khorasan. We will meet him in the final battle." He turned back to us. "Aisha, status?"

"We're in lower orbit now," she answered, "headed to Patrick's drop off coordinates. With the force we packed into that attack, the cloud is probably going to cover Europe with nuclear contamination."

Patrick nodded. "It won't reach as far as we're going."

Where were we going? Before that thought left my mouth, my mind went to all the people—in Geneva, in France and Italy and Germany. How many would this kill?

"You knew this could happen," I said, looking from Aisha to the Mahdi and his men. "Even if your rockets had hit their mark, the cloud would have been a danger to innocents."

"Innocents?" the Mahdi asked.

"Yes." I met his fierce eyes. "Millions might die

because of this."

The Mahdi's mouth was a grim line across his bearded face. "A small price to pay to destroy Dajjal," he said. "Had it been a billion people, it would have been worth it. You saw it as I did—these people *chose* to abandon all that is holy for a virtual world of sin. For that, Allah will sentence them to the fires of *jahannam*."

His passion was unnerving, but he had not seen what I'd seen. "Not everyone chose Babylon," I said. "Some voted against it. Some escape his shadow. You cannot use war and destruction to bring peace. You are feeding into Don's power."

"Don?" the Mahdi scoffed. He looked to Aisha. "Your seer has been corrupted. There will be no peace until Dajjal is burning for eternity."

"And so he will," Aisha said, looking to Patrick. "We've reached the spot. When will we see you again?"

"If all goes well, it should be only a day or so."

"Good. Signal for me and we will arrange the pickup."

"Where are we going?" I asked.

"To Naomi." Patrick's look told me to stay quiet, but I couldn't hold back.

"Where?" I pressed.

"You'll see," Patrick said. "We've got to go now, while Cristo is distracted."

"But—"

"I'll tell you more on the way."

I nodded reluctantly.

"Be careful." Aisha gave Patrick a light hug, then

turned to me. "You too, Eli. Tell Patrick everything you see." We embraced. Her almond eyes looked almost sad.

"Farewell to you both," the Mahdi said.

Patrick turned to go. I caught the Mahdi's eyes—they were dark embers glaring at Patrick. I sensed no love lost.

"Farewell," I said, bowing my head slightly, before following Patrick down the hall to the escape pod.

It was the exact path we'd run together in flight over Morocco. We strapped into our seats in the pod, and Patrick hit the eject button. The force of our expulsion slammed me back against the chair.

"Care to tell me what's going on?" I asked.

"The pact with the Mahdi is complete," Patrick said. "Aisha will still help us, but not because of her leader." He began working at some of the controls, shifting our trajectory north and west as we drifted down.

"What pact?"

"Is your precept off?"

I nodded. "Remember, you did it, you somehow shut it down. How?"

Patrick held up his hand. A translucent ring was on his thumb. "I used this."

"How did you get that?"

"It was Jacques'."

"Jacques didn't say anything to me about it."

"Why would he?" Patrick asked.

I ignored his question. "So how did you get it from Jacques?"

"He sent it to me." Patrick looked away. "Jacques is dead."

"*WHAT?* How? When?" I couldn't hold back the shock, or the questions. "Is Naomi okay?"

He nodded. "I told you, we're going to meet her. That was part of the pact. I helped Aisha and the Mahdi prepare the attack against Don Cristo. They have provided protection for the order's hideaway, and for Naomi."

"Where is she? What happened to Jacques?"

"She's in Scotland. Here, watch this." Patrick tapped a screen on the wall of the pod. He pressed his wrist against it, and Naomi's shadowed face appeared. A video sprang into motion.

"Patrick!" she whispered, frantic. "Where are you? Can you come? Can you bring Elijah?" Her eyes opened wide. "Oh no. *Look.*"

Her face faded and was replaced by a video of what she was seeing through her own eyes. She was hiding beside Camille in a small, dark space. Through a narrow slit, as if peeping through a crack in the floor, I saw what she saw: Jacques tied to a chair. His face was a bloody pulp.

"*Where is she?*" shouted a man. I could see only his back. It was a huge, strong back.

Jacques moaned but didn't say a word.

The man held a gun to Jacques's temple. "Last chance, Jack. I warned you not to wipe your precept. Speak now, or die."

"He will prevail," Jacques said through gritted teeth, "and you will burn for eternity."

"You're useless," the man said.

I heard the gunshot just as Naomi heard it. Then a second gunshot, closer. Then a third.

The screen went black.

Something inside me snapped. Tears came to my eyes. I clenched the cross necklace in my pocket.

"She's in Scotland," Patrick said, "on an isolated island off the northwest coast."

"But—" *My dream. The windswept, grassy hills. That had to be my dream.* "She's not there."

Patrick looked at me with frustration. "She's there."

"How do you know?"

"This message came yesterday. That's where she was when she sent it."

It had to be wrong. She wasn't there. "I've dreamed about this place," I said. "We have to trust my dream. I know she's not there."

"Oh, you think you know?" He glared at me. "Well, I think the Mahdi might be right. The seer everyone loves has been corrupted."

"What does that mean?"

"I think you might be as evil as the rest of them."

"Then why are you here?"

"I told Aisha that attack was never going to work. What were they thinking?" He was shaking his head. "Bombs? *Never underestimate the devil*, I told her. But we have the same enemy, even if our methods differ. So I helped her prepare for the attack, in exchange for the protection."

"You didn't answer my question. Why me?"

"You heard it," he said, crossing his arms over his chest. "Because that's what Naomi wanted."

"You don't seem too happy about it. Why are you doing what Naomi wants? Is it for the order, ISA-7, or something else?"

"Someone asked me to do it."

"And you're not telling me who?"

"Nope."

"So what should we do now?"

His bright blue eyes pierced into me. "Pray with all you got that the Lord comes soon."

An hour later our pod set down on the island in Scotland. "The Isle of Skye," Patrick had said. And I didn't need to ask more—I'd been here in my dreams.

But did that mean Don would be here?

Patrick led me on a hike from where the pod landed. We'd been on foot an hour when we rounded a hillside and caught our first glimpse of a hidden valley amidst the lush green hills. It was the valley from my dreams, and sure enough, a small stone cottage sat by a creek running through the valley's center. Smoke drifted out of the cottage's chimney.

"She's supposed to be in the cottage?" I asked.

"Yeah. Come on. Our landing spot should throw any followers off track, but we have to hurry."

I'd taken ten steps when I heard it. The unmistakable

thrum of a jet engine.

"Faster," Patrick demanded, quickening to a jog through the high grasses of the valley's floor.

We ran side-by-side and were almost within a stone's throw of the cottage when the plane crested the rim of the valley. It flew almost over our heads, its pace slowing. The engines blasted hot air as it lowered. The plane landed just behind us. There was nowhere to run.

Don Cristo stepped out. His hair blew behind him in the wind. "Sorry I'm late," he said, with a knowing smile. "It took a while to settle things after stopping the attack, saving millions, and establishing a new government. I trust you'll forgive me?"

"You've come alone?" Patrick hardly sounded afraid. If anything, his athletic frame stood as Don's equal.

"My forces are at work in other places." Don waved as if dismissing Patrick. "I've come to take what is mine. The time is at hand."

Patrick didn't budge. "You'll never have her."

"Why would I want *her*?" Don replied. "I promised Eli he could have Naomi. And now he's done his part, leading me here."

Patrick glared at me.

Not true, I thought, *she's not here*. But I held my tongue.

"Move aside," Don demanded.

"You can't have her," Patrick said, unmoving.

"So be it." Don walked steadily toward Patrick.

Patrick pulled out a gun and leveled it at Don. "Take another step, and I'll shoot."

Don stopped, raised his hand to Patrick, and shouted out a word I couldn't understand. Patrick suddenly went pale and collapsed.

Don glanced back at me as he stepped past Patrick. "Come on, Eli. Let's see Naomi." His body was tall and regal. The high green grasses swept around him at the knees.

I rushed to help Patrick up to his feet. "We've got to keep up," I whispered. "I still don't think she's there, but if she is, we can't let Don get there first."

Patrick nodded but did not say anything. His gaze was distant and afraid. I slid his arm over my shoulders, helping support his weight. His body was heavy, but together we made our way after Don. The grasses clung to us and slowed our already plodding pace. I started sweating bullets, and not just because of the physical effort.

Please God, I cried out, not knowing what else to do, *let Naomi be gone!*

By the time we reached the cottage, Don had already entered. There was no sound coming from inside. I stepped through the door with Patrick and found the scene just as it had been in my dream. It was surreal but comforting. Naomi was nowhere in sight. A fire was burning bright in the hearth. A man sat facing the fire. I could not see his face.

But things were different, too. Patrick was there, and Don was standing between the man and the fire, glaring down at the man.

"What's wrong?" I asked, breathing heavily as I leaned

Patrick against the wall and rushed to see who the man was.

"Bartholomew," Don growled. "What are you doing here? You are banished from this place."

It *was* him. The large, silver-haired priest. He was wearing a white robe and sitting calmly, looking up at Don.

"Welcome, Abaddon," Bart greeted, with more joy than fear. He looked to me, then back at Patrick. "Elijah, Patrick, good to see you. Don's woman clothed with the sun is not here."

"*I CAN SEE THAT,*" Don shouted. "Tell me where she is, or you will all die."

Bart shrugged. "No clue."

Don bent down and set his face inches from Bart's. "You know what I can do to you."

"I know well," Bart said. "But I can't feel pain after what your dragon did to me."

Don dashed past Bart and dragged Patrick back like a sack of potatoes. "Fine. I'll start with your friend. Maybe something easy first. Should I break a few fingers?"

Bart's face tensed but he spoke calmly again. "Whatever you break, the Lord will mend."

"Let's find out." He threw Patrick's body to the ground but held up his hand. He grabbed his pinky and jerked, ripping the finger totally out of his hand.

Patrick screamed in pain, writhing in Don's grip. I fought back the urge to vomit.

"Have a clue now?" Don asked.

"Don't tell him!" Patrick shouted faintly.

"I really don't know," Bart replied.

"Let's try again. The arm this time." Without hesitation, Don snapped Patrick's arm over his knee. CRACK!

"Stop!" I yelled.

"*NO!*" Patrick groaned, clutching his shattered arm.

"Elijah's the one you should be asking," Bart said, pointing at me.

I forced myself to stay still. It looked like I wouldn't be able to fight Don or escape him, no matter what I tried. I spoke carefully: "Patrick assured me she would be here."

Don nodded. "Eli's telling the truth."

"You think so?" Bart asked. He rose and stood before me. His frame was huge and real. How had he survived?

"Don't touch him," Don ordered.

Bart glanced away from me to Don. "You no longer have power over me, and you know it."

Don scowled. "If you touch Eli, I kill Patrick."

"The same way you tried to kill me?" Bart asked.

"Do it," Patrick said with sudden resolve. "Heal him."

Bart nodded and put his sweaty palms against my cheeks. He closed his eyes in concentration. Even as Patrick shouted in agony, out of my sight, Bart's voice rang pure: "In the name of Jesus Christ, I command you to leave!"

Static flooded my mind, crashing and swirling in my ears and my eyes. All the black and white of organized thought muddled into a painful patchwork of grey. I felt Bart's hand cupped firmly around the base of my skull. "In the name of Jesus Christ!" he shouted, "leave him!"

Tension grew inside my head like a balloon about to pop.

POP.

Something snapped. I felt a sharp pinch on the back of my neck. Then Bart yanked something out. The static was gone, replaced by the cleanest, whitest feeling I'd felt since I'd been with Naomi in the desert.

"What happened?" I breathed out.

"Abaddon touched your mind through your precept," Bart said. "Lightly, imperceptibly, like he has for almost everyone else in the world. The code he injects is evil." He held up his hand and unfurled his fist. Squirming on his palm was a metallic bug, this one with a tail like a scorpion. "And more than the code," Bart said, "his minion implanted this inside you."

"Who? When?" I asked in shock.

"Sven." Bart placed the bug in my hand.

I turned to Don, but he wasn't there. My mouth fell open. Where Don had stood, there was only chaotic shadow. Like what had enveloped the dragon, but complete. I saw no face, no arms, no legs—only waves and ripples of light obscuring and bending around a dark form. I felt a level of fear I didn't know existed. I couldn't bring myself to breathe. I couldn't bear to live in the face of this thing, this blackness, this *evil.*

A sound came from the shadow, like words but unintelligible. It was the same as the sound of the dragon in my dreams.

I looked away in terror. I saw Patrick on the ground, with blood pooling under his motionless body. A flash of pure light crossed before my eyes.

I gasped. I breathed again.

I rushed to Patrick and pressed my ear over his chest. Nothing. No breath. No heartbeat.

"Patrick!" I shouted. I began to press against his chest, but Bart pulled me away.

"Elijah, Elijah!" Bart's words pierced through the sound coming from the shadow. "Think on what the order last said to you about Naomi, and go there. You'll see what to do." He looked down at Patrick with sadness in his eyes. "We will lose many more before this is over. But what Abaddon destroys, Christ will remake. Go, now."

Bart's face and body began to radiate with light.

"Run!" he shouted, moving past me.

The shadow had grown twice in size. It filled the room. Tentacles of darkness grazed my skin and made me shudder in horror.

The rays of light from Bart's frame sliced into the tentacles. The two forms collided as I ran out of the cottage.

I risked one glance back. The darkness was engulfing the light, but the light burned brighter than the sun, hovering over Patrick's dead body.

70

Once outside, I sprinted to the plane that Don had arrived in, but stopped short when I saw two androids guarding it. Armed. Motionless.

I stepped forward slowly, arms at my sides. My fist clenched around the metallic bug. Maybe I could use it, like I'd used my data-chip in Alexi's palace.

I was within a stone's throw before the androids turned their metallic heads toward me. They raised their gun-like arms, but they didn't fire. I kept moving forward, trying to appear unthreatening. These things were probably coded to kill as soon as I did something dangerous...like lift a finger.

When I was maybe twenty feet away, I spoke to them. "Don needs your help."

No response. Guns still raised.

"The President sent me to take the plane."

"Provide verification code," said the androids in unison, in the same hard voice.

"I have the code," I said, uncurling my fist and revealing the bug in my hand. I stepped to the androids. Their lifeless eyes followed me until I was within reach. Then they struck...*hard*.

I couldn't react before they had me on the ground, face down. Or maybe it was just one of them. A vice grip clamped over my wrists behind my back. I lifted my head to try to look back, only to take another blow.

Now something pressed my face into the moist earth.

"The President sent me to take the plane," I mumbled.

Suddenly I was being lifted, feet first.

One of the androids held me up with my ankles together, like a fisherman holding up his catch. The other android had my wrists clamped in its claw. Their other arms were still guns, still pointed at me.

I did not dare squirm, or even flinch.

"Provide the code," they said again.

"Reboot V." She blinked on in my mind. Everything was sharper, clearer, including my thoughts. My connection with her felt pure, untainted again. It was like a breath of fresh air after months in a cave.

From this close, maybe I could hack into the androids, just as I had done in Alexi's mansion.

"Sync," I said.

Their data slammed into me. Where the other robot had been a trickling creek, these two androids were a raging flood. Their coding, their *being*, was more sophisticated than anything I'd ever seen. They had a spirit that dwarfed the capacity of a human mind, and I felt like I was going to drown. Sweating, frantic, I focused on what I knew: V and the bug in my hand. I had no chance of controlling these things, but maybe I could at least slow them. I tried channeling their data back into them, but it wasn't working. They began to pry into V, reversing my efforts, hacking into me.

I panicked. I started thrashing. The bug came to life. It crawled out of my hand, and onto one of the androids.

All at once they dropped me.

"President's code approved," they said.

I jumped to my feet and backed away—toward the plane. They watched me, expectant. "The President needs your help," I said, pointing past the androids to the cottage. "In that building."

They exploded into motion, racing to the cottage. Their movements were in complete unison.

I couldn't believe my luck. Or maybe it wasn't luck. Bart had put the bug in my hand. *Thank you, Bart*, I thought, as I turned and charged into the plane.

It was a smaller version of the disc-shaped planes, and no one else was in it—person or machine. I synced V with the controls and moved to the front.

But where to go now?

Bart wanted me to think of what the order had said. There was nothing about a location, but there was the song. Brie's favorite song about Jerusalem. Chris was the last member of the order I'd spoken to. That had to be it.

Jerusalem. The Captain had given the coordinates of an agent somewhere in the city, and Don said Naomi wasn't there. Was it another ISA-7 agent? At the very least, whoever it was might be able to help. What other option did I have?

As the plane took off, I instructed V to take me to the coordinates. She showed a world map with a blinking red dot on the exact spot, then she had us soaring toward Jerusalem. I puzzled over the clues, my thoughts running in circles and finding no answers. I couldn't bear to think of the blackness that I'd seen around Don. It was like a polar-opposite magnet, propelling me away and into the light.

Patrick had saved me, and now I'd lost him. I had to make his sacrifice worth it.

71

When the plane touched down on a building near Jerusalem's old city, I didn't bother to hide it. V guided me directly from there down a fire escape and onto a street of ancient stones. The coordinates were within a hundred feet. I walked to the spot.

"Destination reached," V announced in my head.

My eyes told me otherwise. I was on a sidewalk among other pedestrians. It was broad daylight and there was no sign of an agent, or anything else of interest. I looked up. I looked down. Nothing, except a nice stone bench connected to the plain stone building behind me.

I sat down. "Coordinates?" I asked V.

"Destination reached."

"Agent's heart rate?"

"Zero."

"When was there last a sign of life?"

"Never."

That was impossible. V had given me the details herself. I'd told the coordinates to Don just a day ago. At the time, there had been a normal heart rate and blood pressure for a young female, in this exact location.

"Recreate precept history until the last change in tracker status," I ordered.

V flipped the screens through my vision like pages in a book. It was the same reading—these coordinates but no vitals. Until the images stopped, then flipped back slowly in the other direction. One of them was different. It was from yesterday evening.

"Full report at that moment," I ordered.

V pulled the overview screen. I'd been with Chris. In that very second, the instant of the different reading from the tracker, he'd been holding his hand over the android, over my tracking sensor, and he'd said something.

"Replay, ten seconds before and after," I ordered.

I saw the scene again from my own eyes. Chris was in the prison room. "…lift the scales from your sight…," he was saying, "just as I found Brie."

"Brie," I whispered. That was the word that coincided exactly with the moment when the agent's tracker had last showed vitals. Chris had picked up on Brie's clue. He'd tried to tell me it was her tracker, not Naomi's.

"Elijah," whispered a woman's voice from above.

I looked up just in time to see Brie's head ducking back inside a window on the second floor.

"Come up," she said, out of sight.

To my left was a door to the building. The handle turned and it opened without resistance. Inside was a narrow staircase. I ascended and found myself in the front of a long hallway lined with doors.

"In here," invited Brie's voice from behind the first door of the hall. It was open a crack.

I stepped through, and she locked the door behind me. It was a plain, tiny room with a tiny bed, a desk, a chair, and nothing else.

"Precept off?" she asked.

I shook my head and her eyes opened wide.

"Now!" she demanded.

I disconnected V. The world went bland again. "But my precept's clean—"

"You cannot connect again. Ever. We must leave soon." Then her face lit up and she engulfed me in a hug. "Oh, but I'm so glad you made it! You must have found Chris. Is he okay?"

"He was locked up, but okay," I said. "I managed to get him out yesterday. How long have you been here?"

"Weeks. I buried the tracker under a cobblestone in the street out there. I've been watching for you."

"Sorry to keep you waiting." I smiled. "Smart move with the tracker. You could've just told me you were in ISA-7."

"My orientation was sixteen years ago. I was your age. Jacques was in my class. We both retired when Don Cristo came to power. Jacques joined the French special forces. I did it to raise my family. But Jacques and I had set the stage for more members of the order to join, to influence, to gather information and technology. You know it wasn't coincidence that Naomi and Patrick were in your class?"

I nodded.

"I'll tell you more later, but we must go now. They'll rush to your last known coordinates."

"Who will?"

"Don's drones, or worse."

"Where are we going?"

"To Naomi."

72

Brie wrapped her head in black cloth so nothing but her eyes showed. As we left the building, she walked in front of me with her shoulders stooped, making her look like a demure servant clearing my path through the winding streets of Jerusalem. I played myself, a wealthy traveler.

We entered a crowded market. Vendors were selling meats and spices, scarves and jewels. The colors and scents were overwhelming, even without my precept's enhancements.

Brie eventually stopped at a small stand with dozens of stacked rugs. She said something in a language I didn't understand to the old merchant sitting on a stool.

He responded in the same language. I guessed it was Farsi, but something about it sounded different.

Brie spoke again. Whatever she said made the man turn

to me with a faint smile. I blinked. For an instant, something bright had flashed at his back. Now there was nothing.

"Elijah, seer of things to come," he said. "Welcome back to your motherland. Jacob sends his best."

"My uncle?"

He nodded. "Your mother's family helps lead the resistance here. I think you will see them before this over."

"You mean, before the world ends?"

"You are learning," he replied. "The light is in your eyes now. This is good, for time is running short. Follow me."

He reached past us and closed a curtain over the entrance to his little merchant stand. Then he slid aside a rug by his feet and lifted a hatch.

Brie and I followed him down narrow steps into a cellar-like room. There was a steel door on one wall. She put her face in front of the panel beside the door. It scanned her and flashed green. The door slid open, revealing a long underground tunnel.

"Tell Naomi what you see," the man instructed, as he waved goodbye. "It will comfort her in dark places. Stay safe."

Brie said something like a command in the foreign tongue. The man nodded, and she used the panel on the other side to seal the door shut.

We rushed down the tunnel. There was nothing modern about it—just a long, narrow path burrowed through hard, brown rock. Brie held a flashlight in front of her, but otherwise blackness surrounded us on both sides. I followed her steps as closely as I could, dodging little stone outcrops on the floor. It took every ounce of concentration. She was moving fast.

I figured we'd been going half an hour when she finally paused and looked back at me. "You okay?" she asked.

My hands went to my knees as I bent over, trying to catch my breath. "How much further?"

"We have no time to waste. Abaddon knows where you took his plane. We're almost to the end of this tunnel. Then we ride." She took off again down the hall.

We ran on, ducking and dodging rocks in the tunnel for a little while longer. We stopped at another metal door. Brie put her face over the panel, and it slid open. She darted out as blazing light shined in. The setting sun.

"Come on. Hop on the back." She had mounted a black motorcycle, and she patted the seat behind her.

I hopped on as my eyes adjusted to the light.

She moved my hands to her waist. "Hold on."

Then she gunned it, leaving me no option but to cling tight or go skidding along the pavement. Around us were the clustered low buildings of a suburb. A few eyes looked at us in surprise as we raced past, but we must have been just a black blur. Brie sped between the buildings as if the motorcycle didn't have brakes.

We turned onto a highway heading south. She was going at least twice the speed of the automated cars around us, zipping between them like they were cones on a racetrack. After maybe an hour she exited onto a smaller road winding its way through more rocky, deserted hills. She didn't slow, though the last light of day faded. A few times she whipped around turns so fast the motorcycle's foot peg scraped the road, setting off sparks.

Then, in the middle of nowhere, we stopped.

"Here we are," Brie said, swinging off.

I climbed off after her. There was nothing to be seen. The road was a ribbon along a steep cliff face, with only stones looming above and a long drop below. I looked at Brie in confusion.

She pressed a finger against her wrist. Just beside the road, a portion of a cliff face side slid open like a door. She rolled the motorcycle in, and I followed. We were in a well-lit garage with three other motorcycles and an armored vehicle.

"The order?" I asked.

She nodded. "Let's join the others."

She led me to stairs at the back of the garage. They went down as far as I could see. I kept up with Brie's quick steps until we reached a cavernous room. It seemed carved into stone, but with a smooth concrete floor and bright lights glowing around the wall. Tiny metal panels lined one of the walls, as if they'd slide away and offer a view outside. It was like some superhero's secret lair.

A large group was sitting at a table in the lair's center. I guessed there were forty men and women. They came to their feet as soon as they noticed us.

A man I didn't recognize approached first. He'd been at the head of the meeting table. He clasped Brie's shoulder. "Well done." He turned to me. His perfect face reminded me of Don. "Elijah, praise God you've made it. An unfaithful man might have doubted you after these months. I'm Michael." He held out his hand to me.

I shook it. "Nice to meet you."

"Elijah!" said a familiar voice. Ronaldo slid into view. "Ya made it, mon!" He swept me into a tight embrace.

"It's been quite an adventure." I couldn't resist a wide smile. I'd missed this guy.

"No doubt, mon, but I see ya got ridda that taint. How'd ya shake Don out?"

"Yes, who healed you?" Michael asked. He was holding his hand above my head, then he glided it down in front of me, as if scanning for something. "Whoever it was had the power of God. You're fully cleansed of Don's touch. No sensor, no foul code." His voice pricked my memory, but I would have remembered if I'd seen his face before.

"It was Bart," I said. "I thought he'd died, but he was waiting in a cottage in Scotland. He and Don were starting to fight, or something like that, when I escaped." I looked down at my feet. "Patrick is dead."

"We know," Brie said. *Right*, she had the ISA-7 data. She would have known when his vitals flat-lined.

"We'll see him again," said Chris, stepping from behind Brie toward me. "In eternity."

"You made it here!" I said.

He clasped my shoulder. "Guided by the Spirit, like you."

I looked around the group again. "Where's Naomi?"

Chris pointed behind me. "Moses and I will take you to her now."

I spotted Naomi's father walking toward me from across the room. Unlike the last time I'd seen him in New York, he had a smile on his face.

"Glad you made it," he said.

"Really?" I remembered his words months ago. "You're the one who wanted me to stay away."

"A lot has changed." His deep voice was quiet. "And she wants to see you. Ready to see her?"

I nodded, and he and Chris led me away from the others. We went through a door and began walking down a long tunnel. Another one carved into stone. It had dim electric lights along the walls. Every step made my heart beat faster.

"Moses is right," Chris said, as we paced together. "Your faith has grown since we first met."

"I've been through a lot." I thought of Brie, of Ronaldo, of Neo. "I've seen how it works for you in the order. Maybe some of it rubbed off on me."

"We believe you've been called from the start," Chris said. "Now you're starting to listen. The Lord is with you."

I thought of Patrick, of Bart, and of how I'd escaped from Don's grasp. "That would explain some things," I said. "I feel like my mind has been a battleground."

Chris nodded as we went around a bend, heading down another tunnel. "I know the feeling. And I must admit, I doubted your plan to return to Geneva to face Don Cristo. I doubted you would hold true. But you did. I'd almost say you're ready for Naomi." His tone sounded like Neo's when he'd spoken of Mara.

"What's that supposed to mean?"

"She could never give you her all if you didn't believe," Moses said. "Even if she wanted to. Her reality is bigger than this world. It's bigger than what yours used to be."

"But like I said, your faith is growing," Chris chimed in. "We can't make you accept the love of Christ. But I believe, deep down, you're close, very close."

"Thanks." I didn't know what else to say. I'd seen enough crazy things to believe that a man could rise from the dead, that a man could be overshadowed with evil, and that a higher power had to be protecting the order from a force like Don. But why would God let Don impregnate Naomi? "Is Naomi doing okay?"

Chris stopped in front of a door. "We think so. She'll be happy to see you."

Moses put his hand on my shoulder. "She's in a difficult place, Elijah. The child grows faster than it should. She has not left her bed in many days. Try to lift her spirits."

"I'll do my best." My pulse was racing as Chris opened the door. I stepped through and he closed it behind me.

73

The room was like a little cave, with a plain bed, a desk, and a wooden chair. Naomi's eyes were closed as she laid on her side in the bed. Her stomach was very large. It had been only six months since Rome, but she looked ready to give birth any moment.

I knelt by the bed and took her hand. Her skin still glowed. She was even more magnificent than I remembered.

"Naomi," I whispered.

Her eyes blinked open. "Elijah!" She turned to me with a smile stretching across her face. "You made it!"

"With a lot of help from our friends."

"We can't do this alone, any of it."

"I know that now." I ran my finger along her cheek. "Are you okay?"

She nodded. "I've been sick. They say it's unusual. It's hard on my body with the child growing this fast. They think Don did something to its DNA. But I still believe this child can be saved."

"So the order has accepted that it's Don's child?"

"Most of them."

"I've talked with Don." I felt horrified at the memory. I hadn't seen him for what he was. I stilled my nerves. "He left no doubt, he thinks the child is his. I think he used a nanobug to implant it in you in Rome."

She pulled up her shirt a few inches from her stomach and pointed to a spot on her skin. "You see the mark?"

"It looks just like the mark left by an ISA tracker after it's installed."

"Exactly." She pulled her shirt over the spot again. "Abaddon has powers beyond ours, but even he must abide by God's laws of nature. His evil vision, though, and his vast knowledge—they enable him to use everything mankind has created to try to thwart God's will." She shuddered on the bed and put her hand over her swollen stomach.

I put my hand over hers. "Don doesn't know everything," I said. "He may have implanted the child, but he did not act last. The other man—I believe it may have been Jesus, like you thought—he could have healed you *and* the child."

"But why would my son be growing so fast?"

"Good genes, tall family?"

She smiled, squeezing my hand. "I've missed you."

"Your dad and sister said you wanted me to stay away."

"Not *wanted*," she sighed. "What I wanted more than anything was to have you with me. I did what I thought was best for both of us. You searching for me would have put us in greater danger."

"Maybe," I said. "Danger found me anyway."

"Doesn't it always?" She laughed lightly. "I sent you my necklace. You know what that means to me. I thought you would understand."

"Part of me did, but it still hurt."

"It hurt me, too." She pressed her eyes closed. "I prayed for you many times, every day. Did you see the light?"

The light. In the cottage. "I think maybe I did."

She put her hand on my cheek. "And that's why it was worth it. I knew the risk. I can't bear to be apart from you again."

I grinned in awe of her beautiful, glowing face. Words came to my lips that I'd said only once before, as she had died on Patmos. "I love you, Naomi."

"And I love you, Elijah." Tears appeared in her eyes. "I was scared you wouldn't…after this." Her hands moved down to her swollen belly again. "Or worse, that Don would corrupt you, even kill you."

"I'm here now," I said, "and I'm never leaving."

I laid down and wrapped my arms around her. It should have been perfect. I should have been nothing but happy. Instead, shame bubbled up inside me. While she had prayed for me, I had run away. First in mourning, then back at school, and all the way to a sailboat at sea, before following what I knew to be right. Now I wanted to run away from my own self, from my guilt. My body trembled, my eyes closed, and I clung tight to her.

"What's wrong?" she asked.

I didn't answer.

"You can tell me."

"I can't pretend I did things right," I said.

"What do you mean?"

"Maybe I saw the light, but before that I ran from it. I let Don tempt me. He led me away from you, and I went where he led. I've been to Babylon."

She paused, our eyes met. "Elijah, no matter what happened, there is forgiveness and grace."

"Can a life of trying to escape, to run from the truth...can that be forgiven?" It seemed impossible.

"That's why God became man and died for us," she said. "Anything can be forgiven. You just have to repent, and accept grace. You can't earn it. You can't *un*earn it."

"Sounds too good to be true."

"It's the truest thing there is." She looked at me expectantly. "Think of all you've seen. Why, Elijah? Why would you see these things if you were not chosen *by Him*?"

I fell into silence. For so long my answer had been that I was crazy, and so was the unraveling world. It had helped me avoid facing the reasons *why*. I didn't want to know *why*. I was scared to know. But was it any more frightening than reality?

No. The dragon. Don. They were real, they were evil, and I couldn't run from my fears. I stared the question *"why?"* in the face.

Why? I shouted inside. *I'm sorry, God. Please, tell me why.*

Elijah, said a voice in my mind. *Did I not choose you?*

It was the voice of the man who had saved Naomi. And I knew him. For the first time, and with more certainty than I knew my own name, I knew his name.

Jesus.

As His name touched my mind, something changed. I could never explain this. Some things can't be explained. Maybe it was like a caterpillar turned butterfly, but it was much more than that. It was a blazing and burning light splintering the darkness inside me into a thousand little cracks. The darkness imploded like the basilica in Rome, only this time I was wrapped in this light of warmth and peace, and the light was God.

I chose you in the beginning, said His voice.

Why? I wondered again.

All that the Father gives me will come to me, and whoever comes to me I will never cast out. I didn't have to respond. He knew me, and He knew I understood, because He was the reason why. He *was* the whole answer. *My time is at hand,* He said. *My Spirit is the light, and now it dwells in you. Now you will see. Love your enemies, do good to those who hate you, bless those who curse you, pray for those who abuse you. Let them give you quarter. In the moment when the world listens, tell the world I am coming. I am coming soon.*

The words wrapped around me like a cocoon of light.

Energy penetrated my core, and I said aloud, "Yes, Lord."

"What?" Naomi's voice was full of hope and surprise. "What happened?"

My eyes opened to see Naomi's beautiful, excited face. "I believe," I said, overwhelmed, through tears of joy. "I see it now. Jesus is the reason why. I heard His voice."

"You heard Him?" she asked. "Jesus?"

I nodded. "You were right. He was the one who brought you back to life."

A knowing look passed over her face. "He saved me," she said in awe, putting her hands to her belly.

I told her then what He'd said, and every ounce of me believed it. He would come again soon.

74

Naomi and I talked for hours. I told her everything—first about the return to Washington with Patrick and Aisha, about the Captain and my father, and about sitting *shiva*. It was hard to talk about that week and the ones after it. They were dark in my memories. The people were like shadows. The sailboat was a prison, not an escape. It started to change with Ronaldo. I told her about how he'd taught me. I told her about my decision to go back, and how I ended up with Neo and the order in Montana. Then came Geneva, the Captain, and the Omega Project. By the end, I could hardly believe I'd made it here. It was like something had guided me along the way. Maybe that was part of faith.

Then Naomi told me her story. Jacques had found her in the desert outside Zag. He'd taken her back to the camp—to get Camille and supplies, and to burn it to the ground. From there they trekked north. They'd met Patrick in Casablanca, where Jacques had ordered the message be sent to me. Then they traveled by sea to Scotland. They *had* been in the cottage. That was where one of Don's henchmen had found them. He'd killed Jacques.

"Camille lost it," Naomi said. "We were safe, hidden beneath the floor. I think we could have made it out after Don's man left. That's why Jacques sacrificed himself. But Camille couldn't restrain herself." Naomi paused.

"What happened?" I asked.

"She had a gun. Right after the man shot Jacques, she fired through the crack in the floor. He fired back. We sprang out of the hiding spot. I took a bullet in the arm. Both Camille and the man died. I fired the last shot."

I glanced at her arms in disbelief. I saw a faint, long-healed wound on her left forearm. "When did this happen?"

"Two months ago."

"But," I swallowed. "But I just saw the video today. Patrick showed me on our way to Scotland. I thought it was from yesterday."

Naomi was nodding, sympathetic. "Patrick had to do it that way. He came to me and brought me back here after Jacques and Camille died. We thought of the plan then, to save the video until the time was right. How else could he convince Don to come? Remember, your precept was infested. Don was tracking you."

"How much did he see?"

She shrugged. "Don't know. Probably as much as he wanted to."

After he'd extracted the metallic thing from my head, Bart had said "Sven." Had Sven implanted it during my first return to ISA-7? That meant…New York, Brazil, Montana…Don could know where I'd been. And maybe more. Maybe he had shaped the words that had come to me in my speech before the reporters in New York. Maybe he had goaded me on at school and at sail. Had Ronaldo known? Or Neo? I thought of the order's school in the mountains. Don would know about it now.

"One of the order's leaders, Neo," I said. "Have you seen him?"

"Yes. He visited this base a week ago."

"What did he say?"

"He told us about your visit to his school, and your determination to travel to Geneva and face Don. He asked us to pray for your safety, for your mind and body and soul."

"What about the school? Is it safe?"

"Yes, as far as I know. Neo moved it to a different hideaway immediately after you left. Even though Neo had his ring activated, there were too many risks."

"Good," I said. "Patrick had a ring outside the cottage. It didn't stop Don. It didn't stop his androids."

"Don's true form is being revealed. The time is coming when he will no longer need the mask of technology for his power. Bart expected that." Naomi paused. "That's why he wanted us to bring Don to him."

"So it was a trap? Patrick knew Don was going to come, and that's why Bart was waiting?"

Naomi nodded. "Only a few in the order knew. We suspect another traitor in our midst."

"Sven? He betrayed us."

"No, Sven betrayed the Captain and ISA-7. We know that now, but we never relied on him. He was never on the order's side. This might be another leader. Another Gregory."

I remembered Don's words: *two of their leaders joined me.* As I told Naomi what Don had said, my mind returned to Gregory and his fight with Bart in the plane over the desert. "What happened to Bart?" I asked. "I thought the dragon killed him."

A distant look passed over Naomi's face. "He spoke to me in a dream. It must have been like your dreams. It felt so real. We think the Lord might have brought him back, kind of like He brought me back." She glanced past me, to the table beside her bed. "Can you grab that Bible?"

I handed the book to her.

She opened it to a page with a bookmark. "We don't know everything, but listen to this:

'Your dead shall live; their bodies shall rise.
You who dwell in the dust, awake and sing for joy!
For your dew is a dew of light,
and the earth will give birth to the dead.
Come, my people, enter your chambers,
and shut your doors behind you;
hide yourselves for a little while

until the fury has passed by.
For behold, the Lord is coming out from his place
to punish the inhabitants of the earth for their iniquity,
and the earth will disclose the blood shed on it,
and will no more cover its slain.'

She stopped and met my eyes. "So Isaiah wrote, bodies shall rise...and we must hide."

"Don will not give up until he finds us."

"I know." She looked exhausted, her face wearing weeks of pain and uncertainty.

"You should rest." I kissed her forehead.

She pulled my head down and kissed my lips.

The weeks apart vanished. It was only us, together now. Every lost hour, every fear, every passion released in our lips' touch. When she pulled away, I couldn't hold back a little laugh.

"What?" she asked, suddenly shy. "Did I do something wrong?"

"Not at all. It's just hard to believe this is actually happening."

She smiled and whispered, "I prayed you would see."

He will see...she'd said those words in my dream. Now I could see: Naomi had loved me then, and so had God. He'd been leading me to this moment all along.

75

After a while, Naomi and I fell asleep on her bed.

Then I stood alone in a burning desert. It was flat as glass, with nothing but pale, yellow sand as far as I could see. But over the sand, fires raged—red and orange, white and gold, dancing and playing. The flames made the cloudless sky glow like a sunset. They rolled toward me with ever-rising heat. They came from every direction, as if I were a deserted island surrounded by tidal waves—only I'd be submerged in blazing pain, not water.

I would give up everything for water. I was going to be scorched, and I would die, when the fires reached me. These were my last moments. I was alone. Where was Naomi? Where was God?

Elijah, said a man's familiar voice in my head.

I spun around. No one was in sight.

Look up.

I did. A light was descending from the sky. It was a light with form. As it came lower, I could see it was a throne. It seemed bigger and brighter than the earth.

"What is it?" I asked.

The Great White Throne, said the man.

The flames began to sear my skin. I looked down in terror. The fire engulfed me. There was nowhere to run. I smelled my flesh and my hair burning. I screamed out in pain.

Look up.

When I did, I woke up. Naomi was no longer beside me. The morning light streamed through a narrow slit in room's the stone wall. It was shining hot on my face.

I rose, took a few deep breaths to collect myself, and went to the door.

Ronaldo was waiting outside. "Mornin'," he greeted. "Ya look like a new man."

"I feel like one, too," I said, stretching my arms.

He guided me to the main cavern. Naomi and the orders' members were seated around the large table. This time they did not rise to meet me. The smell of fresh bread tickled my nose, but as I walked to the table, my breath caught.

Wings. The man named Michael had wings.

There was no mistaking it. Real, honest-to-god wings—they looked soft as silk, light as light. It hit me all at once. This was the one who had spoken to me in my dream. He was not a man. He was an angel, as Jezebel was a demon.

"What's wrong?" asked Chris.

Michael's eyes met mine. They were blazing fires. "Naomi said you heard the Lord speak to you," the angel's voice rumbled. "What did he say?"

I told him every word, down to the last line: *I am coming soon.* The group listened attentively, and then they looked to Michael.

"What of your dreams?" the angel asked me. "Do you remember? Did Bart lift the taint from the seer?"

That's what Michael had said in my dream—*lift the taint from the seer*—as I'd laid beside Naomi on the stone slab. "I remember you," I said.

"I would hope so. Tell us what you have dreamed of the dragon. Tell us what you have seen, and what you see now."

"Okay." I thought back to the dragon. "In a dream, I saw its huge black form on a mountaintop. It flew away as the sound of bombs came. I think that dream was about the attack on Geneva, and how Don and the dragon stopped it."

"The media is reporting on it as a miracle," Chris said. "They say President Cristo saved millions of lives by stopping the bombs. He's using it as an excuse to bring war against the Persians."

"It wasn't a miracle," I said. "It was the dragon."

"What else?" Michael urged me on.

"I had another dream where the dragon was smaller. It rose up from the water and swallowed a digital, earth-like sphere with ten satellite rods. The rods became horns on the dragon. I think it had something to do with Babylon."

"Of course it does." A man stood from the table. I'd never seen him before. He looked dignified, and his accent was Spanish. "I told you we should attack it."

"Attack what?" I asked.

He leaned forward and fingered his mustache. "The city Cristo rebuilds and Michael ignores. The city of Babylon."

"A direct attack on the devil is suicide," Ronaldo objected. He pointed to his head. "I know ya got the brains, Vicente, but Babylon's in here."

"You underestimate Cristo," said the man.

"Maybe," I said, "but I think Ronaldo's right about Babylon. I've been there. It's a virtual city that allows you to have whatever you desire, but Don controls it. There's something consuming and twisted about it."

"Then what about the city he's building in these lands? Vicente challenged. "Have you seen that, too?"

"No."

Excitement filled his face. "I saw it yesterday, while I scouted the area. The androids work on it relentlessly. They will have it built in days. The tower at its center rises higher than the one in Geneva." His eyes seemed to flicker like lights during a storm.

"Who are you?" I asked.

Vicente leaned forward, putting his elbows on the table. "I am a leader of the order," he said. "My counsel has been followed since before you dreamed your first dream."

"I still think this city is a ruse," interrupted Brie.

"The devil doesn't care about the physical world," Chris agreed.

"Why don't we ask Elijah what he cares about?" asked an elderly Asian man. He held the hand of an Asian woman with long white hair. "You spoke to him, right?"

I nodded, as all eyes in the room turned back me. "I think he wants dominion over both worlds. He can pacify the people and make them worship him through Babylon, and then his chosen few can reign in the physical world or in Babylon as they desire."

"See!" Vicente stepped forward. The air seemed to ripple around him. "I told you, we must attack the city Cristo is building."

I rubbed my eyes—*help me see, Lord*—then opened them again. A shadow had unfurled behind Vicente, billowing though no wind blew in the room. I staggered back.

"What do you see?" Michael demanded.

"Shadows," I said. "Who is he?" I pointed at the man.

"Vicente?" Ronaldo said.

Before the name had left Ronaldo's lips, Michael had struck. He flashed like lightning over the table, slamming into Vicente. He pinned the man to the floor and held a sword to his throat. He glared down at him in fury and said, "Another betrayer."

The man tried to yank free but Michael held firm. "Help me!" the man shouted.

The others at the room looked at the pair with confusion and fear. The man jerked on the floor again. Michael planted his boot on the man's face.

"Don't move, demon," Michael ordered.

"Michael is the liar," groaned the man. "He's the demon. Look at him. He attacked me for no reason. Have you ever seen a man move like that?"

Ronaldo put his hand on my shoulder. "Tell us what ya see." He sounded uncertain.

I should have known. They couldn't see. "Michael has wings," I began. There were gasps in the room.

"His wings are white as snow. They glow brighter than Naomi's skin." I looked to the man on the floor. The shadows behind him had solidified into wings, but of a very different kind. "The other man, Vicente, he has wings, too. They are dark as shadows."

"He is a demon," Michael said. "Lucifer sent him to twist Gregory's mind, and to report on our movements. And now he will die for his rebellion."

"You will all die!" shouted the demon, from the ground. "Even you, Michael. You know you cannot stand against my master."

Michael drew a sword and raised it high. The demon went into a frenzy as the sword flashed down and pierced into him. The body convulsed harder, forcing Michael back. The demon snapped to its feet and its eyes looked into mine with hate. Tentacles of shadow began oozing out of the wound in his chest. The eyes stayed locked on me until, an instant later, Michael swung again and its head fell to the floor.

The body crumpled. No smoke, no mystery. Just death.

"It's time to flee," Michael said, wiping ink-black blood

from his blade. "Our position is compromised. I'll take Naomi and Elijah with me."

"Where?" Naomi asked, as a wince of pain crossed her face. Her hands clasped over her stomach. "How far?"

"We will go to the wilderness." Michael turned to the room. "Chris, Brie," he said, "you lead the others back through the tunnel." They nodded like soldiers taking orders. "Ronaldo," Michael continued, "you stay and report on what comes. See this body is burned." Ronaldo nodded, as solemn as I'd ever seen him.

Michael faced the rest of the room. "All of you, pray continually for those in Jerusalem. The enemy's armies are descending now. A host of my kind is gathering to meet them, but more suffering comes before it ends." With a last wipe of blood, the angel sheathed his sword. "This begins the last battle."

END OF BOOK TWO

Ω

AUTHOR PAGE

Want to see how it all ends? Visit **www.jbsimmons.com** for a free preview of the final book, *Great White Throne*.

If you enjoyed *Clothed With The Sun*, please post a review on Amazon. It can be just a few lines. Every review is digital gold. And please help spread the word. I've shared my best with you, and I hope you'll want to share it with others.

Thank you! Email me at jbsimmons.light@gmail.com about anything else. I'd love to hear from you.

*   *   *

J.B. Simmons lives outside Washington, DC, with his wife, three little kids, and an intriguing day job. He writes before dawn and runs all day. His secret fuel: coffee and leftover juice boxes. Learn more at www.jbsimmons.com.

ACKNOWLEDGMENTS

Thanks to Lindsay for asking all the right questions, especially the hard ones. Thanks to my family and friends for providing the love and support from which art can grow. Thanks to The Falls Church Anglican for offering a glimpse of what a light-filled community is supposed to be. Thanks to the fantastic beta-readers: Anne, Michael, Danny, Grace, Ryan, Jean, Gigi, Eric, and Laurel. They helped push this book to another level.

OTHER WORKS BY J.B. SIMMONS

Light in the Gloaming
Breaking the Gloaming

In the *Gloaming* books, J.B. Simmons weaves political philosophy into fantasy, like *A Game of Thrones* with a C.S. Lewis twist. The characters champion history's great thinkers, from Machiavelli to Locke to Nietzsche, and bring them to battle, even in the darkest of underground cities: The Gloaming.

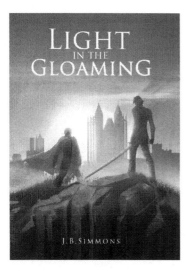

"Tightly crafted . . . a real triumph to creative literature and well deserving of its stars."
Sara Bain, Ivy Moon Press

"A great mix of fantasy, adventure, and allegory." Sunshine Somerville, author, *The Kota Series*

"The characters were outstanding . . . The story was excellent . . . [E]very part of the world is more brilliant in the way the author describes it."
Two Reads Blog

Available on Amazon. Preview at www.jbsimmons.com.

Made in the USA
San Bernardino, CA
19 November 2016